BLOOD GOLD

A Michael Drake Thriller

MARLENE CRONKITE

*This novel is dedicated
To the men and women who
struggle daily with Post Traumatic
Stress Disorder*

CHAPTER 1

THEY CALLED HIM Mr. Lucky. He walked with a limp, but what the hell—the guy in the next room had his legs blown off.

Mr. Lucky, that's me... tell it to my dead buddies.

First to fight, always faithful, the few, the proud, the Marines—he lived it, he breathed it, he consumed it for seven years.

Now, he stared at the design on the sterile hospital floor waiting to be discharged from Landstuhl Medical Center in Germany. The time had come for change; a new direction, a new life. A new what? He didn't know.

A nurse with fiery red hair whizzed into the room pushing an empty wheelchair. "There's a call for you, Mr. Lucky." She pointed to the phone across the room from where he sat in a dark corner. "Do you need help?"

His chest elevated. "No, I can manage… and please, how many ways must I say it? Don't call me *Mr. Lucky.*"

"I'm sorry Michael, but you *are* one of the lucky ones. You just don't know it yet. Give a buzz when you're finished with your call, and I'll wheel you down to the lobby. You're good to go. Don't forget to use your cane."

As soon as she left the room, Michael rose to his feet and let the cane drop to the floor. "Who needs the damn cane?"

He limped his way toward the phone until the cold tile met him in the face like a wall of steel. He tried to get up, but his leg felt wedged between two giant jaws.

Guilt dictated he should be as lifeless as his dead buddies killed in the chopper crash. He could not fathom why his life was spared.

When the pain in his leg subsided to a dull ache, he forced himself back up and took two steps before he fell again. Images of his buddies flashed across his mind. *Pete, Joe, Adam, John. They lost their lives. The least you can do is stand up on your damned two feet.*

He crawled to the bed, grabbed the sheet hanging down on one end, and pulled until he grasped the mattress. Ignoring the pain, he forced himself to his feet.

When the nurse poked her head in, her eyes trailed from Michael to his cane and back again. She crossed the room and picked up the cane off the floor. For a moment, she studied him then moved to his side. "Doctor's orders," she said, handing him the cane.

He stared at her in silence as he latched onto the eagle's head of his walking stick.

She looked down at the blinking phone. "The call's been waiting a long time, Mr. Luc… Michael." Her eyes smiled as she turned and left the room.

At least they saved his leg and didn't amputate. Now, he wanted to get the hell out of there. After six months in a hospital you lose your self-respect.

The call was probably from Clint, discharged a few weeks earlier from the same platoon. They had agreed Michael would pay two-hundred dollars up front to sleep on his couch until he could make other arrangements. He sat on the edge of the bed and lifted the receiver. "Yeah, Michael here."

The deep voice on the other end echoed in his ear. "Hello, son… this is your father."

Michael nearly slammed the receiver down, but he couldn't resist blurting out the words he'd recited in his head for the past seven years. "*I don't have a father.*"

"Son, please… I know how you must feel."

"You have no idea how I feel."

His father had disowned him. He'd grown to accept it. At twenty-four, he had seven years behind him in the Marine Corps. The thought of going home went against every cell in his body.

"I'll make it worth your while. Son, I need you here."

Here comes the old power play. His father had been successful at just about everything he touched. From business ventures to the stock market, he oozed wealth like a succulent orange renders juice. The old man didn't mind sharing the juice as long as you played by his rules. A powerful man and he let everyone know it. Sooner or later he wanted something in return.

Michael heaved a sigh. "Don't try to buy me. I see through it."

"I'm not trying to buy you. You are my son. I may not have much time left…" He paused a moment and mumbled something under his breath.

"Speak up, I can't understand you."

His breathing was labored. "All right, damn it! Some bastards are trying to kill me. I need your help. Don't make me beg."

Michael noticed the quiver in his voice, something he'd never heard before. "I'm not asking you to beg. I've made other plans."

"Michael, you've changed."

"Yeah, I've changed. I've spent the last seven years fighting a fucking war—what do you expect? No one asked you to call."

"Look, you little jerk, let me make it up to you. I'm sorry, I—"

"Sorry doesn't cut it." Michael slammed the phone down. "Manipulative bastard." He turned toward the window. The orange and rust colors of tall oaks stood out in the distance against the blue sky. It reminded him of home. He pushed away the nostalgia.

The nurse poked her head in just as the phone rang. "Michael, you have another call. I'll be back."

He let it ring. Then flinched and lifted the receiver to his ear. The voice on the other end took over. "Michael, it's Aunt Jo, I understand you're being discharged today?"

"Yes, I'm—"

"Well, Michael, we've missed you. I wasn't going to tell you this—I wanted to surprise you. We all love you. So much so that a few of us got together and planned a welcoming home party."

"Aunt Jo, I can't—"

"Nonsense, you wouldn't want to disappoint your friends, would you? I didn't invite Trish. No way would I invite that two-timing bitch after the Dear John letter she wrote you; yeah, I heard about it. This party is exclusive. And it's all going to take place on your father's new yacht. Isn't that exciting?"

Michael's body shook with anger as he took control of the conversation. "No, I'm not coming home." Images of crushed bones and body parts flashed across his mind. Celebrate a homecoming while his Marine buddies were still warm in their graves? Inconceivable. He swallowed hard. "As I told Dad, I've made other plans."

"Now, wait a minute. Forget the party. Your father needs you. I need you."

"Aunt Jo, I've always appreciated you. You've gotten me out of more trouble than I care to imagine. But when did my father ever need anyone, especially me?"

"Your father is a complicated man."

Michael scoffed. "That's his problem."

Aunt Jo's voice was strong and convincing. "I understand how hurt you were after he threw you out, and right now he's suffering for it. He's sorry. I explained to him you didn't take part in the drug smuggling. I told him you were an innocent bystander on Big John's yacht the night of the drug raid. But, by the time the charges were dropped, your father was long gone on his annual business trip to London."

Michael sat on the edge of the bed and massaged his throbbing leg. "Aunt Jo, my father's an asshole. He believed the worst of me, and I have no desire to be in his company. I'm starting a new life now."

"You've been through a lot. I'm thankful your life was spared in this damn war." Her voice cracked. "But your father is fighting his own war. He's ill. And that's not the half of it. Believe me when I tell you, someone is out to kill him, and he needs your help. I don't want to go into details over the phone."

"What do you mean someone is out to kill him? He mentioned something about it, but are you sure this isn't another one of his manipulations? He's good at mind games."

"Like I said, I can't discuss it over the phone. But he needs your help. I can only do so much."

Michael searched his soul. Even if he hated the old man, he couldn't deny him help. If it were true someone was out to kill his father, bum leg or not, he'd kick some ass if he had to. He had plenty of experience over the past seven years.

"Okay, I'll return home on one condition. I won't stay at the Drake Mansion; that's out of the question."

"Fine, where do you want to stay?"

"I'd like to stay at the old cabin by the lake. Is it still available?"

"Yes, but are you sure? You can stay at the mansion and have all the amenities your heart desires."

"My heart desires the cabin by the lake."

"As you wish; your dad will meet you at the airport in Los Angeles. The Drake Learjet will be waiting to fly you home."

CHAPTER 2

MICHAEL HOOKED HIS cane over one arm, grabbed the handrail, and followed his father up the steps of the Learjet. As he walked past the high gloss wood cabinetry, he almost didn't recognize his own reflection. The desert green fatigues he'd worn for the past seven years were a thing of the past. He looked like any other guy on the street dressed in faded blue jeans and a red polo shirt.

He trailed his father to the center of the plane, steadying himself with his cane. They stopped in front of the window-seats. "Let's sit here," his father said. "Would you care for a drink? We have an espresso machine if you want coffee."

"Water's fine." Michael looked into the face of a thinner, more humble man. His father was a person who had done two things well in life, make money and screw women. Somewhere, Michael's birth mother fit into the mix. Who she was and where, he had no idea. But the old man looked pale. As much as he resented his father, he hated to see him lose his edge on life.

He sank down into the beige leather seat as the jet engine geared up for takeoff. His leg pained him, and his gut told him to get the hell off the plane. He sniffed the air.

Damn, am I going out of my mind? The smell of burning flesh, where did it come from?

He braced his head against the backrest of the leather seat as images of charred bodies eclipsed his brain. Their screams came from the depths of hell. He balled his fists so tight, his nails dug into the palms of his hands.

Minutes later, when his mind cleared, he peeled an eye through the window of the jet as it flew above the clouds. *What in hell just happened?*

His father stood over him holding drinks. "Are you all right, son?"

"I'm fine." He gulped down the water his father handed him and set the glass on the extension tray.

"I popped Chicken Alfredo into the microwave in case you're hungry. It should be ready in a few minutes."

Chicken Alfredo... somehow he had linked the smell to burning flesh in his mind. "No thanks. Where's the head?"

"Just down the aisle to the left. What's wrong? Your hands are bleeding."

Michael looked at his hands as if they belonged to someone else. "I'll be right back."

He hurried to the toilet and vomited into the commode. When he returned, he stared out the porthole as the jet soared above red and greenish-blue discharges.

His father's eyes were full of concern, something Michael wasn't used to. "You can talk to me anytime, you know."

Michael's jaw stiffened. "No, it's okay. I've been under stress, that's all."

I lost my buddies. I should be dead too. Doesn't anybody get that?

There was a long gap of silence between them. After a while, Michael asked, "You said someone's trying to kill you? Do you want to talk about it now?"

"Now, is a good time, I guess." His father set his paper plate on the extension tray and took a sip of his vodka tonic. "Let's just say, unusual happenings have made me more than a little suspicious. Perhaps that's the point; whoever's doing the dirty deed is trying to drive me nuts."

Glad to think about someone else, Michael turned toward his father and noticed the strain in his eyes. "I can see something or someone is putting you through hell. Tell me about this dirty deed."

His father took a swallow of his drink and set the glass on the tray. "It began a few months ago on my yacht. I think the poison was planted just to scare the crap out of me." He breathed deeply and exhaled like he was glad to get it off his chest. "The rat poison appeared one day. I found the container in the pantry among the nutmeg and other spices. A small container, similar to a cinnamon can. I questioned the staff. No one knew anything about it. I had all the food on the yacht thrown out."

Although there could be a good explanation for rat poison, Michael thought, it didn't enhance any stew he'd ever chowed-down on. "You mean not even the kitchen staff knew anything about the poison?"

"No. They said they didn't. The cooks were off duty when I found the stuff one evening. I made myself scrambled eggs and bacon, and I almost mistook the rat poison for pepper. Since then, I've hired a security guard full-time on the yacht." He took another gulp of his vodka tonic.

"No wonder you're upset. Rat poison could do you in."

"That's not all." Perry's voice trembled. "I've received numerous harassing phone calls. The voice is disguised."

Michael shifted in his seat and repositioned his leg. "My God, what's going on in your world? Tell me about the disguised voice."

His father placed his head back against the cushioned seat and closed his eyes. "It's what the voice doesn't say. That's what worries me. The person doesn't come right out and say he will kill me. It's a recording because the message repeats the same phrase in a low rasping voice. *Come on, deep pockets, hurry up and die, die, die. Join the dearly departed."*

Michael leaned into his father. "How long have you received these calls?"

"Every night, around midnight for a week; the message is never long enough to trace. I'm beginning to think I'm a nutcase."

"No one can blame you for being scared. You have good reason to be?"

His father raked his fingers through his salt and pepper hair. "That's not the half of it. I was having lunch at the Mile High Chinese Restaurant the other day. I go there every Wednesday after golf. I ordered my usual Almond Chicken. Later, when I opened the fortune cookie, it read…" He closed his eyes a moment and then opened them, *"Come on, deep pockets, hurry up and die, die, die. Join the dearly departed."*

Michael shook his head. "Chilling… I hope you saved the message from the fortune cookie."

"No, I was so rattled; I paid my bill and rushed out of the restaurant like a fool."

Michael's concern grew. "Damn. Do you have any idea who wants you dead?"

"I'm certain my wife is behind all this."

Michael pictured Ida. He was never fond of his father's second wife, but he never saw her as a killer. "How about the police, did you report this?"

His father toyed with his thick, white mustache and shook his head. "No, I was stunned at first. Then I was afraid I sounded crazy because I had no proof."

"But why would she try to screw with your mind like that?"

"It's all about greed, son. It's like Gandhi once so wisely put it: *Earth provides enough to satisfy every man's need but not every man's greed.*"

"Ida is doing this to you out of greed? I always pictured her as a bitch but never a killer."

"No, Ida was in a car accident that left her in a coma. She died two years ago. A lot has happened since you've been away, son. I remarried a much younger woman—a beautiful woman. I thought I loved her. She turned out to be a tramp after my money. I'm almost sure she had something to do with Ida's death."

"My God, Dad. What kind of woman did you marry? What's her name? Do I know her?"

His father's took a small flask from his pocket and poured vodka into his glass then swirled it around in the ice. "No. I don't think you know her. Her name is Nicole Hunt. She moved to Lakeport when you were just a boy. She went to work for me, and before long she was practically running The Rock."

"You say you're suspicious she murdered Ida?"

He snickered. "Well, I always wondered why the hell Nicole's diamond hair-barrette got tangled in the bed sheets shortly after Ida was pronounced dead. It doesn't make sense. Nicole never visited Ida—she hated Ida. She wanted to take Ida's place at the mansion. Yes. I think she murdered Ida."

Michael pondered on his father's predicament. He seemed naïve—not like the man he grew up around. "Why didn't you go to the police? Why did you continue to see this woman?"

"I don't know. I must have been going through a midlife crisis. I was so blinded by love, I couldn't see past it." He gulped down his drink and shook his head.

"Damn! You really allowed yourself to be played. Hey, I know the feeling. I received a Dear John letter while I fought the war in Afghanistan. But that's nowhere near what you're facing now. Tell me, is Nicole the sole beneficiary of the Drake fortune?"

"Not for long. Believe me I've come to my senses. I have an appointment with my attorney Monday morning. I'm changing my will; you and Jo will be the sole heirs of everything I own."

Even if his father were a fool over a woman, something had changed him from a selfish bastard to a more thoughtful human being. "You know I'm not after your money, don't you?"

He smiled. "Yes, I know. It took the Jaws of Life to get you to come home."

"Does Nicole live at the mansion with you?"

"Yes, but we sleep in separate bedrooms. She has her own apartment on the third floor of the mansion."

"Were there any other incidents?"

"Yes, the day I received the message in the fortune cookie. On my way home from the Chinese restaurant, Nicole followed me in her red BMW. I spotted the personalized license plate through my rearview mirror. She pulled up next to me at a traffic light. I looked in her direction, and she smiled at me." His father shifted in his seat.

"Her smile made you suspicious?"

"She has an evil smile. Don't you see? She's laughing at me. She's trying to bait me." He downed his vodka drink.

Man oh man—the old man was in deep shit. "Don't tell me there's more?"

"One more incident."

Michael scrunched his brow. "Let's have it."

"This morning, I went out to drive the Ferrari to the airport. I stepped in brake fluid as it ran down the sidewalk. My gut feeling says the line on the Ferrari didn't break on its own."

It didn't take a genius to figure out that someone was screwing with his father's mind. Michael stared out the window of the plane. The power hungry jerk needed him now. He leaned his head back against the cushion; his eyes grew heavy with sleep.

Minutes later, his father broke the silence. "You should know son, this isn't just about the Drake fortune." He reached into the breast pocket of his sports jacket and drew out a yellowish looking document.

Michael eyed the crude piece of paper. The top of the page was torn on one side and taped together. The whole bottom half was spotty with what looked like coffee spatters.

"This may not look like much, but this beat up piece of paper is worth a fortune."

Michael imagined his life getting more complicated by the minute. He dreamed of getting a place on the beachfront where he could meet chicks and get his love life going. But here he was on a jet, flying north at a good clip, right into a new war-zone filled with more landmines than he cared to imagine.

"There's a story behind this map." His father went on. "This old piece of paper touched many lives as it was passed down by a family of lawmen close to my ancestors. They guarded it with their lives. This happened during the gold rush days in a place not too far from Lakeport. They call it Rogue's Hollow."

Michael squinted at the document. "I remember Rogue's Hollow. It's an old ghost town isn't it?"

His father nodded. "Yes, a dangerous ghost town. Some people have gone there never to be seen again. During the Gold Rush days the settlement was known as Lode City. After the miners sucked all the gold out of the area they left town with their money. All but one person remained. A big Swede by the name of Goldie buried his gold worth millions. Today's market would bring in an unimaginable fortune."

"Why didn't Goldie cash his gold in like everyone else?"

"Goldie was an old miser who lived in a ratty shack in the hills. He did the only thing he knew to do—bury his gold like any good hoarder."

"How do you know any of this is true? Suppose it's all a lie, an exaggeration made up by bull-shitters? And even if there is truth to the legend, how do you know one of the so-called lawmen didn't dig up the gold and take off with it?"

"I don't know, son. As Napoleon Hill once said—*money without brains is always dangerous*. Here's what I do know. Con artists and criminals between Lakeport and Mexico City have been killing each other for years searching for this buried treasure. That's why they changed the name of the ghost town from Lode City to Rogue's Hollow. Every lowlife and his brother moved there." His father paused a moment and reached into his pocket. "Mind if I smoke?"

Michael wondered if his dad's cigarette smoking had led to health issues. He wanted to tell him not to chance it, but how could he object after all the weed he'd smoked in Kandahar? "Go ahead."

His father fired up, took a drag and continued, "There were four brothers in the family, and they all became lawmen. The lawmen helped Goldie draw up the map. One brother, the youngest of the four, was considered the black sheep. The other brothers refused to give him the map. Before the elder brother died, he gave the map to me for safe keeping."

"So what happened to the younger brother, the black sheep? Is he still around?"

"Yes, when he was a young punk, he used to hang around the pool halls back in the days when I shot pool for a living—that was before I invested my earnings into stocks. His name is Dillon Hobbs."

"So you know this dude?"

"Oddly enough, I just found out he's my wife's new lover. I knew she was having an affair, so I had her followed. This bastard's been screwing my wife and trying to weasel his way into my money. Problem is, he's the sheriff of Three Lakes County and hard to touch."

His father's face tightened as he stubbed out his cigarette. Michael observed the gauntness in his face. Seven years is a long time. He had worry lines and creases that weren't there before. He still wanted to turn and run in the opposite direction, but the words slipped out of his mouth… "What can I do to help?"

"First we have to get you settled at the lake cabin. Are you sure you don't want to stay at the mansion? For what it's worth, your old room is waiting for you, plus you'll have the run of the house and all its amenities."

"No thanks. I'll feel more comfortable at the lake. I need to be alone for a while."

"I understand. I did a stint in Vietnam. It takes a while to wrap your brain around war and it's worse if you lose friends. As I said, if you need to talk, I'm here to listen. I know I wasn't there for you when you were growing up."

"It's okay—it's in the past, let's leave it at that."

"Fine, I'll get the cabin ready for you. It hasn't been lived in for years."

They were silent for a while. Michael wasn't sure he could leave the past in the past.

"Before we land, I want to give you this." His father folded the map, placed it in an envelope and handed it to Michael. "Keep it in a safe place, Son."

CHAPTER 3

THE LEARJET MADE a smooth landing at Three Lakes Regional Airport. Michael tried to shake the feeling he should be anywhere but Lakeport. He empathized with his father, but his gut told him he hadn't resolved his anger issues. Maybe he never would.

They stood face to face at the small air terminal; tears glistened in the old man's eyes. Michael could barely hear him over the planes taking off and landing. "How about we go out on the houseboat tomorrow and take in a little fishing?" His dad's voice rose over the roar of the jet engines. "Something we should have done long ago."

Michael didn't trust the old man, but he sensed a new openness. He nodded. "Okay. I'll see you tomorrow at the lake. We can get caught up"

"Thanks, Son."

Michael watched his father walk away. He recalled his eighth birthday; how he waited until sundown for his dad to meet him at the houseboat to teach him to fish. He never showed.

€€€

Michael rented a Jeep and took off for the twelve-mile drive into the woods toward the lake cabin. Nature was far more satisfying than the cold empty rooms at the Drake Mansion. The huge house inflamed too many memories of his adoptive mother, Nora. He'd been the center of her love and attention for the first eight years of his life. She died of leukemia and left a void he never quite got over.

He figured he'd stay three or four weeks at the cabin, then head for unknown territory in search of a new career. Too much time in Lakeport kept him away from his dream of opening his own Dojo in San Diego. By that time, he figured he should be free of the cane and his gimpy leg.

He shifted the Jeep into a lower gear and climbed the potholed, two-lane blacktop. Cool, fresh air stroked his face, and the scent of verbena hung in the air like sweet vapor. His mind wandered to the war in Afghanistan. Too bad his Marine buddies weren't alive to enjoy the freedom with him. He wondered where they were in the scheme of things.

Then intrusive phrases played a game of ping-pong in his head. Back and forth, over and over, like an old broken record…

Your buddies will never breathe the open air—never enjoy the scent of verbena—in fact, they can't even breathe…

The sweet scent of verbena morphed into the foul smell of burning flesh. Michael pulled over in an abrupt stop along the roadside.

He grabbed his cane and hobbled to the bushes. "Oh sweet Jesus," he cried out as he retched. "Will this never end?"

When the ordeal stopped, he sat on a rough patch of ground and leaned his back against a rock. Life took on a flash of the past in a Cobra helicopter as it spiraled to the ground. One by one, their faces floated toward him. He called their names: "Pete… Joe… Adam… John…"

When the flashback ended, he stared at the ground and spotted a lone red ant carrying a load of debris up to an ant hole. The insect reminded him of his aloneness. Funny how old memories pop back into your head, he thought. As he watched the ant, he recalled something he read by O'Rourke: *But people are not ants or bees. We do not reason or love or live or die collectively. We are individuals.* Still… guilt ate at his core.

He rose and limped back to the Jeep. Beads of sweat dripped into his eyes as he rested his face on his arms against the steering wheel.

He lifted his head in time to see a black and white police car pull up behind him. He watched through the rear-view mirror as a cop strode to the driver's side of his Jeep. The badge pinned to his khaki uniform said Sheriff of Three Lakes County. The shitty grin below the handlebar mustache had *gotcha* written all over it.

His tone had an edge of authority. "Driver's license and registration, please."

Michael slid his driver's license out of his wallet, grabbed his insurance and rental contract from the glove compartment and handed them to the officer.

The cop studied the license. "Drake? Your name Michael Drake?"

"Yes, sir."

"Any relation to Perry Drake?"

"My father."

Oh, oh, here it comes.

"So you're the infamous Perry Drake offspring? Are you in his good graces now after he dumped you?"

Michael wanted to smack the insidious grin off his face. He ignored the insult. "Just down for a visit."

"Last I heard the DEA arrested you on Big John's yacht for drug smuggling."

Michael kept a stone face. "The charges were dropped."

The sheriff pinched his brows together with gloved fingers. "Oh, yeah, now I remember. You joined the military and became a big bad Marine."

Michael's adrenaline jumped through his veins. It took every ounce of self-discipline to stay cool.

"Yes, I joined the Marines." He looked at the cop and gave no evidence of anger, interest or amusement.

The sheriff stared at him. Michael wished he could see the guy's eyeballs behind the mirrored sunglasses.

"You're parked in a no parking zone—did you know that, boy?"

"No, I didn't know. Sorry."

"Ignorance of the law is no excuse. You know that, don't you, boy?"

"Yes, sir."

"You got eyes, don't you? Did you hear me, boy? You got eyes?" He leaned in, inches from Michael's face.

"Yes, sir."

"Don't they teach you in the Marines to open your eyes? There're all kinds of no parking signs along this route. Did you even see one of them?" He took a deep breath and fingered his lip foliage. "Well did you?"

"No, sir."

"Had to take a leak? Is that why you pulled over?"

"Yes, sir." Michael was glad the cop thought of it.

"Where're you headed?"

"Just taking a casual drive around the area, it's been a while since I've been home." Michael didn't want him to know he planned on staying at the lake cabin. Unless there was more than one sheriff in the county, this self-important dude could easily be his father's number one enemy and rapidly becoming his own.

He handed Michael back his license, insurance, and registration. "From now on, if you gotta take a leak, hold it, boy."

"Yes, sir."

Michael was surprised the cop didn't write him a ticket. He watched the sheriff through the rearview mirror, strut like a stuffed pigeon, get into his police car and speed away. As soon as he disappeared, Michael grabbed his cane, jumped out of the Jeep, limped a few feet into the bushes and took a leak.

€€€

Several miles ahead, Michael climbed a narrow road that seemed to go on forever. When he reached the top, he had to admit, he'd forgotten the beauty of the setting sun as it spread a kaleidoscope of color across the lake. Regardless the circumstances it felt good to be home.

As he turned onto the dirt driveway, he spotted a black Ford pickup parked in front of the cabin. It could be a squatter, or worse, someone from the ghost town ten miles up the road. He hoped it wasn't part of the welcoming home party Aunt Jo promised to cancel.

He turned off the Jeep engine and coasted into the driveway. He climbed out of the Jeep, grabbed his cane and approached the cabin. The front door stood ajar a crack. He pushed it open.

In the dim light, he saw a faint figure of a man bent over an old trunk in the far right corner of the cabin. He hooked his cane over his left arm and crept up behind the intruder, prepared to place him in a choke hold.

The man turned his head just in time. "Michael, no!"

"Bruno?"

Bruno held a hand to his chest and found a chair. He gasped between words as he sat down. "Michael, you nearly gave me a bloody heart attack. Don't you know better than to sneak up on a person?"

"I'm sorry, Bruno. What are you doing here?"

"Your father called on me to help get you settled."

Michael considered Bruno part of the family. He'd been the butler at the Drake mansion ever since he could remember. Bruno the Brit ran the place with an iron fist and a heart of gold.

Michael held out his hand. "Well, my friend, it's good to see you. I'm sorry I frightened you."

"It's okay, I'm happy you're back." Bruno shook his hand. "I hardly recognized you—you've grown into a man."

"Yeah, I guess that happens when you become a Marine." Michael grabbed a chair and sat across from his friend.

"I must say, that's quite a beastly haircut. You look scalped." Bruno raised his bushy white brows.

Michael laughed and rubbed the top of his flat cut. "You don't like my high and tight snatch patch?"

Bruno grinned. "Yeah, well it's okay for a jarhead, I guess."

Michael enjoyed Bruno's British humor. "Just for that, I will grow my hair to my shoulders." He recalled how they argued night and day about his long hair when he was sixteen.

"Oh, no, not long curls again? You had girls chasing you, dying at your feet just for your hair."

"Now, for sure I'll grow it hippy style."

For the next couple hours they laughed, drank beer, snacked on cheese and crackers, and talked about the good times.

Michael asked Bruno to stay the night. The cabin was equipped with a bedroom and a half. The half amounted to a supply room with a cot. He insisted he'd take the cot and Bruno take the bedroom. "I'm used to sleeping in foxholes," he argued.

Later, Michael grabbed his cane and ambled out about fifty feet from the cabin. It was time to kick back and listen to the crickets. The bed of grass he stretched out on satisfied Michael's need to be detached from the rest of the world. He studied the vastness of the Galaxy and in a few minutes fell asleep.

At dawn, he awakened to a blanket of fading stars. For the first time in six months, he'd slept through the night with no nightmares. The whole idea of sleeping forever appealed to him, and he dozed off again.

He opened his eyes as the sun peeked over the horizon. The raw beauty of deep gold and red patterns spread across the lake. Life seemed so simple right at that moment.

Then a sudden gust of cold air bit through his windbreaker, reminding him of reality. He folded his arms across his chest to ward off the chill. The war taught him many things; mostly that life is a crapshoot. He opened and closed his fists. Right beneath his skin he felt angry—angry at the war, angry at his buddies for dying, angry at himself for not dying with them—just angry enough to track down any bastard out to hurt his father.

He'd taught advanced Karate in the Marine Corps. Even with his leg injury, he was in better shape than most. He would never start a fight, nor introduce someone into a violent encounter. But if the occasion arose, he'd kick ass if he had to.

He grabbed his walking stick and stared at it. *If it's the last thing I do, I'll get rid of this damn cane.*

The breeze softened and brought with it the aroma of freshly brewed coffee. He forced himself to his feet and limped to the cabin.

Inside, coffee percolated on an old wrought iron woodstove. Bruno stuck his head out from behind the pantry door. His full crop of unruly white hair gave him a wizardly appearance.

"Good morning, Michael. You must be a wreck after sleeping in the cold all night."

"No problem, not that bad at all."

Bruno strolled out of the pantry and poured himself a cup of coffee. "I imagine it's bloody good to be home, no matter where you sleep. War is such an ugly racket."

"Yeah, it's a mean scene over there." Michael hoped Bruno didn't want to discuss the war.

Bruno's wise old eyes didn't flicker. As always, his timing was on the mark. "There're clean mugs on the shelf over the stove. There's plenty of food in the fridge."

"Thanks." Michael grabbed a cup and poured himself coffee. As he sipped on the steaming liquid, he looked around at the surroundings he'd chosen over the mansion. His great, great grandparents had built the cabin when they moved to California in 1901. Along with the rustic wood stove, the cabin had its original furnishings.

A knotty pine coffee table was centered in the living room between two beige leather couches. The prominent picture window displayed a panoramic view of the lake. A floor to ceiling rock fireplace covered the opposite wall and held a roaring fire in the hearth that Bruno had built.

"I'm leaving now. I'll be back in a few days." Bruno headed toward the door. "Cheerio, try to stay out of trouble."

"I'll do that! Thanks for helping me get settled and stocking the cabin with grub."

"Don't thank me, thank your father, he pays me well." Bruno smiled dryly.

Michael laughed to himself. Eccentric as hell, Bruno the Brit always went the extra mile. Yeah, he did it for the money, but he also did it because he cared.

After Bruno left, Michael sat by the fireside and drank his coffee then strolled through the cabin. The place portrayed a warm atmosphere with old family portraits decking the walls, some with smiling faces, and others showing their starchy side. He thought about the treasure map tucked away in his pocket. Was there a place in the cabin worthy enough to hide the old piece of paper?

He sat on the couch and gazed out the window at the blue body of water. The houseboat in the distance appeared cool and inviting. He looked forward to fishing with his dad the following day. Memories flooded his mind. He thought of Nora, his stepmother, and the family gatherings they'd had as they cruised the lake. They always tied a couple motorboats to the side of the barge for water skiing, and then the fun began. If Nora were alive today, she'd want him to help his father. She'd insist on it.

He stared across the room at a portrait of one of his ancestors hanging on the wall in the dining area. Nora told him once he was named after his great, great grandfather, Michael G. Drake, the third.

He walked over to the rendering for a closer look. It was like staring into a mirrored image of himself.

What would his great, great grandfather do about the map?

He lifted the painting off the wall and studied the back panel. Then the answer came.

In the kitchen, he found a small plastic bag and placed the map inside the protective covering. After searching every drawer in the kitchen, he found duct tape in a junk box in the pantry. Careful not to damage the old rendering, he removed the painting from the frame, and then taped the plastic bag containing the map to the underside.

Once the map was sandwiched between the picture and back panel, he hung the painting back on the wall. Now the map was safe until he could rent a security box at the bank. He stood back and whispered the battle cry, "Oorah..." Grandfather Drake, the third, smiled his approval.

CHAPTER 4

SHERIFF DILLON SQUINTED against oncoming headlights as he climbed the two lane stretch that led to the old ghost town. His cell phone pulsed and Nicole's name popped up on the screen. He placed the call on speaker-phone. "Yeah, baby, what is it?"

"Dillon, I'm worried."

The tone of her voice set him on edge. "About what, sweetie?"

"Perry's son flew home today. He's staying out at the old Drake cabin."

"Yeah, I had a run in with him this afternoon."

"What happened?" Her tone struck a sharp chord.

"Just a parking violation, that's all. Try to calm down, will you?"

"You gave him a ticket?"

"No, it wasn't that big of a deal. The map is the important thing. We need to find it."

"Well, who's got the damn thing?"

He didn't need or want her bitchiness. "We can only hope Perry locked it away somewhere. If he's given the map to his son, that will complicate matters. The important thing is to keep calm and stay focused."

Nicole snickered. "Staying calm isn't my best quality, you know that."

Dillon held back his impatience. "Look, if you want a ten-figure fortune, then I suggest you get a handle on your emotions."

Nicole breathed into the phone. "Easier said than done; the map to the gold is not the only problem."

Dillon sensed she was on the verge of tears. "What do you mean?"

"Perry has an appointment with his attorney on Monday. I'm sure he will replace me in his will and give the estate to Michael."

Dillon pulled to the side the road and turned off the engine. The Drake fortune was worth at least seventy-five million, alone. "Do you think Perry is suspicious of us?"

"He's suspicious of everyone."

"I mean of you and me?"

"He's never singled you out or said anything about you."

Dillon smiled to himself. "Okay, I have a plan."

"Oh, really. What plan?"

"Not over the phone, baby. Let's have dinner tomorrow night. I'll take you to Dino's and tell you all about it."

When the conversation ended, Dillon realized he had his work cut out for him handling the Drake bitch.

As the sun fell behind the mountains, the headlights of Dillon's unmarked police car lit up the pot-holed road. Soon he would cross the threshold and enter the old ghost town. Chills coursed through his veins as he drove past the bullet-ridden sign that read, *Welcome to Rogue's Hollow.*

The population of criminals ran amuck, most of them after the buried gold. If the thugs found out he was a cop, he wouldn't live long enough to enjoy the money.

He turned onto a side road and parked out of sight in a woodsy area near the edge of town. The Boomtown Saloon was known for barroom brawls; no one thought twice about dropping a bullet into someone's gut. He figured the gold was worth the risk, but he needed to play it extra safe.

From under his black leather jacket, he slid his Beretta out of its shoulder holster and chambered the round. Good, the magazine was in place ready for any bastard who wanted a piece of him. He took off on foot in the direction of the saloon. The less anyone knew about his presence the better off he'd be. Everyone hated dirty cops, especially the bad guys.

Cody knew he was a cop, but Cody wasn't running from the law; he defended the ones who were. Cody was a rattlesnake, mean as they come. But smart. He got his degree in criminal law at Folsom Prison. The slippery bastard must have had something on the judge because somehow he outfoxed the legal establishment; they dropped the felony rape and drug charges so Cody could practice law in California. Dillon didn't trust the man, but he needed someone like Cody to come up with a scheme to help him outsmart Perry Drake.

He adjusted his black over-sized Stetson, hoping it helped conceal his identity and pushed through the swinging doors of the Boomtown Saloon. He stood near the door for a moment until his eyes adjusted to the darkness. The smell of mold and stale beer wreaked havoc with his allergies.

Damn-it, he thought, as he tried to resist the urge to sneeze. What a way to make an entrance. The sneeze of all sneezes irrupted from his gut. But the saloon was almost empty and no one seemed to notice.

Dog, the bartender wiped down the countertop as Dillon stepped up to the bar and ordered a draft. He wondered how the bartender got a name like Dog. He'd heard the guy was a real son-of-a-bitch—maybe that was the reason. "Is Cody around?"

"Who wants to know?"

"A friend."

"What do you want with Cody?"

"I'm supposed to meet him here, not that it's any of your business."

Dog placed his long snout into Dillon's face. "Look, you, in the big black cowboy hat with the purdy blond curls round yo neck. I don't know who you think you are. You don't give your name; you don't say your business. You don't say shit. This is my bar, and I run the show here! Get it?"

The guy had a pit-bull face with two black bullet shaped eyes, and Dillon pretty much figured where he got the name Dog.

"I told you, I'm a friend of Cody's. Isn't that enough?"

Dillon felt someone slide up next to him at the bar.

"Yo, Dog! He's with me."

Dog glared at Dillon, then walked down to the other end of the bar and grabbed a bottle of whiskey. "I'll fix your usual," he muttered.

Dillon stared at Cody, relieved. "I thought for a minute you weren't coming, man."

Cody's tanned face cracked a lopsided smile. "Don't mind Dog, he's a gentle lamb. The bouncer quit and all hell breaks loose in this place if he doesn't take control. Let's talk in private, over there." He pointed to a table at the back of the bar.

Dog brought Cody a bottle of whiskey and Dillon another draft. "On the house," he said as he lit the lantern on the small table. The semi-dark room brightened as they settled in.

Cody poured whiskey into a glass and took a swig. "Let's not waste time. Tell me about the map."

Dillon squinted at his new partner. "Not much to tell. It's a simple map leading to the buried gold."

Cody shot an intense stare. "Can you give me a little history? I heard rumors an old miser buried the gold in 1850, during the Gold Rush days."

"Right, an old miser named Goldie. He lived in the hills in a shack near here. It was rumored he had millions in gold he didn't cash in."

Cody arched his black brows. "Do you know who's got the map, now?"

"Yes, I know who's got the map. But before we go there, I'd like to talk about your cut of the payoff."

Cody took another swig of whiskey and set his glass down hard on the table. "It's a cool fifty percent."

This guy's off his rocker, Dillon thought. "Don't insult my intelligence." He got up and started for the door.

"Wait, what percent did you have in mind?"

Dillon turned to face him. "Twenty percent. Take it or leave it. I may throw in an extra five percent depending on how hard you work for it."

Cody studied Dillon for a few moments then nodded. "Okay, deal."

They shook hands. Dillon sat back at the table and downed his beer then signaled Dog for another.

Cody shifted his gaze to Dillon, his black eyes unshakable. "So who's got the map?"

"He's a high roller that lives in a mansion at Lakeport."

"What's his name?"

"Perry Drake."

"Yeah, seems I've heard of him. How'd he get his hands on the map?"

"That's a long story. Do you need to know that?"

"It's not important, just curious."

Dillon didn't want Cody or anyone to know how or why Drake had the map. The whole thing embarrassed him. The valued piece of paper had been in the Hobbs family for years. His grandpa was the cartographer for the old miser and had kept the document under lock-and-key for a couple decades. Before his grandpa died, he willed the map over to his pa. Before his pa croaked, he gave the map to Perry Drake. Dillon vowed he'd get back what was rightfully his.

"So, tell me about Perry Drake," Cody went on. "I understand you're banging his wife."

Dillon's jaw dropped. "How in the hell did you know?"

"Someone saw you together at Dino's. Word gets around. Suggest you be a little more discrete if you want to keep your love life a secret." Cody's lips parted in a half-smile.

"Damn!" Dillon wondered how many others knew about his affair with Nicole.

"Okay, back to Perry Drake. How sure are you he's got the map?"

Dillon paused a moment before he spoke. "Let's put it this way. I'm not as sure as I was before his son came into town."

Cody drummed his fingertips on the tabletop. "Then you don't know who's got the map, do you? Could be the son, could be the old man—could be ghost riders in the sky. What do you mean till his son came to town?"

"I'm saying there's a slight chance Drake gave the map to his son."

"Slight chance? Well, I don't like surprises. What's his son's name? Where does he live?"

Dillon held back the urge to punch Cody's wise-ass face. "His name's Michael Drake. He was discharged from the Marines and flew home today. He's staying out at an old cabin by the lake, about ten miles from here."

"Aren't you even a little worried this may complicate things?"

Dillon felt like he'd just stepped into a big piece of shit and wondered how he could shake it off. He finally said, "He's just a young punk. What's the problem?"

"He's a jarhead, fresh out of Afghanistan, that's the problem. He's a killing machine. And you'd better hope this young punk, as you call him, doesn't get possession of the map." Cody knocked back a shot of whiskey. "I'm thinking we ought to kill him tonight and get it over with. Save us grief."

"You're not serious?"

He didn't answer, but Dillon sensed he sat across from a man who wouldn't blink an eye at murder. "He's not much of a threat. He's lame. A helicopter crash left him with a wounded leg. I saw a cane in his jeep when I stopped him today for illegally parking on the side of the road."

"A leg injury won't hold back a good Marine. They have their ways."

Dillon squinted at Cody and downed his beer. "I think you're wasting time worrying about nothing."

Cody stared hard at Dillon. "I hope you're right."

Dillon leaned into Cody. "Let's focus on Perry Drake and forget about his son. We can always set up plan B and resort to it if we need to."

"I'll go along with plan B if it means we kill the little prick the minute he enters the picture."

Dillon shook his head. "Look, I know it's a crapshoot but come on, let's outsmart the bastards, and leave murder as last resort."

They remained silent a few moments, avoiding eye contact. Cody finally said, "The first thing you need to do is follow Perry Drake and check out his habits. Follow him everywhere he goes. And since you're tight with his wife, find out if she knows anything about the map; maybe a safe deposit box at a bank or a lockbox in the mansion. Check all that out then let's meet back here on Monday."

Dillon thought about Perry's appointment on Monday with his attorney. If Perry named Michael as beneficiary and left Nicole with nothing, then this affected the status of the Drake Estate, as well as the map. He'd keep his lips sealed for now. "I have personal business to take care of Monday. Let's try for Tuesday."

Cody nodded. "Okay, Tuesday." He pushed aside his empty whiskey glass and signaled Dog for another round.

The place filled up. Billiard balls crashed and split apart as Johnny Cash hit the airwaves with Folsom Prison Blues. The song reminded Dillon he was in a saloon filled with people who would sell their own mother for a price, and it would serve him well to watch his back.

He figured he wasn't much better than the lowlife in this bar. If his pa knew he'd turned dirty, he'd kick up dust from the grave. But growing up wasn't easy knowing you were the big joke in the family. Even today, he felt the shame. His pa and brothers were tough lawmen with sun-baked skin and muscular bodies. Dillon had dimples, blond curls, and blue eyes, just like his ma. Even after he grew a thick mustache, his kinfolk still considered him a pretty boy.

He gazed across the room through a haze of cigarette and marijuana smoke. A tall skinny dude with heavy black brows stood out—he couldn't quite place him. He watched the guy chalk his cue stick and lean over the billiard table for a shot. His long dyed hair hung over his face in strands of red and black.

Then the name Red Robin popped into his head. How could he forget? They called him Red Rob. He was an ex-con from Soledad Prison. Dillon had put the guy away for drug smuggling and domestic violence—a mean son-of-a-bitch, who almost killed his own girlfriend. Yeah, Dillon recalled, that was back when he took the job of sheriff to heart.

"You seem on edge." Cody's black brows wedged together. "How about a game of pool to take your mind off things?"

"Nah, I gotta go." Dillon guzzled his beer and rose to his feet.

"Hey, I just ordered us another round. Come on, kick back."

Dillon kept an eye on Red Rob and ignored Cody's offer. "Got any preference where we meet next week?"

Cody looked around the saloon as he spoke. "What's wrong with right here? This joint's got everything—booze, broads. Okay, so the broads are whores, but they ain't bad once a man's liquored up. And it's private. Ain't nobody going to get past Dog." His lips curled into a smile. "Don't you like it here? Or maybe you're just afraid one of the ex-cons you put away might recognize you. Is that it?" His laugh had an irritating edge to it.

Dillon didn't answer the obvious.

"Okay, have it your way. Let's meet at my trailer out on the edge of town. You can't miss it parked next to my red pickup truck."

Dillon nodded and stared at the sawdust on the floor. "Fine."

"I'll see you Tuesday, man," Cody said. "But remember, the minute the Marine shows signs of butting in, he's a dead man. If killing ain't your style, just leave it to me, I'll handle it."

Dillon didn't answer and headed for the back exit. The more he thought about it, the more he realized taking Cody on as a partner might prove to be the worst decision of his life.

CHAPTER 5

NICOLE PRIMPED AND twirled and dropped her lace negligee to the floor. The mirror didn't lie. Not one wrinkle since cosmetic surgery. No traces of sag or flab in her nude reflection. At age forty, Nicole Drake had the face and body of a twenty-year-old.

The tap at her bedroom door came as no surprise. Maggie Fellows, her secretary, on time with the morning paper and the day's schedule.

She slipped back into her negligee and sat on the edge of the bed. "Come in," she called and watched Maggie head for the drapes to let the morning sun fill the room. "Not yet, Maggie, I'm not quite ready for the light. Would you make a pot of coffee first?"

"Of course, Miss Drake, as you wish." Maggie made a quick detour into the small kitchenette off the bedroom.

Nicole had things on her mind—private things. Things she couldn't share with anyone. Perry's phone conversation with Michael gave her good reason to worry.

For years, the mere mention of Michael had thrown Perry into a rage. This was the son he never wanted to see again—the son he had disowned. Now, everything had changed. Perry's thoughts centered on

Michael, the Marine, the hero. Michael could do no wrong, and she was sick of it.

Her cell phone rang, and Dillon's picture smiled at her from the screen. They had a dinner date for later that evening. Calling her at the mansion was off limits.

She placed the phone to her ear. "Hello, Dillon?"

"Sweetie, are you alone?" The minute his voice came on the line she relaxed. Everything about Dillon pleased her. The sex was almost as good as Perry before he got old and sick.

She stretched her body out on the bed and propped her head with one arm. "No, I'm not alone. My secretary is in the kitchenette making coffee. You know it's dangerous to call me here. If you must, call back a little later."

Perry had found out about her little fling with the chauffeur and paid him to leave the country. Poor Kurt had no idea about Perry's wrath. She wanted to spare Dillon the same end.

"So you can't talk now?" Dillon asked.

She spoke in a whispered tone. "I can't take the chance. Maggie may be listening as we speak—Perry has spies."

"All right, let's meet at noon. I have something important to discuss with you."

"At Dino's?"

"No, Dino's is off limits. Someone spotted us there. We need to be careful. Let's meet in Two Lakes at The Hungry Bear. The restaurant is private and out of town."

"I know the place. I'll be there."

After she hung up, she smiled. Her body tingled with passion. Since Perry's illness, he offered little in the way of sexual pleasure. Things hadn't been the same between them for a long time. No parties on the yacht. No wining and dining at high-class restaurants. No expensive gifts, like the BMW she'd received on Valentine's Day. She hadn't counted on him finding out about her chauffeur. Now, she had the distinct feeling Perry intended to disinherit her from his will.

She grabbed her rag dolls and curled up in a fetal position. She held their frayed bodies close to her heart and rocked back-and-forth. Nobody would take away her dream. Nobody. Not now. Not ever.

She'd gone to great lengths to keep her dream alive. She even helped poor Ida out of her misery. Perry might not be grateful if he knew about the mercy killing. He may not understand that placing the pillow over his wife's face was an act of kindness. The old gal had been comatose for months after her car accident. Nicole just speeded things along.

Besides, with Ida out of the picture, I could become Mrs. Perry Drake and claim my right to the mansion and the wealth.

She hugged her ragdoll's tight as she thought of her latest affair with Dillon. He was an attractive man, but she'd stop seeing him if things got too risky. She'd be damned if she'd allow the Drake fortune to be inherited by Michael or anyone but her. Her attempts to drive Perry nuts only pushed him closer to Michael. *Too bad the rat poison didn't kill him.*

She laid her ragdolls aside and sat poised on the edge of the bed. Maggie brought in coffee and sweet rolls and read the day's schedule. "Since today is Saturday your schedule is fairly simple. All you have to do is pick up the art for the Drake Missing Children's Fundraiser. The exhibition is held next week."

Nicole gave Maggie a sober look. Shooting orders at her secretary gave Nicole simple pleasure. Her tone was autocratic. "Call Big Ben. Have him pick up antique sculptures and oil paintings at the lake cabin for the children's fundraiser. I'm sure the Drake forefathers would be delighted to have their art used for a good cause."

"Yes ma'am, I'll call Big Ben right away." Maggie flipped her long dark hair behind her ear. "Is there anything else?"

"Yes, the exhibition is an all-day affair served with champagne and hors d'oeuvres. You are in charge. Make sure you order the finest. Then, report back to me."

"Yes, ma'am."

"That will be all." Nicole stared at Maggie coldly. "By the way…"

"Yes, ma'am?"

"After this, wear your hair pulled back in a bun. I don't like the looks of your long tresses. And get rid of that pink rose in your lapel. You work for me, just remember that." She held Maggie's gaze for a moment. "That will be all."

Maggie lowered her eyes. "Yes, ma'am."

After Maggie left, Nicole dressed in blue jeans and an aqua-colored silk blouse. She wore her favorite diamond rings and bracelets, with a jeweled belt at her waist. When she slipped into her black stiletto sandals, she looked like a young model. Roberto's beauty salon was down the hall of the third floor. She had just enough time for a brush-out before she drove across town to meet her lover.

€€€

Nicole removed her sunglasses and pushed through the doors of The Hungry Bear restaurant. Once her eyes adjusted to the dark, she spotted Dillon sitting at a small table near a stone fireplace. She loved how he rose from his chair the minute he saw her. A man's ardent attention seemed to go to the core of her being. Her psychiatrist told her it was part of her sexual compulsive disorder.

She strode up to him, licked her lips and smiled.

He kissed her neck and helped her get seated. "You look ravishing."

She gazed at him over the top of a lighted candle. Just being in his presence aroused her.

"What would you like to drink, my love? Your usual Martini?" He reached for her hand across the table.

The warmth of his touch sent shivers through her body to her groin. She flipped her long, blond hair back with the tips of her fingers. "Yes, make it a double, with two olives. I need to unwind."

Dillon flagged the waiter and ordered their drinks.

Nicole liked the way he took charge—she needed that in a man.

Dillon's blue eyes questioned her. "I take it you're stressed. Why so troubled?"

"I'm worried about what Perry will do when he meets with his attorney."

"Do you think he will write you out of his will?"

"Yes, I think so. He's a powerful man and usually gets what he wants. He accused me of having an affair with the chauffeur. I haven't seen poor Kurt since Perry paid him off to leave the country."

"Were you having an affair with the chauffeur?"

She kept a straight face. "Of course not; I'd hate to think what Perry would do if he found out about you and me."

Dillon took a drink of his Scotch. "That's what I wanted to talk to you about."

"You mean about Perry?"

"Yes, Perry. We need to talk about what to do with him. He's big trouble."

"What to do with him? What are you suggesting, murder?" She was glad he brought up the subject. Now she'd let him take the reins.

Dillon looked around. He spoke in a whispered tone. "Quiet, someone may hear you. Yes, to put it bluntly. Somehow, we need to make him ride off into the sunset and never return."

Their drinks arrived. Nicole downed her Martini and reordered another double.

After a few moments of silence, Dillon reached for her hand. "Does Perry have a wall-safe at the mansion?"

Nicole felt titillating vibes. "Yes, it's behind a painting in the library."

His brows shot up. "Do you have access to the combination?"

"No, he's never shared that with me?"

"Have you ever heard him discuss a map that leads to buried gold?"

"He's never talked to me about it, but I've overheard things."

Dillon leaned forward. "What kind of things?"

"His sister and the butler are privileged—he trusts them and tells them everything. I overheard him informing them about a map."

Dillon spoke in a hushed tone. "That's the map I want to get my hands on."

"He told them he may hand the map over to Michael for safe keeping."

"Damn! That complicates things."

"Michael also stands to inherit the Drake fortune if Perry has a mind to write me out of the will."

"We need to act fast."

"What do you think we should do?"

"Don't worry, sweetie, I'll take care of everything."

CHAPTER 6

DILLON SAT AT the bar in Big Red's Saloon with a watchful eye on the door. He was surprised Perry had agreed to meet him at a place with a reputation for bar brawls and sleazy women.

But, if he remembered right, Perry had a thing for wild, crazy behavior. He couldn't have been married to Nicole without it. In fact, Nicole had bragged several times about having sex with Perry in elevators and risky places where they might get caught. She said the risk added to the excitement. According to Nicole, all they did the first few years was fuck around in out-of-the-way places.

Even for Dillon, she was over the edge when it came to her sexual appetite. He would handle her as long as he needed to. The map that led to the gold was top priority. After he got his hands on the gold, he'd dump her.

His pa had trusted Perry enough to give him the map for safe keeping. So Dillon figured Perry would trust him enough to talk about old times and open up after a few drinks. The guy wasn't stupid—just older now and perhaps a little demented, which comes with age.

Murder was the last resort, but the plan was in the works. If Dillon didn't place a call to Cody by 11:00 pm., Cody would plant the bomb in Perry's car.

He ordered another draft and lit a stogy. Then he saw the tall, refined-looking man enter the saloon. In some ways, Perry favored Sean Connery in his later years. But in Dillon's mind, Perry was past his prime, far too old for Nicole.

He signaled, and Perry walked toward him. Dillon rose and reached for a handshake that wound up so painful he wondered if the bones in his hand were still intact. Dillon kept a stoic demeanor, but when Perry let go, Dillon let out a relieved sigh, hoping he didn't show the hurt too much.

He clenched his fists and tried to hold back his anger. "That's some handshake you've got there."

"Sorry," Perry said. "Sometimes I don't know my own strength."

Dillon rubbed his fingers and had the feeling Perry wasn't the least bit sorry. He pointed to a booth at the far end of the saloon. "Mind if we sit over there? It's quiet."

"Fine." Perry led the way.

As they settled in the booth, Dillon detected anger in Perry's eyes. *He must know something.*

"Hello, boys. Hold on a moment while I light your fire." The cocktail waitress leaned over and lit their candle. "Now, what can I get for you?"

"I'll have scotch on the rocks." Dillon glanced at Perry. "How about you?"

Perry rutted his brow as he eyed Dillon. "I'll have a draft."

"So how's everything going? Are you still into stock car racing?" Dillon asked, thinking he'd start with something they both had in common at one time.

The long span of silence made Dillon uncomfortable. He offered Perry a cigar.

Perry shook his head and reached into his pocket for a cigarette. "No thanks, I don't smoke cigars."

The waitress brought their drinks and Dillon paid the tab. Damn, he thought, where do I go from here? The guy just stares at me. He decided to try light talk. "It's great to meet up with you again after all these years." The minute he spoke, he realized it sounded phony.

Perry fired up a cigarette before he spoke. "Okay, let's cut the bullshit. What I can't figure is why you invited me here tonight. Did you think I'd fall for that crap about long-lost buddies?"

Dillon's voice had a sudden edge that took on a tone of authority. He'd practiced it many times on the criminals he'd arrested. "What do you mean? We raced cars together, played pool together, bet on the ponies. You were a little older than me—kinda like a father figure. We used to be friends."

"Let's get to the bottom line, asshole. I know all about you and my wife."

"I'm not sure I follow."

Perry took a drag off his cigarette and squashed the butt out in the ashtray. "I'm sure you follow just fine. Try to be more discreet next time. You're too easy."

Dillon felt the undertones of Perry's wrath. He'd let him have the floor. "If you've got something on your chest, go ahead, get rid of it, I'm listening." He ordered another scotch, lit a cigar and kept quiet.

"This conversation won't last long because I only have one thing to say. Listen and listen well. Nicole is not getting one penny of Drake money." Perry leaned across the table, his eyes dark pits. "And neither are you, lover boy."

Dillon stayed calm. "I assure you, I am not interested in your money."

Perry rose to leave. "Well, that's good because as of tomorrow Nicole will be penniless."

Dillon followed Perry out the door and watched him walk to his car. He checked his watch. 11:10 P.M. As soon as Perry drove off, Dillon reached for his phone and punched in Cody Roark's number. "Did you plant it?"

"Yeah, the job's done. He'll feel it right about Peak's Cliff."

Dillon snapped off the phone and rubbed his fingers.

That's the last time that bastard will ever shake hands with anyone.

CHAPTER 7

THE MORNING SUN sprayed golden red patterns over the surface of Lake Crystal as Michael sat on the front porch of the cabin and took a sip of freshly brewed coffee. He listened to the faint sounds of wildlife in the nearby woods—a nice change from the battle cries of war.

In a few hours, he'd hang out with his father. They'd fish off the side of the houseboat. He promised to place his anger on hold and view the old man from a fresh perspective. In spite of their shaky past, he found himself wanting to bond.

His stomach growled, reminding him he hadn't eaten much since he returned home. He walked inside the cabin to the pantry and dug around in the freezer. When he wasn't gunning down Taliban in Afghanistan, he dreamed of sinking his teeth into pepperoni pizza slathered with mozzarella—one dream he didn't mind coming home to.

As he delved through the frozen food locker, a faint cry in the distance tweaked his attention. He could have sworn he heard the sound of a whimpering child coming from under the pantry floor.

He found a flashlight on top of the freezer, pushed aside the oval braided rug on the pantry floor and discovered a hidden trapdoor. The soft cries became louder as he raised the hinged cover. A blast of cold, musty air hit him in the face like a smelly meat locker—just enough to trigger the reek of burnt bodies.

One by one, his buddy's faces appeared and disappeared into the black hollowness of death. He slammed down the trapdoor and for the next hour the pantry floor became a Marine's battlefield of horror.

Little by little, as his head cleared, he recalled the war zones in Afghanistan. How he'd walked for miles in wind and sand in a desert filled with IED bombs. How he'd gunned down Taliban from the door of a Cobra Helicopter. Questions flooded his mind... *after all you've been through, are you going to let a little door in the floor panic you? What would your buddies think? They'd call you a Marine who can't perform under pressure. They'd call you a wimped out jarhead.*

He raised the lid. The same musty cold air blasted him in the face—this time he sucked it up—this time he peered down into the black opening belowground. He slipped the flashlight into the pocket of his windbreaker, hooked his cane over one arm, and ignored the familiar pain in his leg as he lowered himself down the ladder stairway.

Darkness hemmed in around him as he flashed light about the room in search of a wall switch. He picked up obscure glimpses of what appeared to be rows of dusty wine bottles tucked into little grooves. He leaned against a shelf with vessels that poked him in the ribs. His cane kept him steady. Unless he could find more light, he promised himself this little journey would end soon.

What can go wrong, will go wrong, he thought, as his flashlight flickered and died. Noise from across the room fueled his adrenalin and his combative drive kicked in—he stood motionless.

There it was again, louder this time. *Maybe a rat?* He waited for another sound. Nothing came.

Like a blind man, he tapped his way through the dark in search of a light switch. Something strange tickled his nose. *A crawling insect? A spider?* "What the hell?" He swiped at the air grabbing at nothing. "Damn-it, get off me!"

Then he touched what felt like a chain to a light fixture hanging in front of his face. He pulled on it. "Oorah, light up my life!"

As his eyes grew accustomed to the brightness, he squinted at the small figure standing in front of him.

A kid of about twelve, gripping a wine bottle stood ready to strike. "Stay back!" he warned.

After his initial surprise, Michael spoke to the boy. "Hey, come on young man, lay down your arms, I won't hurt you."

The boy cringed and stepped back, prepared lash out with his weapon. Michael figured the kid had stowed away in the wine cellar for a couple days. "You look like maybe you haven't eaten in a while. How about some grub?"

The boy's eyes flickered.

"Hungry, huh; thirsty too, I bet?"

He nodded—his jaw clenched.

"I'll put some food together for us. I'm hungry too. But first lay down the wine bottle, okay."

"Okay, but don't hurt me," he said, setting the bottle on the floor.

"Thanks, that's better. Of course, I won't hurt you. Now, tell me what you're doing down here?"

He pointed overhead. "Somebody locked the trapdoor."

"And you just happened to be down here, is that it?"

"Well, no, I was hiding down here."

"Hiding? Who were you hiding from?"

The boy shook his head. "I don't know; whoever locked the trapdoor. I got stuck down here, and there was no way out."

Michael saw the kid held back tears. "That's not too cool is it, to be stuck down in a wine cellar?"

"No, it's not." The boy wiped his runny nose on his dirty t-shirt sleeve. "I need to get home. My gran will be worried."

"Let's get some chow, follow me." The boy whizzed past Michael, scaled the ladder, leaving him in the dust.

Topside, Michael handed the boy bottled water and sat him on a stool in the pantry while he rummaged through the freezer. He glanced over at the boy. "You like pepperoni pizza?"

The kid nodded between gulps of water.

Michael dug out two pizza pies. "Come on, let's sit in the kitchen. Grab a chair." Michael popped the pizza in the microwave, then opened two cold root beers and set them on the table.

The boy guzzled down his drink and burped. "Excuse me."

"Taste good, huh?"

He nodded and smiled shyly.

Michael opened another soda and handed it to him. They sat at the kitchen table in silence while they ate. Then Michael served ice cream with chocolate fudge syrup and nuts.

"Okay, what's your name?"

The boy looked up at Michael as he ate the last bite of his ice cream. "They call me Nash, short for Nashoba. I'm a half-breed from the Muwekma Ohlone Tribe."

"Who's they?"

"My grandmother and the shaman elders."

"Why were you locked in the wine cellar?"

His brow wrinkled, and he spoke with conviction. "Someone locked the little door and caused me to get stuck down there like a prisoner."

"Is this one of your usual hangouts? Why were you in the wine cellar in the first place?"

He didn't answer. His big brown eyes revealed nothing. "I have to go now. My gran worries." He got up to leave. "Thank you for feeding me. I'll pay you back."

"Hey, not so fast. You can't just run out and not tell me where you live—it's not polite." Michael locked eyes with the boy. "Can we be friends?"

"Yes."

"Okay, friends help friends. You owe me nothing."

"I live up the road." He gestured toward Rogue's Hollow.

"You mean in the old ghost town?"

Nash nodded. "Have you ever heard of Heoma?"

"No, can't say I have. Is that a person?"

"My grandmother. She is Heoma, Medicine Woman. She'll be worried, I gotta go now."

Before Michael could answer, the boy disappeared.

€€€

Michael sat on the porch and waited for his father. He checked his watch. It was past Noon.

One o'clock came, two o'clock. He waited and watched the dirt road in the distance for any vehicle. Old feelings of rejection mounted.

Surely the old man wouldn't forget…

At three o'clock, he'd just about given up when a Mercedes drove by—stirred up dust—then circled back and pulled into the driveway. Michael squinted to see who it could be. It didn't look like a car his dad would drive.

The Mercedes sat idle for a minute in the driveway. Then the door on the driver's side opened and Aunt Jo got out of the car. Bruno slid out on the passenger side. Michael's gut said something was wrong. He hurried over to them. Jo walked up to Michael and wrapped her arms around him. "So glad you're home."

"Good to see you, Aunt Jo." He stood back and studied their faces. "What's going on? Where's my father?"

Jo clasped her hand in Michael's big mitt. "Let's go sit on the porch. I'd like a glass of water."

They sat at the redwood table on the front deck. Michael served Aunt Jo ice water and Bruno cold beer

"Where is he?"

Jo swallowed and took a deep breath. "Your father…"

Michael arched his brows. "What's happened to my father?"

"Well, we don't know for sure, but—"

"Damn it, Aunt Jo. No disrespect, but please spit it out?"

"What she's trying to say," Bruno broke in, "is that your father's car crashed over the guardrail at Peaks Cliff."

"Well, damn…" Michael shook his head—tears welled in his eyes. He was silent a moment, then pounded on the redwood table. "Damn it all to hell!"

"The thing is," Bruno went on, "There's no sign of his body."

Michael's eyes widened. "Then he must be alive."

"That's what we hope," Jo said.

Bruno rutted his bushy brows. "But, it's best not to jump to conclusions. His body may have been thrown from the vehicle into the lake. We just don't know…"

"Any sign of foul play?"

"The police are ruling it an accident until further investigation." Bruno shook his head in disbelief. "They think he may have fallen asleep at the wheel on his way home from Big Red's Saloon."

"That dump? That's not a place my dad would hang out. Who said he was there?"

"The police reported him leaving the place around eleven last night," Jo said.

"Sounds suspicious," Michael said. "My father may be guilty of raunchy behavior, but one thing I know about him—he would not hang out at Big Red's Saloon. Not unless he had good reason to be there. Back when I was a crazy kid, I knew enough to stay away from the place."

Jo nodded. "All we know is what the police tell us."

"I'll check it out."

"Be careful," Jo said.

"Aunt Jo, I just got back from fighting a war in Afghanistan. I have a Black Belt in Karate. Do I look like I can't take care of myself?"

"No, but I'm concerned about your injured leg."

"My leg is fine."

"You don't have a phone here at the cabin. We need to keep in touch."

"I'll get a cell phone."

Jo reached into her purse, dug out her cell phone and handed it to Michael. "Take this one."

"That's okay, I'll get one tomorrow."

Jo smiled. "Just take it until you get one."

"If it makes you happy." Michael took the phone and stuck it in his jacket pocket. "Always looking out for me, aren't you?" He patted her hand gently.

"Someone has to." She stood and kissed him on the forehead.

"Before you go, Dad said something about his wife—I believe her name is Nicole?"

"Ah, yes. The Vamp, we call her." Jo sat back down.

"She lives at the mansion, right?"

"Yes, the whole third floor is hers—hers and her entourage."

"Who's her entourage?"

"Several people come to mind," Jo said, looking over at Bruno for help.

Bruno smiled dryly. "There's Maggie Fellows, her secretary—more like a gofer. There's Roberto her hair stylist. Then there's Big Ben Kowalski, her bodyguard—brute of a man. I'd hate to tangle with the bloke."

"Do they live at the mansion?"

"Yes, they have their own rooms on the third floor with baths and kitchenettes built at Nicole's request."

"Don't forget, Kurt Redding, the chauffeur," Jo added.

"The chauffeur is no longer in the picture," Bruno said. "Perry became suspicious that Nicole was having an affair with the chap.

Next thing we know, poof, Kurt vanishes. Your father can be very persuasive if you know what I mean."

Michael nodded. "Yeah, I know what you mean—probably offered him an ultimatum he couldn't refuse, like get the hell out of Dodge or your ass is dead."

Michael remembered the conversation he'd had with his father on the plane trip home; *this bastard's been screwing my wife, trying to weasel his way into my money. He's also the sheriff of Three Lakes County.*

"Do either of you know if Nicole is sleeping with anyone else now?"

Bruno shook his head. "She probably is, but with whom, I couldn't say."

Jo rolled her eyes. "I've seen her sneak out late at night a few times. It's a big mystery."

Michael recalled the sheriff that pulled him over on his way up to the cabin. "I think I know who our mystery man is."

Jo and Bruno spoke in unison, "Who?"

"I'll tell you when I'm sure."

CHAPTER 8

THE FOLLOWING MORNING, Michael practiced Tai Chi on a knoll near the shore of the lake. The pain in his leg subsided and more mobility returned as he focused on each designated move

Later, he sat on the ground, leaned against an aspen tree and relaxed into a sleepy state of mind. When Aunt Jo's cell phone rang, he hated to break the spell.

He grabbed the phone from his jacket pocket and placed it to his ear. "Yeah, Michael here."

"Hey, how's my handsome Marine?"

Michael's heart hammered against his ribs. "Who's calling?"

"Come on, Michael, you know who this is." The catch in her throat always turned him on.

Michael sat up straight, pushed back his feelings and gained control. "How did you get this number?"

"One of your old friends said your Aunt Jo gave him the number. I didn't think you'd mind." Her tone was low and subtle.

Images of moonlit nights on the shore of the lake flashed across his mind. He wanted to cut her off. "What do you want?"

"Oh, just to say hi for old-time sake."

There it was again, the catch in her throat. He swallowed hard. "There's no old-time sake between us. At least nothing I want to remember."

"My, how you've changed." She laughed in her sultry way. "Not even a little bit?"

"No. Don't call again!" He snapped off the phone as words from her Dear John letter burned in his brain. *Sorry, Mikey, I've found someone new* The women of his dreams—his first love—turned out to be a bitch.

Love and hate mingled in his mind like yin and yang smoldering on an open flame. He tried to regain his relaxed state of mind, but everywhere he looked, he saw Trisha.

Colorful patterns and shapes danced across the water reminding him of how they made love under the stars—how they awakened to the sun on the horizon and made love all over again. When she learned he'd been disowned by his father and no longer in the Drake will, she dumped him for an ugly dude who had tons of money.

His father's sobering words by Gandhi, came to mind: *It's about greed, son. Earth provides enough to satisfy every man's need—but not every man's greed.* Or woman's, Michael thought. Seems everyone wanted Drake money, including Trisha.

He needed to get her out of his head. He walked over to the houseboat. His dad must have hired people to keep the vessel in tip-top shape. It appeared in excellent condition. He stepped up on the deck and recalled his father's instructions: *The blower should always run for a few minutes until all gas odors have left the engine compartment.* Michael started the blower, then stood at the helm and reached for the binoculars.

Crisp blue water rippled against purple and red flowers as he scanned the area across the lake. He had almost forgotten the beauty of nature as images of war-torn Afghanistan flashed across his mind.

Then he saw movement and magnified the binoculars. She plunged off the large rock—the same flat rock he used to swim to and play on when he was a kid.

Her beauty took his breath away as she climbed up on the rock and dried her wet body with a yellow towel. Her long, wet hair hung down her back in auburn ringlets. Her body glowed in the sun like a tanned enchantress. Thoughts of Trisha disappeared like a falling star.

Criminals from the nearby ghost town often traipsed through the woods. A dangerous place for a woman to be alone, he thought. Then he noticed her horse tied to a limb and the leather scabbard with the rifle poking its head out. He smiled. Maybe she'd blow their brains out if they messed with her.

She strolled over to her horse and gave him a pat and a treat. Then turned and gazed across the lake in his direction. She couldn't see him with the naked eye at such a distance—still, he felt awkward. No doubt she sensed someone watching.

€€€

After a hot shower, he studied his face in the mirror. He wondered if the girl on the rock would find him attractive. In the interest of sex appeal, maybe he'd get rid of the high-and-tight haircut and let his hair shag around the edges of his neck. He tried to smile at his reflection. But all he saw were two icy brown eyes staring back. Somehow he found it difficult to get past his anger—even to smile.

He dressed in jeans and a blue polo shirt, then put on tennis shoes, grabbed his cane and headed out the door.

He'd check with the police first to locate his dad's crash site. Then, time to pay a little visit to the lady on the third floor of the Drake mansion.

ϵϵϵ

Michael pushed through the oak doors of the Lakeport Police Department. At the far end of the corridor, he saw a police clerk with a fat neck and droopy eyes sitting behind protective Plexiglas. Michael laughed to himself. Maybe he's expecting The Terminator.

He strode up to the window. After a good three minutes, the clerk shifted his gaze toward Michael. "Yeah, what can I do for you?"

"I'd like to speak to the detectives handling the Perry Drake case."

"Who wants to know?"

"Michael Drake, his son."

The clerk cut Michael a hard stare, then reached for the phone and punched in a number. "There's a guy here who claims to be Perry Drake's son." He paused a minute. "Okay, fine." He hung up and pushed his glasses up on his nose. "Your identification card?"

Michael reached for his wallet in his back pocket, slipped out his military ID, and shoved it through the small opening of the Plexiglas.

The clerk bit the flesh of his bottom lip and scowled at the photo. "I thought you looked familiar. You were here a few years ago up on drug charges, weren't you?"

Michael wondered how the guy could remember a face from seven years back. "The charges were dropped."

"Yeah, amazing what a little money will do. Looks like the military straightened you out."

Michael envisioned his fingers wrapped around the guy's throat, squeezing the oxygen from his rotund body.

The clerk's eyes widened as if he felt Michael's wrath. He lowered his head and quickly handed back the identification card. "Detective Fox will be out to see you in a moment."

Michael took a seat on an orange, hardback chair against the wall. He tried to focus on his father's disappearance; but a chill ran through his body as he recalled the pain of being disowned, and the fact that his dad never stuck around long enough to learn the drug charges were bogus.

He could still see the shitty hang jaw expression on the drug officer's face when he admitted to Michael they had arrested him in error.

He would never give up the seven years he'd spent in the Marine Corps—not for all the money in his father's bank account. But when the old man forced him to join the military at age seventeen, he felt the same fear a stray dog must feel when hauled off to the pound.

Michael's stomach growled. The peanut butter on toast wasn't enough to stick to his ribs. Ten minutes later a tough looking cop of about forty with graying sideburns and leathery skin walked toward him. The business suit he wore of charcoal-gray with a maroon colored tie did not cover up his aura of cop persona.

He held out his hand to Michael. "Hello, I understand you're Perry Drake's son. I'm Detective John Fox with homicide."

"Homicide?" Michael rose to his feet and shook his hand. "Then my father was murdered?"

Fox lowered his voice. "As you probably know we haven't found a body yet. We're covering all bases. There's a possibility of foul play. Come to my office, and we can talk in private."

The detective led Michael into a room filled with file cabinets, two desks cluttered with papers, and two computers. "Have a seat." He pointed to a side chair next to his desk. "Can I get you water, coffee?"

"No thanks." Michael sat down.

The detective poured coffee for himself from the pot across the room, then pulled a folder from a cabinet and took a seat at his desk. His expression showed little emotion as he thumbed through the file and took a sip of coffee.

He reminded Michael of an older version of his drill sergeant in the Marine Corp. His voice had a flat impersonal tone. "I'd like to ask you a few questions."

"Fine." Michael thought; he'd like to ask questions too. Like where in hell was the location of the crash site? That's what he came for—not to take a vacation.

"When did you last see your father?"

"Friday, two days ago—we flew home together on his jet from Los Angeles. We planned on meeting Saturday and go fishing."

"Did your father give you any kind of hint he felt threatened by anyone?"

Michael didn't want to divulge too much. His father told him plenty in confidence. The stakes were too high to let it all out until he knew who he could trust. "We hardly had a chance to talk. I hadn't seen him in seven years. Like I said, we were going to meet Saturday, take in a little fishing and talk about old times."

"I understand your dad cut you off."

Michael's jaw tightened. His brown eyes grew darker. "What do you mean, cut me off?"

"Shall I draw you a picture? I mean—wrote you out of his will."

Michael stood and gave the detective a fixed stare. "This questioning session ends right now."

"Sit down! I'm not through!"

"You're through as far as I'm concerned."

"Look, we treat everyone like a suspect—especially family members."

Michael folded his arms across his chest. "Are you saying you think I killed my father?"

"I'm saying I don't know. Your father may be walking around alive somewhere, for all I know."

Michael's nostril's flared. "I came here to find out the location of the crash site and any clues, like blood at the scene. But I don't need you. I can read the daily newspaper and find out that information."

"Sit down, and I'll pour you a cup of coffee."

"Don't placate me—you've wasted enough of my time." Michael turned to go.

"Wait, maybe we can help each other solve this thing." Fox wrote on a notepad and handed it to Michael. "That's the location of the crash site. Meet me there at 3:00 P.M. today. I don't usually do this, but it's better than having you stumbling around out there on your own, screwing up evidence."

"I don't stumble around." Michael snatched the note from Fox's hand.

"No, I'm sure you don't. You're fresh out of the Marine Corps, right?"

"That's right. Gunnery Sergeant, Afghanistan. "

"Takes one to know one." The detective smiled. "Semper fi."

Michael pointed at Fox. "You?"

"Desert Storm, 1991."

"Well, I'll be damned." Michael laughed. "I might have known the way you were barking orders."

"So let's meet at the crash site and go from there. Sound like a plan?"

"I'll be there." Cool, Michael thought. You could always count on a Marine to watch the back of another Marine.

Fox gave Michael a knowing grin. "One more thing… If Afghanistan was anything like Iraq, memories can play hell with your head. How are you doing in the stress department? After I came home from the Persian Gulf, it took me over a year to stop fighting the war."

Michael stared at Fox not knowing how to answer—the words stuck in his throat.

"That's okay," Fox went on, "no need to explain." He reached for a business card on his desk and handed it to Michael. "I facilitate a group of Marines who suffer from Post Traumatic Stress Disorder. If you ever feel the need to talk, just drop in—you are welcome anytime. We meet once a week."

Michael tucked the card into the zippered pocket of his jacket. He turned to leave, swallowing back something in his gut he didn't understand. "See you at the crash site."

CHAPTER 9

MICHAEL PARKED BEHIND a black Mercedes Benz, grabbed his cane, and slid out of the Jeep. The eighteenth-century statue of Timothy R. Drake appeared majestic as it stood near a waterfall within the circular drive of the Drake Mansion. Michael laughed to himself and wondered if the present generation met the elite status of the Drake name.

He found it hard to believe only a few years back he called the place home sweet home. Swallowing back nostalgia, he remembered climbing the walls of the mansion after all night boozing and weed parties on Big John's yacht. Aunt Jo seemed to possess a sixth sense about his activities and chewed his ass out more than once.

He walked toward the rose garden where Bruno kept the spare key hidden in a red flower pot. Then he stopped in his tracks. After all this time, how could he stroll into the house as if seven years of his life had never existed? He climbed the steps of the mansion and rang the doorbell.

Within a few seconds, Bruno answered. "Michael, what in bloody hell are you doing ringing the doorbell?"

He needed to take it slow. This is where Nora, his stepmother died. This is where love ended and emptiness began. Stepping inside the mansion squeezed air from his lungs. Michael didn't want Bruno to know. But, then again, the old wizard seemed to know everything.

Bruno arched his bushy brows, his eyes reflecting humor. "My dear ole chap, the key is where it's been hidden for years. Don't you recall? The family decided no one would suspect a mansion worth millions to have a house key hidden in a lowly red flowerpot?" He smiled wryly.

"I should have remembered, but after seven years fighting a war in a sandbox, somehow it slipped my mind."

"Well, don't just stand there, come in. Let's have tea and discuss the balderdash. I'll make lunch."

He spoke to Bruno's back as he followed him through the mansion. "It's important that I question Nicole."

"Fine, we need to find privacy first. Follow me."

Michael tucked his cane under one arm and grabbed the handrail as Bruno led the way up the marble staircase. Michael remembered it well—the pathway to the Drake Room—a spacious second-floor with a view of Lake Crystal and the yacht harbor. The decorations alone would make any European swoon at the French motif with flowers and tasteful art. Michael's heart quickened as his eye caught a portrait of Nora holding him in her arms when he was a baby.

They entered the large, luxury kitchen that sported marble countertops with contrasting cabinets. Then they made a sharp turn into a cozy messy den with a round table used as a break room for Drake employees.

"Have a seat and get comfortable. Most of the kitchen staff is on vacation, so this room will be private. I'll make us a pot of tea, or do you want coffee?"

"Tea, thanks," Michael said, recalling how he and Bruno shared tea and English muffins right in this room. He wasn't sure of Bruno's age, but he'd been the butler at the mansion ever since he could remember. Bruno's strength and ingenuity were the glue that kept the Drake family together.

So how could things have gone so wrong?

"Are you hungry?"

"Starved!"

"I think I've got your favorite sandwich makings in the fridge." Bruno disappeared around the corner. Michael sat back and felt a sense of peace for the first time since he arrived in Lakeport.

During lunch, they discussed Nicole. "What I can tell you about Nicole is that she displays a tremendous amount of interest and admiration in herself."

"She never had my father's best interest at heart, did she?"

Bruno shook his head and lowered his eyes. "I'm afraid not."

"One thing is certain; she can't collect on the Drake fortune until a body is found." Michael pointed out.

Bruno nodded. "Quite."

Michael chomped down on ham and cheese loaded with mayonnaise, lettuce and tomato between two huge slices of French bread. He wiped his mouth with a napkin. "You are aware we're dealing with more than the Drake fortune, aren't you? Much more."

"Oh, yes. There're millions in gold buried out there and the map shows spot-on where it's hidden. I take it the map is in your possession?"

"Yes, for the time being."

Bruno got up and poured more tea. "What's the first thing you'd do to track down the doer's of the dirty deed? What's your plan?"

"Plan?" Aunt Jo entered the room. She smiled and kissed her nephew on the forehead. "If we're talking plans, I want to be in on it. May I sit at your round-table?"

"Yes, by all means," Bruno said, placing another cup on the table. "I'll pour you tea."

Michael got up and pulled a chair out for his aunt. "Glad you joined us, Aunt Jo."

"Thanks, guys." Jo smiled sliding her petite body onto the chair. "Good to see you again, my darling nephew. I'm so glad you came home to Lakeport. How's my cell phone working out for you?"

"Great, thanks, Aunt Jo. I'll get it back to you as soon as I shop for a new one."

"Don't worry about it." She patted his hand. "I bought two new ones—the latest Galaxy. It keeps me out of trouble—like a toy. Here is yours." She pushed the phone across the table to her nephew. "All programmed, ready to use."

"Well, thank you." He smiled, placing it in the pocket of his jacket. "But the last thing on my mind is a phone."

"I'm aware of that. That's why I bought it for you. I knew you'd never get around to it." She smiled. "So, what have you learned about Perry? Anything?"

"I've been to the Police Department this morning and met with the detective handling my father's case. I've set up an appointment for this afternoon to meet him at the crash site."

Jo gazed over the top of her horn-rimmed glasses. "Sounds as if you are on the right track—but I worry…"

"Why?" Michael reached for his cup and took a swallow of tea.

"Because, I don't want to lose my nephew, that's why. Ruthless people are after your father and his money. Are you sure you want to put yourself in that kind of jeopardy?"

"If memory serves me, you begged me to come home to protect my father. Now, I'm here, and I'll give it my best." Michael reached over and squeezed his aunt's hand. "Not to worry. I can take care of myself."

"Yes, I coerced you into coming home. But I've had second thoughts. I want you home safe. We're not sure what Nicole is up to. She and her cohorts might do anything to get their hands on the Drake fortune. For all we know, your father is lying at the bottom of the lake right now. I hate to think the same could happen to you. The Drake fortune and the gold aren't worth your life."

Bruno broke in. "I agree with Jo. This whole thing could get ugly. There are hoodlums living in Rogue's Hollow near where the gold is buried. The old ghost town has become a melting pot for every criminal imaginable—from parolees to outlaws wanted for murder."

Michael pressed his lips together. "What would you have me do?"

"Be prepared. Develop a plan of action. You've fought a bloody war for seven years, but that doesn't make this thing at home any less dangerous."

How ironic, Michael thought. Fight a damn war in Afghanistan only to fight another one on the home front. In the meantime, he didn't want to worry his family. His eyes crinkled in a smile. "Hey, with the two of you as my allies, how can I go wrong?"

Jo took a sip of tea and gazed at her nephew lovingly. "You have my blessings. Just be careful."

"One of the first things I want to do is meet Nicole and question her. Is she home?"

Jo frowned and shook her head. "I saw her leave early this morning. She's a hard one to keep track of."

"Do you have any idea what her habits are? What time she might return?"

Jo leaned forward and whispered. "I have a spy in the mansion that may know something."

Michael smiled—he loved his aunt's shrewdness. "Do I get to meet your spy?"

"No..." Her eyes widened. "The identity of my spy remains anonymous—I call him Snoops."

"Okay, but tell me, does Snoops know Nicole's habits?"

"I'm meeting with Snoops this afternoon. I'll let you know what I find out."

They visited a while longer then Bruno walked Michael to his Jeep. "Just remember to be cautious and watch your back. There are plenty of blokes out there who would love to do you in."

CHAPTER 10

MICHAEL DUCKED UNDER the yellow crime-scene tape and followed Fox down a dirt path to the bottom of the embankment, about three hundred feet below.

When they reached the floor of the cliff, Fox pointed to red stains on the gravel near the water. "Notice the blood here in this dry area on the rocks?"

"My father's blood?" Michael asked, dreading the inevitable.

"Don't know yet. We should hear from forensics anytime now with the answer."

Michael scowled into the sun and placed dark glasses on his nose. He stared at the bloodstains and tried to process the scenario. "Assuming this is my father's blood—he must have been thrown from the vehicle and landed in this spot."

Fox nodded. "Yes, and as far as we can tell, he wasn't wearing a seatbelt."

"Sounds like him." Michael remembered how Nora nagged him to buckle up. "How did his body slip past the airbags?"

"Good question." Fox said. "Your father drove a convertible with the top down. Forensics found traces of bomb fragments in and around the car. According to the bomb squad, the device didn't completely detonate, but we think enough of the explosion forced his body past the airbags."

"So, someone tried to kill my old man?"

"I'd say so." Fox pointed to the shoreline. "From here, he may have dragged himself into the lake. It's only a few feet to the water."

"But, why? Why would he do that?" Michael gazed out at the massive blue body of water. "Why would he make matters worse for himself? Wouldn't he wait for help?" He stared at the blood for a moment. "Unless…" The answer slowly sank in as his eyes connected with Fox's.

"Yeah." Fox nodded. "Unless someone was trying to kill him, and his only option was a quick exit into the lake."

Michael's face flushed with anger. Someone tried to make certain his father wasn't around to change his will, and he was damn sure who it was. "So, here's the scenario. They targeted my old man from the beginning. He knew they would follow him down here to the crash site to check his pulse and make sure he was dead."

"Sounds reasonable."

"By now they are aware he either escaped or his body is somewhere at the bottom of the lake." Michael looked over at the pile of wreckage that was once his dad's red Safari convertible. "Is there any chance he freed himself from the wreck and crawled over to this spot?"

"No, there's no blood trail, no footprints or drag marks. And, it would be near impossible for a person to get free from that tangled mess."

"What about other evidence found in the car? Can we walk over there and look around?"

"I suggest staying clear of the vehicle until the crime lab is finished. They've gone over every inch, but they haven't given the word yet they're done. We'll know more when the report comes out."

"When will that be?"

"I'm not sure. Sometimes it's a slow process."

Michael took a deep breath. "What are you doing to find my father? Assuming he found his way into the lake, and he didn't make it, have you searched for his body?"

"Yes, divers dredged the lake. This lake has strong rip currents. His body could be anywhere from here to the Canadian border by now."

Michael raised his brows. "Or, he may be alive."

"Right. But whether he's dead or alive, more to go on would help. He must have told you something. Is there anything that seemed suspicious about your dad's life up to this point in time? Was he afraid of someone?"

Michael wanted to open up and tell Fox everything. But could he trust the guy? So he was a Marine—they had that in common. But before he divulged anything, he needed to meet Fox's partner. Partners share everything, and he wanted to make damn sure he wasn't dealing with dirty cops. Word traveled fast in Lakeport, and there was too much at stake. "If I think of anything, I'll let you know."

€€€

As Michael parked in front of the cabin, a big bruiser with paintings under each arm stormed out of the door and bolted down the stairs. Michael grabbed his cane and slid out of the jeep. "Hey! Where're you going with that stuff?"

The guy stopped a few feet from a dirty brown van parked near the cabin. "I'm following instructions from my boss." His red face scrunched into a scowl. "You got a problem with that?"

Michael's six-foot-two stature looked like a leaf in the forest next to an eight hundred pound gorilla. He stepped in front of the big man's path. "I don't know you or your boss, but I'm telling you to take a hike back into the cabin with the loot."

The bruiser walked around Michael. "Yeah, gimp, who's gonna make me? You?" He laughed.

Michael grabbed the hulks arm and bent it behind his back so fast he didn't see it coming. "Big guys fall hard, you know. Now pick up the paintings like a good boy and take them back inside the cabin where you got them."

"Okay." He grunted. "Let go, and I will."

Michael loosened his grip. "First, tell me who you are?"

He didn't answer.

Michael squeezed, applying pressure to the shoulder joint.

"All right, let up will ya? My name's Benjamin Kowalski. They call me Big Ben."

"Who's the so-called boss that ordered this?"

"Nicole Drake. I'm her bodyguard. You must be Michael, the old man's son. She told me about you."

"Oh yeah, like what?"

"You don't want to know." He snickered.

"You think this is funny?" Michael forced Ben's hand upwards, toward his neck.

Ben gasped. "No, it's not funny. She said you were a son-of a-bitch. I happen to agree." He groaned as Michael squeezed harder.

"Like I said, pick up the paintings and put them back where they belong. I expect any booty that found its way into your van returned to the cabin."

He let go and Big Ben picked up the paintings. "Nicole will be pissed when I don't bring this stuff in."

"Too bad."

"It's a shame. It's for the Drake Abused Children's Fundraiser exhibition, held tomorrow. Those poor kids… like I said, Nicole will be pissed." He stood with a painting in his hand.

Michael didn't see it coming. The painting crashed down on his head with the force of an ape. For a moment, Michael lost equilibrium. Then the toe of the big man's boot swung around and slammed into his face. Michael dropped to the ground, warm blood gushing from his nose.

Ben stood over him with the broken painting in his hand. A nasty smile formed on his lips. "What's the matter, Gimp? Can't get up?"

For a split second, Michael caught a glimpse of the heavy boot aimed straight for his face. He jerked his head away in time for the foot to meet the dirt. Michael used his only choice of defense and dug his fingers into the bruiser's tree-trunk leg, squeezing the sciatic nerve with all the force he could muster. The man screamed and hit the ground like a ton of wet earth.

"Take that, you gargantuan bastard," Michael said, spitting blood in his face. Then Michael felt the rock collide with his skull and a million lights blaze in his head.

Kowalski scrambled to his feet and kicked Michael's cane out of reach. He smirked. "Have a nice day, Gimp."

Dazed, unable to move, Michael watched Big Ben load paintings and sculptures into the dirty brown van and kick up dust as he barreled out of the driveway.

Bathed in blood, mixed with dirt and grime, Michael struggled to his feet, found his cane, and hobbled inside the cabin. As he leaned against the wall for support, the first thing he noticed were the barren walls. He limped into the dining room and stared at the blanched out area where his great, great grandfather's painting once hung.

Damn! The bastard got the painting and the map.

€€€

The following day, the Drake Fundraiser was held outdoors in the gardens of the Lake Rosalie Hotel. Michael stood in the shadows of a tall Yucca Palm disguised in a white Panama hat. He hoped the hat and sunglasses hid the bruises and cuts around his eyes.

Auction crews set up the stage with several pieces of artwork from all over the country. Some of the wealthiest people around Three Lakes County filled the seating area.

As the auction began, paintings and sculptures were sold to the highest bidder. One small antique bust sold for over one-hundred-thousand. Bruno had access to the Drake bank accounts and signed a blank check over to Michael.

After thirty minutes, Michael wondered if the Drake art would ever appear. Then he saw Big Ben stroll on stage. An easel held one of his ancestor's paintings; then two more pieces were carried in. The portraits auctioned as the first settlers of Lakeport, and the bids drew in a hefty amount of cash. Michael felt a void in the pit of his stomach as his forefathers disappeared into the hands of total strangers. He didn't see his great, great grandfather Drake anywhere in the mix.

Keeping a low profile, he pulled the hat down over his eyes and edged to the seating area for a better view of the stage. A spry little lady with silvery hair held opera glasses in her gnarled fingers and smiled up at him. He picked up a pink shawl that had fallen to the ground. He noticed an empty seat next to her. "Is this shawl yours, Ma'am?"

"Oh, yes it is. Thank you." Her eyes twinkled. "How nice, to see a young man with such good manners."

"May I sit next to you and borrow your opera glasses." He smiled showing his dimples.

"Oh, please do, I'm happy to share." She handed them over to him, her wrinkled face lit up into a smile.

Michael removed his sunglasses and peered through the eyepiece. Grandpa Drake's portrait had finally arrived. The introduction came. Then the auctioneer's thick voice called out, "Do I hear one-thousand?"

The silence was so profound, the waterfall surrounding the gardens sounded like Niagara's cascade. Then the auctioneer enticed people to bid. Little by little the price edged higher. Within seconds, the painting was up for seventy-five grand.

Going once—going twice… Michael moved his pinky, and the bid jumped to eighty-five thousand. Going once—going twice—sold, to the man in the white Panama hat.

Michael handed the opera glasses back to the little lady. "I can't thank you enough."

She nodded and smiled sweetly. "The painting you just purchased of that Michael Drake fellow—I got a good look at him. I must say, when I look beyond your beat up face, you could almost pass as twins." She sighed. "But what do I know? I'm eighty-nine years old, and I'm probably seeing double. My name's Alice Smith, by the way."

Michael grinned. "Nice to meet you, Alice."

Her eyes twinkled. "And your name is…?"

"The name's Drake. Michael Drake."

For a moment, she looked puzzled. "Oh, my, now, doesn't that beat all. Now I'm wondering if I should believe in angels or ghosts." She chuckled. "Please, stop by for tea sometime, won't you? I live at the Lake Theresa. It's a village for rich old people like me. I'll serve tea in my best china, provided I live that long."

"I'd love to." Michael held both her withered hands in his and looked into her eyes. "It's a date, Alice."

€€€

At home, he unsealed the map from the back of the painting and placed the age-old document in the top pocket of his black leather jacket. He had to stay one step ahead of the bastards at all times.

He pondered calling his Marine buddy, Clint. Two retired Marines worked better as a team. He and Clint could take care of the matter within a few days then he could be off to live his life.

The eighty-five thousand dollar check he'd written to the Abused Children's Fund with Drake signature would wave a red flag under Nicole's nose. It was just a matter of time before she and her cohorts figured out why he bought the painting back.

He found Clint's number in the bottom of his unpacked duffle bag and punched it in on his new cell phone. Clint picked up the call in a matter of seconds, and Michael explained the whole rotten scenario. "I've never seen you turn down the chance to kick ass, and I do need your help."

"Sorry, old buddy, but I just started a new job. And would you believe I met the sweetest girl. She's hot, she's fun, and she can even cook. I'd like to help, but…"

Michael's face dropped as he listened. "Yeah, okay. I get it. Good luck! I'm glad things are working out for you." He hung up the phone and stared at the lake through the picture window. What now? Go it alone? He flinched as he ran his fingers across the cuts and bruises on his nose and face.

Once in shape again, I'll get rid of the damn cane—that's a promise.

He dozed off on the couch and fell into a dark dream. Each time he grabbed for his father, the old man slipped away into a sea of foam. The knock on the door jarred him awake; out of habit he reached for his Beretta. Damn, he missed that gun.

Detective Fox and an unfamiliar face with long, dark hair tied in a ponytail stood at the threshold; their sober faces said they had news. He invited them in.

"This is my partner, Robin. She has something to tell you about the blood found at your father's crime scene."

Her big, brown eyes were serious. "The results came back from the lab. We thought you might like to know the blood at the scene belongs to Perry Drake, your father."

"You're sure there isn't something you want to tell us about your dad?" Fox asked. "Something you're holding back?"

Michael stiffened. "I told you, I'll let you know." The sheriff of Three Lakes County was dirty. For all he knew so were the local police.

Fox eyed Michael's face. "That's a bad bruise around your nose and eye. Looks like someone kicked the shit out of you."

"Just a barroom brawl—you know how it goes, some people hate Marines."

Fox shrugged. "If you say so, but just remember, you're not in this thing alone. If you're worried about my partner, you can trust her. She was an intelligence specialist in the Marine Corps. She's back from Afghanistan, now one year, and we've solved more than a few crimes together."

Michael wanted to talk to Nicole first before he revealed too much. Besides, he liked doing things his own way without police interference. He'd keep the map under wraps. Maybe give Fox a little information at a time to get him off his back. "Do you know the sheriff of Three Lakes County?"

"Yeah, Dillon Hobbs, a real bastard. What about him?"

"He's having an affair with my father's wife. This could be a motive." He wasn't lying—he just wasn't elaborating on the rat poison and the other threats toward his father. He'd go into detail later. He watched their faces.

Robin kept a stoic expression and didn't speak. Fox's brows flexed. "The guy thinks he's a real lady's man, so I wouldn't put it past him. We'll look into it."

Later, Michael slept outside near the shoreline of the lake. A baseball bat would do for protection until he shopped the following day for a firearm.

CHAPTER 11

SHERIFF DILLON SLOWED his unmarked police vehicle to a crawl as he strained to see Cody's RV in the semi-darkness. If the directions were right, the motor home should be tucked in a grove of cypress with a red pickup parked in front.

He drove a mile or so down the two-lane road, made a U-turn and cruised back. His eye caught a glint of light bathed in the shadows of Cypress trees. He made a quick turn onto a dirt road and parked in back of Cody's motor home. His paranoia over goons discovering his cop status had become an obsession. Even though his car was unmarked, he needed to take every precaution.

He crossed through heavy shrubs and stepped up to the front door. The wooden plaque on the outside wall stood out prominently: *Cody Roark, Attorney at Law*. His status as Rogue Hollow's hired gun impressed and comforted the criminal element. Dillon smirked. *I may need the shyster myself after last night.*

He knocked on the steel frame.

The door opened and Cody, dressed in a yellow button-down shirt and jeans, sprang into view. "Yeah, come on in."

The late model 5th Wheel had all the amenities of home. A lot safer than the Boomtown Saloon, Dillon thought. He wanted to make the meeting quick. His dinner date with Nicole at the Bear Mountain

Inn couldn't be placed on hold. Her propensity for trouble did not fare well with a long wait.

Cody walked to the fridge. "What's your pleasure, beer?"

"Beer's fine." Dillon sat at the kitchen nook.

Cody planted a cold Bud in front of Dillon, poured himself whiskey over the rocks, downed it then poured another. "So, have you heard any news? Has Perry's body turned up?"

"No, still missing." Dillon nursed his beer.

Cody cocked his brows and scowled. "I thought being the big sheriff around these parts you'd have access to more information."

"Not if local detectives are working the case. They keep things under wraps. I'll nose around and see what I can come up with. We both checked right after the crash and didn't find his body." Dillon couldn't keep the anger out of his voice. "Maybe if the damn bomb you planted hadn't been a dud—"

"So, I'm no bomb expert. But the device detonated enough for Perry's car to swerve and go over the cliff and crash, didn't it? I'm sure he's kissing the bottom of Lake Crystal by now. My worry isn't so much Perry, but his jarhead son. What's the latest on him?"

"From what I understand, he got into a fight with Nicole's bodyguard at the lake cabin over some paintings."

"What happened?"

"I'm not sure. I'll know more tonight after I talk to Nicole."

Cody downed his drink and stared at his partner. "You don't know a whole hell of a lot about anything, do you?"

His sarcastic tone got under Dillon's skin, and something about his black snake eyes unnerved him. His blood pressure rose as he stood to leave. "You can bow out of this partnership anytime you fucking want."

Cody laughed. "Come on, sit back down. Have another beer. Geez, can't you take a joke?"

"Joke? I'm dead serious." Dillon jutted his jaw. "I have no time to pussy around with you."

Cody leaned back in his chair and stared up at Dillon. "All right, chill out. I get it."

Dillon went on. "When I find out more, I'll tell you. But if you want to remain, my partner, I don't want fuck-ups. I thought you knew what you were doing. The car bomb's failure may cost us."

"Okay, I screwed up. It won't happen again."

"Okay, I'll call if I find out anything. And get this straight—you ain't runnin' the show here—I am."

€€€

Thirty minutes later, Dillon pulled into the parking lot of the Bear Mountain Inn and parked next to Nicole's BMW. It occurred to him to inform her to use a different vehicle without signature license plates.

He pushed through the restaurant doors and saw her waiting in an overstuffed chair by the fireside. Her hair flowed long, blond and beautiful against olive skin. She smiled when she saw him. He walked over to her.

"Hello, my love." She smelled of lilacs as he leaned down and kissed her neck. A woman with many appetites, and he appreciated all of them. But he could never be completely honest with her—his feelings were more for the love of gold and the Drake bank account.

The maitre d' led them to an intimate table near a river rock fireplace. Dillon ordered fresh drinks, and for a while he enjoyed moments of sultry eye contact over candlelight. He hoped her seductive tendencies didn't get out of hand. She saw a psychiatrist for sexual compulsive disorder. The dysfunction he didn't mind as long as she kept it in the bedroom. But part of her compulsion was to have sex in elevators and out of the way public places.

She leaned toward him, her green strapless dress revealing two plump breasts. "I need you." She breathed heavily. "Let's go into one of the bathroom stalls and do it. I don't think I can wait till later."

"Didn't your psychologist advise you to slow down and take deep breaths? Have you been taking your Yoga classes? Come on, Nicole, you're better than a bathroom stall, aren't you?"

She pouted and took a sip of her Martini. "Perry would do it for me. Perry would do it anywhere I wanted."

Dillon pitied her. "Yeah, well, Perry's not here. We murdered him last night, remember? His body, we hope, is somewhere at the bottom of Lake Crystal by now. Until his equipment went south, Perry's sexual addiction resembled yours in many ways. Come on, I think you've had one too many Martinis. Let's have dinner." He signaled the waiter.

The waiter spoke with a French accent, "Oui monsieur, may I take your order?"

"Yes, the lady will have shrimp cocktail, chateaubriand, and baked potato."

When their food arrived Nicole pouted. "I want you." Her eyes hungered as she pushed her plate away. "I want to make love with you—now." She breathed like she would climax at any moment. "Oh, god, oh, god, it's killing me. I want you, now." She scooted over close to him, reached and squeezed his penis through his jeans.

He wanted to ask important questions about the map. But he'd have to have sex with her first before she would open up and talk to him about anything. He removed her hand. "Let's go to my place."

He signaled for the check.

€€€

As they stepped into his condo, she pushed him against the wall and ripped off his shirt. She unhooked her strapless gown and let it fall to the floor exposing her beautiful body. She kissed his chest, then unbuckled his belt and pulled his pants and skivvies down around his ankles. He stepped out of them and felt his manliness grow larger as she hiked up her body and straddled him. She pulsated against him as she clawed at his back. "Oh… Oh… Oh…" she moaned. Then with a mighty shudder, she dropped to the floor like a ragdoll.

He picked her up, carried her into the other room, and placed her on the bed. They made love until she cried and fell asleep.

At two in the morning, she wanted sex again. He obliged her until he was exhausted. "Can we talk now?" He wanted to know, holding back his frustration.

"I'm so hungry," she said.

"How about some eggs?"

"Sounds good."

He got up, slipped into a pair of blue jeans, and found a big white button-down shirt for her to wear. In the kitchen, he made scrambled eggs, English muffins, and coffee. They sat at the breakfast table.

She scarfed down the food like a hungry child. "You are a wonderful cook—did you know that?"

She didn't look a day over twenty. But Dillon knew she was a forty-year-old, emotionally disturbed woman with recent cosmetic surgery. So, maybe he was a greedy piece of shit and now a self-proclaimed murderer. But he still had feelings for puppies and children, and he couldn't help feel sorry for her. That didn't make him any less a bastard. When the time came, he knew he'd leave her flat, broken and alone.

He cleared their plates from the table. At last, he could ask his long awaited questions. "So what do you know about Michael? Anything new?"

She lit a cigarette and took a long drag. "Never met the guy, but there's plenty new."

"Oh, like what?" He poured more coffee into their mugs, then sat across from her and fired up a stogie.

She stared at her cup on the table then lifted her head and made eye contact. "Like an eighty-five-thousand dollar check made out to the Drake foundation."

He took a drag off his cigar and eyed her. "What in the hell is that all about?"

She sipped coffee for a thoughtful moment. "First of all, our Marine wasn't too pleased when my bodyguard went out to the lake cabin and helped himself to the artwork—under my call, of course. They got into a big fight, and Big Ben beat him up bad."

"Well, that's not saying much since the guy is lame and walks with a cane. What's this got to do with the check?"

"I'm coming to that." She took another gulp of coffee and dragged long on her cigarette. "Michael went to the Drake fundraiser where they held the auction and bought back one of the paintings for eighty-five grand."

"One painting?" Dillon's eyes widened.

Nicole nodded. "Just one. I'm curious to know what was so special about that one painting of his ancestor."

"Good question." Dillon winked and took a swig of coffee. "Maybe the time has come to pay a little visit to the Drake cabin."

CHAPTER 12

AS THE SUN ROSE to meet the day, Michael opened his eyes to glowing color that reflected sunrays across the lake. He sat up in his grassy bed and gazed at the beauty and then remembered all the crap he faced. He reached inside the top pocket of his leather jacket and touched the frayed edges of the map. The little worn piece of paper had become an obsession among thieves and murderers, and he aimed to do something about it.

The top deck of the houseboat was large enough for fishermen, sunbathers and lovers gazing at the stars. It also served as a perfect spot for Tai Chi.

He popped his favorite music into the CD player, rested his cane against the wall of the stairwell, and begun the slow meditative physical exercise.

He could barely hear the small voice above the music. "Can I do that, too?"

Michael looked over his shoulder and saw two large, inquisitive eyes gazing up from the shoreline. The Ohlone Indian kid had returned. He flipped off the music. "Nashoba, good to see you."

The boy smiled.

"Sure, come on up."

Quick as a fox, he was on the roof. "You remembered my name."

"How could I forget? Your name means wolf in your native language, right?"

"Yeah, but not too many remember." His lips creased into a slight smile. "You can call me Nash if you like."

Michael turned the music back on. "Okay, get behind me, Nash, and do what I do."

The boy raked his fingers through his dark shoulder length hair and followed Michael's lead.

When Tai Chi ended, they did pushups and sit-ups. Then they dove into the lake and swam laps out and back. Nash labored with the pushups but swam like an otter.

When finished, they drank tons of water, and Nash copied Michael's every move. When Michael rested his back against the stairwell, the boy found a spot next to him.

"Do you have brothers and sisters?" Michael asked.

"No, it's just me and my gran."

"And your mom and dad?"

The boy lowered his eyes. "They were both killed by the some bad men."

"Oh, I'm sorry."

Nash fell silent.

"Care to talk about it?"

His black eyes connected with Michael's. "I'm a half-breed, doesn't that tell you something."

"What's your breed supposed to tell me?"

"My father was Ohlone, my mother white."

"You mean that's why they were killed?"

He nodded. A single tear ran down his cheek.

Michael understood why the kid showed so much fear in the wine cellar. He handed the boy a bottle of water. "Those prejudices still exist today?"

"They exist in Rogue's Hollow."

"How do you survive—you and your gran?"

"My gran is an Ohlone healer."

"Does that mean she's a doctor?"

"People know her as Heoma, Medicine Woman. Many come to see her when they get sick. They pay her." Nash pressed the bottle of water to his lips and guzzled.

"Yes, I recall you saying your gran was a medicine woman." Michael wondered why the boy and his grandmother lived in the ghost town. "I understand Rogue's Hollow is a hangout for crooks and parolees. Are you safe living there? Isn't this where your parents were killed?"

"The elder shaman protects my gran. If anything happened to her or me, there would be much to pay. Not too many come up against my gran."

"Oh, why is that?"

"They understand what can happen if they cross her. Besides, they need her to mend gunshot wounds or whatever else ails them."

The old west thrived right in Rogue's Hollow in the twenty-first century, Michael thought. "What happened to the bad men that killed your mom and dad?"

"Gran took care of them," Nash spoke with confidence. "One of them is paralyzed all the way down his right side. He's the one that pulled the trigger that killed my parents. The other man can't talk.

Something scared him speechless. He's the one that said bad things about my mom and dad."

"So, you think your gran placed a spell on these men?"

The boy nodded. "It's best not to doubt my gran. Her power can call on evil spirits whenever she needs them."

"Powerful woman, that gran of yours."

"Yes, she is."

The boy sounded well versed on the subject, but Michael didn't believe in witchcraft. "Where do you go to school?"

"My gran home schools me and I study courses online. Can I come back tomorrow and exercise with you?"

Michael smiled. "I hope you will."

Michael thought about the boy after he left. Trust was hard to come by—he guessed that's why his circle of friends had dwindled. But he felt certain he'd made a new friend in Nash.

Michael scanned the lake with binoculars. On the other side, a large wooded area hugged the edge of the water. Anyone could spy from any point. Whoever torpedoed his father car, knew by now he had the map. He didn't like wearing a sign as an easy mark for the enemy. If he could scan the other side of the lake, so could his opposition. But he doubted they'd kill him, at least not until they got their hands on the map.

He made another wide sweep then panned over to the flat rock where he used to play when he was a kid. There she was again, her auburn hair ruffling in the breeze. His lips curled into a big smile—she stared straight back at him with her own binoculars.

ƐƐƐ

Michael drove into Castle Rock with one eye on the rearview mirror watching for flashing red. If the sheriff and Nicole were lovers, then it wasn't too far off the scale to figure the guy hungered for the Drake fortune and had a hand in his father's cookie jar. According to his old man, greed for the gold had led to the deaths of many for decades, and it wouldn't end anytime soon.

If he were a scoundrel, he'd take possession of the gold right now—after all, he owned the map. But somehow, blood gold just didn't interest him. When the time came he'd donate a hefty portion to charity.

Meanwhile, wherever he hid the little-worn piece of paper, the bastards wouldn't give up until they found it. They'd run circles around him unless he changed the rules of the game.

He pounded on the steering wheel. *That's what I need to do. Alter the rules.* It wouldn't take much to scan the map into a computer and create encrypted code. He'd simply change the algorithm. Even if someone got their grubby fingers on the flash drive, they wouldn't understand the codification. The more he thought about it, the more he liked the idea.

The only person who could break the code would be his friend, Thomas. They grew up together and were as close as brothers until Thomas moved to Europe. Thomas was fourteen and Michael thirteen when they hacked into Lakeport Yacht Works. They called themselves the Shadow-Hacks. They did it for fun and challenge, not to hurt anyone. When Aunt Jo found out, his hacking days suddenly came to an end. But the knowledge stuck in his brain like dormant buds of magic code ready to burst at any moment.

When he arrived in town, he bought a laptop and a scanner at the Shopping-Mart then made a quick detour to the mansion. Everyone was out. He went to the game room in the lower level where he knew his father's arsenal was stored. The Beretta M6 and a Sig P226 looked good to him. He had no desire for violence. But if the thugs tried anything, he'd be prepared.

He'd carry one with him and keep the other at the cabin. He loaded the Beretta and placed the piece on the inside pocket of his leather jacket. After careful thought, he took an AR15 rifle for the houseboat and then grabbed plenty of ammunition to go with the stash.

Anxiety ate at his gut. For all he knew, the old man could be wandering around delirious somewhere in need of medical care. The sooner he secured the map, the sooner he could focus his attention on finding his dad.

εεε

Back at the cabin, he setup the laptop and the scanner on the kitchen table and read the map into the computer. It didn't take long to convert the language into encrypted code and then copy the same data into a flash drive. After a few tests, he found his alternative worked perfectly. He deleted the computer file and then took a match to the original dog-eared yellow piece of paper.

This would piss plenty of people off. The map alone was worth big bucks. The little piece of ratty paper had belonged to a family of lawmen for nearly a century, and his father had possessed it for many years after. But what will be, will be—it had to be done.

He hoped his father would understand as he watched the age-old document go up in flames. The diagrammatic representation to the gold's whereabouts was alive and well, reborn into secret code and nobody need be the wiser. He smiled cynically—no trace of the original map. *The idiots will knock themselves out for nothing.*

He drove to the bank and placed the flash drive into a safe deposit box. The key went around his neck, along with dog tags under his shirt. Mission accomplished.

Cane in hand, he walked out of the bank toward his Jeep parked a few blocks down the street. He stopped a moment to tie his tennis shoe. As he raised his head, he saw a reflection of a man in a store window across the street. When he gazed over his shoulder, the man ducked into a department store.

Michael picked up his pace. As he got closer to his vehicle, two girls he remembered from senior high loitered outside Sammie's Bar and Grill smoking a cigarette. They were his age, but they didn't look too much older than their high school days. Now was not a good time for hot chicks and fun nights. He tried to move passed before they recognized him.

The tall blond called out, "Hey, Mikey baby, what's the rush? No time for old friends?"

Michael smiled and waved but kept walking.

The brunette rushed over and grabbed his arm. "Come on, lover boy. Don't you remember me? That night on Big John's Yacht before you joined the Marines? We kissed and—"

Michael looked into her eyes and shook his head. "No, I don't remember you. Can I have my arm back?"

"How rude." She raised her voice. "Is that what they teach you in the Marines, to be so rude?"

He couldn't seem to control it. People irritated him and he wound up pissing everyone off. Hating to make a scene or hurt her feelings, he peered at the other girl, then back at the brunette. He noticed the guy across the street watching every move. If he ducked into the bar with the girls, he could leave via the back entrance. Maybe the girls were a blessing in disguise. He tried to smile. "Now I remember you. I'm sorry—I didn't mean to be rude."

The blond stubbed her cigarette out with the toe of her shoe and strolled over. "Why not make it up to us, Mikey—buy us a drink?" A big smile crossed her face. "Maybe you just needed to be reminded. I'm Jolene, and this here is my best friend, Beth. We suffered through math class together, remember?"

I have no time for this shit, Michael thought, but smiled through his antipathy. "Sure, now I remember. I'd love to buy you girls a drink." He opened the door to Sammie's Bar and glanced over his shoulder before he followed them in. The tail had disappeared.

The band hadn't arrived yet, so music played from the jukebox. The dance floor had a few people moving around trying to mimic a rendition of Dirty Dancing.

Michael was thankful for the darkness as he walked up to the bar. A quick drink for the girls, then he'd split. There were no seats available, so they stood in a circle. He tucked his cane under one arm. "What are we having," he asked as pleasant as possible.

The girls gave their order to the bartender and pressed against Michael so he couldn't leave without breaking through their hold. "Aren't you going to have a drink with us?" Jolene wanted to know.

"No, I'm sorry, I have other commitments."

"Oh, there you go again, being rude. Can't you stay for just one?"

"Another time." He smiled politely and scanned the faces of the surrounding people. He looked for the tail or anyone else who might cause him trouble.

Beth draped an arm over his shoulder. "Come on Mikey baby, let's boogie."

"Look, I apologized for any rudeness on my part. I agreed to buy you both a drink, but that's where it ends."

Jolene stood back. "This sucks, Beth, let him go. There're plenty of guys around that would be happy to spend time with us."

"No," Beth leaned against him, "I want Mikey."

"You are both beautiful girls, but I…"

He turned to pay the tab and glanced in the mirror over the bar. The face of the man who had been following him appeared and then vanished in a flash within the crowd. Michael placed money down on the bar, bid goodbye to the girls and headed for the back exit.

€€€

Michael crouched behind a large trash bin and waited for the backdoor of Sammie's Bar to open. He hoped the guy would bypass him, pick up his feet and move on down the alley.

Michael saw part of a tweed jacket between the wall and the trash bins. As he braced himself, his cane slipped to the ground and skidded across the alley.

The man turned and walked toward the sound. Michael wrapped an arm around his pudgy neck, forcing him to bend forward in a headlock. "Who the hell are you?"

The guy choked out the words, "Let go."

As Michael released him, he prepared to lay him flat at any given moment. "What's your name?"

"Luis," he coughed and sputtered. "Luis Silva."

"Why are you following me?"

Luis reached under his coat.

Michael drew his M6. "I wouldn't do that."

"Sweet Jesus, I'm only going for my identification."

"Do it slowly."

He showed his ID.

"So, you're a cop—figures. Did Fox send you?"

"Unfortunately, yes." Luis put his detective's badge back into his pocket. "His orders were for me to follow you and make sure you stayed out of trouble." He rubbed the back of his neck. "Looks like you are trouble."

"Sorry, I had to rough you up," Michael said grabbing his cane off the ground.

"Fox seems to think you're lame and may need help. He worries too much. I'd say you handle yourself just fine."

"Tell Fox to stay out of my business."

"I'll do that." He started to leave then turned back. "Oh, by the way, Fox has news about your old man. But since you don't want the police in your business, I won't give you the latest."

"Spit it out, Luis? What is it?"

Luis stared at the ground in silence.

"Damn it, what do you know about my father?"

Luis cleared his throat. "Someone saw a man that fits his description near the outskirts of Rogues Hollow, by the lake. According to the source, the guy looked pretty beaten up."

Michael puffed out a sigh of relief. "Well, there's a chance the old man is still alive, then. Thanks."

Luis coughed and rubbed his neck again. "Don't mention it."

"Tell Fox I'll be in to see him as soon as I can."

Without answering, Luis wrinkled his forehead and walked down the alley toward the main drag. Michael waited a few minutes then followed the same path toward his vehicle. Once in his Jeep, he drove straight to the Drake mansion—this time to visit his father's wife.

€€€

Bruno served ham and cheese sandwiches outside by the pool. "Tea, coffee or beer?"

"Tea, please." Michael took a bite of his sandwich. "Mmmm, this is good, I'm starved."

"You're always starved." Bruno disappeared a few moments and came back with a bowl of potato salad and napkins. "Cook made this yesterday." He set it on the table then sat across from Michael and poured tea for the two of them. "What's this news about your father? You say he may be alive?"

"Someone may have seen him."

"Where?"

"On the outskirts of the old ghost town, near the water's edge. I'll get more specifics from the detective after I leave here. But I want to talk to Nicole first. I haven't met her yet, and I have plenty of questions."

"Looks like you'll get your chance; there she is now. Be careful what you say around her. She can be a bit cheeky."

"Yeah, I'll be careful. But I'll hold her responsible for anything that happened to my father."

Nicole stepped up on the springboard and plunged into the pool with a perfect forward dive. When she came up from the water she swam to the edge where Michael and Bruno sat.

"Hi, Bruno, who's that with you? Oh, it's the gorgeous Marine everyone's talking about." She laughed, dove under the water and swam back to the other end of the pool.

"I'd better warn you. She has an obsessive disorder of a sexual nature."

Michael laughed. "How do you know this, Bruno? Did she hit on you?"

"That would be the bloody day." Bruno grimaced. "Your Aunt Jo's spy keeps us informed."

"Are you referring to Snoops?"

"Yes. I've always been curious as to who Snoops is. Could be a housekeeper, maybe Nicole's secretary—Jo keeps mum." Bruno gazed across the pool. "Here she comes again."

Nicole's hips swayed as she walked from the opposite end of the pool deck. She strode up to their table, her bronze body glistening under a yellow bikini. Wet locks fell to her shoulders as she sat down and removed the tieback from her hair.

"You're Michael, aren't you?" She smiled. "Well, I've been dying to see you up close." Her fingertips ruffled her damp hair as she spoke. "The name's Nicole, I'm your daddy's wife; you can call me, Mom."

Michael gave her a cutting stare.

She went on. "My, you're a quiet one, aren't you? Okay, just kidding about the Mom stuff."

"I'd like to talk to you about my father. I have some questions." His face showed little emotion.

"Oh, sure," she laughed nervously, "what would you like to know?"

"When did you see last see him?"

"Hmmm, let me think… the last time I saw Perry was…" she stared out at the pool. "Oh, yeah, that would have been two nights ago when he said he was going out."

"Was that the night he disappeared?"

"You know, you remind me an awful lot of your father. You're good looking like Perry when we first met." She reached over and laid a warm hand on his arm.

Michael shifted in his chair and drew away. "Do you mind answering the question?"

"Oh yeah, about your father… now, what was it you wanted to know?"

Michael held back his annoyance, wondering what his dad ever saw in the woman. "The night he disappeared; you said two nights ago when he went out, right?"

Her eyes grew wide. "Well, yeah, I guess so."

"And he didn't give you a clue where he was going?"

"No, he never said a word." She jumped out of her chair. "You know what? I'm getting bored with these questions."

"Why?" Bruno asked. "Do you have something to hide?"

"Of course not; but I'd feel a whole lot better if you talked in the presence of my attorney."

"Well, we're not the police, Nicole. We're family. Michael here is concerned about his father."

"I know, but..." She licked her lips. "It sounded an awful lot like he was giving me the third degree."

Michael caught Bruno's look, which he took to mean soften up. "I'm sorry Nicole," Michael said. "Tell me anything you might remember about my father that will help."

She sat back down. "Sure, I'll tell you what I told the police detective."

"That's good," Bruno said.

"Well," her eyes darted from Bruno to Michael, "Perry was in that awful crash over on Peaks Cliff, you know, and they never found his body. That's all. I told the same thing to the detectives."

Michael wanted to keep a civil relationship for later questions so he let her get away with lying.

She rose to her feet and giggled. "Why don't you come up to my studio, Michael? I'm on the third floor of the mansion. I'll show you around. After all, as Bruno said, we are family."

Michael glanced at Bruno and saw him shake his head.

Bruno didn't have to worry. He had no intention of going to her place. He wanted to catch her off guard when she least expected it. "Not today, Nicole, maybe another time."

"Oh, shoot." She bent down and kissed him on the lips. "I was so hoping we could…" She smiled. "Well, another time."

They watched her walk away, her hips swinging to a rhythm of her own music.

"You weren't thinking of visiting her studio, were you?" Bruno asked.

"No, of course not, but I need to find out all I can. I know she's involved in my father's disappearance—the closer I get, the more I can draw out of her. She's involved with the sheriff, and I'm pretty sure he's using her to get close to my dad's money and the gold. He's the scoundrel in this mess, although there may be more. I want to know everything, and I believe Nicole is the key."

Bruno raised his brows. "Seriously, old chap, you know she'll attempt to seduce you, don't you?"

"She's my father's wife, Bruno. I would never allow it. Besides, she's not my type. But sometimes the enemy must become your friend. I can play her just as hard as she plays me and get what I want."

Bruno smiled. "Yes, I need to realize you're all grown up. But remember, I'm here if you need me, and I'll be watching your back."

CHAPTER 13

ANNIE SADDLED KNIGHT and prepared for her morning ride into the woods. A low mist had formed just above the meadow as dew condensed from the morning sun. More and more, she looked forward to her secret getaway. If she left early enough, she would ride Knight through the woods and arrive in time to take a dip in the lake at her favorite spot. Later, she would sunbathe on the flat rock.

She hated to disobey her family—her brothers had her best interest at heart. But she was twenty-one years old now and deserved time to herself.

She patted Knight and turned to see Zack standing at the barn entrance. His expression told her she was in trouble.

"Up earlier than usual, aren't you?" He walked into the barn and stood in front of her. "I take it you're going on another ride into the woods?" It was more of a statement than a question.

"Yes, that's my plan." She tightened the cinch under the horse's barrel.

She loved everything about the ranch. Pa and her two older brothers were her world. They had been her heroes from the start of her life. She hated to think what might have happened if Zack hadn't rescued her from that old Chevy parked alongside the road.

A shudder moved through her body. Pa found her alone kicking and screaming in the car seat. There were a lot of questions in her mind; like what happened to her mother. Did she abandon her along the roadside? Was her mother assaulted?

After searching for her parents, the Maguire boys, as they were known to the townsfolk, legally adopted her. Some of the ladies in town stared right through her when she walked into the church. They whispered she was *a love child* of the devil. But Annie stood straight and proud just like Pa taught her.

Although she had fantasies about her birth mother, Zack, Jonas, and Pa were her family, and they treated her like a princess. But the time had come when she needed space. Her brothers just didn't understand her newfound independence.

"You need to know the dangers," Zack went on. "There are bears and bobcats in those woods. Remember, the Walker family lost a son last year to a rabid mountain lion. Besides that, you can never be too sure when an unsavory character may come down from the old ghost town."

Jonas walked into the barn and joined the discussion. "I agree with Zack. Your willingness to tempt fate could lead you into danger."

"I'm not a child," Annie spoke with conviction as she smoothed out the saddle blanket that Zack had given her on her last birthday. Her brothers should have more faith in her. "You boys have taught me how to handle myself."

"It's true, we taught you well." Jonas stood in front of her blocking the way. "You can ride like the best of us. In fact, the way you handle yourself on a horse and shoot a rifle, I pity the poor bastard who tries anything with you. But we still don't like you going out there alone in the woods—and Pa agrees."

"It's only a few miles out. I'll be careful." Annie buckled the flap on her saddlebag. "Besides, I've got my cell phone. I'll call if I run into trouble."

As she mounted Knight, Jonas stepped aside. She turned and waved to her brothers then followed a dirt path toward a grove of eucalyptus trees. The horse responded as if he knew the way.

When Annie reached the wooded area, the morning breeze kissed her face, and she enjoyed the fragrance of wild flowers and earthy scented plants. She rode along a narrow horse trail for a few miles and stopped to rest at a small creek that ran across the path. Her eye for beauty triggered a desire to capture the surrounding trees and wild blossoms on her sketch pad.

She dismounted Knight, sat down with her back against a rock and sketched the nature surrounding her. Her drawing moved fast across the pad using pastel chalk. A scene with green plants and yellow poppies came to life. In the background, she caught the rush of the creek washing across stones.

The woods were alive with wildlife and birds and strange noises. Tingling skin and a rush of adrenalin warned her that someone or something watched and that the sounds she heard were more than gnawing little animals moving around in the trees and bushes. Probably a squirrel scurrying in the underbrush, she thought, but when the crunch of twigs got louder, her fear became more pronounced.

"Is someone there?" she called out. Stillness washed over the forest, and for a second or two even the birds stopped chirping.

She packed her equipment in her saddlebag, then mounted Knight and took off for her secret getaway. Every so often she looked over her shoulder. Zack and Jonas did a good job pounding fear into her, she thought. It was likely nothing more than a squirrel or rabbit.

A few miles later she reached the entrance—enough room for her to ride Knight through the narrow opening between two enormous boulders. Once on the other side, the magnificent blue lake came into view, and the magic of another world unfolded.

She slid off Knight and guided him along a rocky path, which really wasn't a path, but the route she took to get to her special getaway. She reached the opening through dense shrubbery and secured her horse to a nearby limb. A cool breeze caressed her body as she undressed and slipped into her bathing suit.

The flat rock that hovered over the top of the lake, not only made a perfect place to sunbathe, but a diving point. Crystal clear water felt velvety soft on Annie's skin as she snorkeled and swam and played.

Exhausted, she climbed onto the rock, grabbed an apple from her lunch box and fed Knight. He nickered, and she patted his head—then the same feeling she'd had earlier washed over her. This time she sensed eyes watching from across the lake. She wondered if her fear was an overreaction to what her brothers had planted in her mind. She turned to gaze toward the distant shore. If someone was watching it was too far for her to see.

She grabbed her carryall, climbed on top of the flat rock and pulled out her binoculars. She scanned the shore across the lake. Same trees, same lake cabin, same houseboat. She was just about to sunbathe and read her latest romance novel when a man came into view. He walked across the top of the houseboat.

She magnified her scope. "Oh, my… Now, what do we have here?"

CHAPTER 14

BY THE TIME Michael arrived home, it was late afternoon. He parked in front of the cabin and stiffened at the smell of trouble. The front door stood wide open. From the rip in the screen, this did not look like a friendly visit.

Sweat slicked his brow as he grabbed his cane and climbed out of the Jeep. His leg burned like an evil fire, but adrenaline propelled him up three steps to the porch. He hooked his cane on the doorknob and drew his Beretta in a two-handed grip. With the toe of his shoe he nudged the door wider. Inside, he proceeded slowly, stepping over debris until every room in the cabin was combed.

He snatched his cane off the doorknob and waded through a trail of demolition. In the kitchen, swarms of flies buzzed around food strewn in every direction. Michael surmised they went to an awful lot of trouble to trash the place—almost as if they had a vendetta.

War on the home front looked an awful lot like chaos in the Middle East. His gut rolled into a knot as he eyed the paintings and sculptures of his ancestors. The slashed sofa could be replaced, but except for what sold at the fundraiser auction, the balance of artwork belonged to yesterday.

He'd been away from the cabin since midmorning—six hours. This meant someone had watched him and knew his moves. He reached up and touched the key hidden under his shirt—he had encrypted the map none too soon.

As he pondered on what to do next, footsteps creaked behind him and he spun around aiming the Beretta at a silhouette standing in the doorway. "Who goes there? Speak up, or I'll put a bullet through your skull."

"Stand down, Marine!" A gruff voice commanded.

Michael grimaced as the barrel of a Glock leveled straight for his head. The man stepped through the door out of the shadow, and Michael breathed a sigh of relief. "Fox, damn it, you shouldn't sneak up on people. It could get you killed."

The detective holstered his gun and coughed a dry laugh. "Okay, quick draw. What the hell happened here?"

Michael bagged his gun in the shoulder holster under his jacket. "I arrived home, and this is what I found."

"You better talk to me, buddy. No one rips a place apart like this unless they are looking for something of value, and I think you know what that something is. I'm also wondering why you are so well armed—legally, I hope."

"As legal as it gets." Michael shot him a blank stare. He didn't have time to worry about trivial matters. If he were fined or thrown in jail for taking possession of his father's stash, he'd deal with it when the time came, but he wasn't about to go unarmed.

He thought it damn suspicious that a good detective like Fox, an ex-marine, would be in the dark about the buried gold. Perhaps he knew more than he let on and saw him as a pawn in a fishing expedition to find out the map's whereabouts. Maybe the detective was part of the whole damn conspiracy.

He placed Fox on the defensive. "Look, I don't know what the fuck you think I know, and frankly I don't care. But I'm getting damn tired of you trying to pump information out of me. Furthermore, I don't appreciate you sending your dogs out to tail me."

Fox frowned. "Yeah, well I have to agree the whole thing with Luis was counterproductive."

"Don't you have something more important for your men to do?"

"He gave you information about your father, didn't he?"

Michael bristled. "Come on, man. Do you think I need a tail on my ass to tell me about my old man? You could've called."

"Look at it this way—Luis was acting as your bodyguard. You've got an injured leg. You were beaten up pretty bad the last time I saw you. I thought you might need help. Luis followed you under my orders in case you got into trouble."

"I don't need your foot soldiers for protection."

"Yeah, so I heard. My lead detective is still grumbling and rubbing his sore neck." Fox walked over and placed two kitchen chairs upright. "I'd like to talk about something else." He pointed to one of the chairs. "Sit."

Glad to take the weight off his leg Michael obliged. "Make it quick. I don't have a lot of time. I need to clean up this mess."

"Touch nothing until the crime scene team does a thorough investigation."

"How long will that take?"

"My advice is to find new digs for the next couple days so forensics can do their job."

"I'll sleep in the houseboat."

"Suit yourself." Fox turned the other chair backward and sat opposite him. "All right, there's been a little thing like gold-fever going on around these parts for quite some time—many years, in fact."

Here it comes, Michael thought. "Yeah, I heard something about it."

Fox went on. "There's a map that leads to a pot of gold buried in the hills."

Michael didn't lie, just avoided telling what he knew. "It's probably an old gold miner's fable, more like legend than anything else."

"No, it's very real." Fox grimaced. "My gut tells me that's what these boys were looking for today." He gestured toward the debris. "And whether you know it or not, you're in danger because they think you're hiding it."

Tell me something I don't know, Michael thought, wanting to laugh at the irony. "Look, I don't have it—whatever it is. When you get more news on my father let me know. In the meantime, I hate to be rude, but I've got things to do."

Fox rose to his feet and strode to the door. "Okay, but remember, if you know anything at all about the map, which I suspect you do, these men will do anything, kill, maim, torture, to get it. From one Marine to another, watch your six. And, by the way, the post traumatic therapy sessions open next week. I hope to see you there."

Michael shook his head. "Nah, that's okay. I'm doing all right in that department. See you around."

€€€

After the detective left, Michael punched in the mansion's number on his cell phone. A familiar voice answered, "Drake mansion."

"Yeah, Bruno. I ran into trouble."

"Blimey, what happened?"

"The cabin's been trashed. Everything is in a state of chaos."

"The bastards, I hope they didn't find what they were looking for."

"No, I saw to that. It's hidden where no one can find it."

"Well, why not stay at the mansion. Your room is just like you left it."

"No, I'm staying at the houseboat. The crime scene detectives will be here soon to dust for prints and investigate. After that, we've got to think about hiring someone to clean the cabin and put things back together. They even ripped some of the walls out. I'd like to have security cameras in place as soon as possible."

"I'll make some calls and get someone out there to take care of it. We've got furniture in storage. No problem there."

"Wait a few days for forensics to dust for prints and search for clues. Maybe they'll find answers."

"Damn well hope so," Bruno said. "I'll be over in a while to stock the houseboat with food."

"Cool. Oh, and Bruno. Check Dad's gun cache. I need two more rifles and one more pistol."

"Sounds like you expect a bloody war."

"Only if they start it."

€€€

The following morning, after a quick shower, Michael dressed and climbed to the top deck of the houseboat. Nash climbed aboard just in time for morning exercises.

Michael was glad for his company. "Ready for Tai Chi?"

Nash planted a big grin across his face. "My gran said you are a good man for teaching me an ancient art. She wants to meet you and has invited you to our cook-out."

"Tell your gran I'm eager to meet her. When is this cook-out?"

"Tomorrow night. Don't forget."

"What time?"

"Be there at sundown."

Michael smiled with humor. "I remember what you said about your gran's ties to supernatural powers. I guess I'd better make sure I attend."

They both laughed. Then Nash drew a straight face. "It's no joke. She can heal the sick with her powers. She also calls on evil spirits when she needs them."

Michael was in no mood to argue black magic or psychic forces. He wanted to get past the morning exercise and focus on locating his father.

He turned to the built-in CD player and switched on Moonlight Sonata, then eased into the slow and even tempo of Tai Chi. Nash cloned his every move.

At the end of the session the ache in Michael's leg had subsided. They went through their push-up and sit-up routine, then dived into the cold lake and raced fifty laps out and back. Once again, the boy out swam Michael by two laps.

After they guzzled water, Nash asked, "Do you know Karate?"

"Yes, I taught martial arts in the Marine Corps."

"Can you teach me? I know a little already from Karate for Kids at the gym, but Gran couldn't afford it, so I dropped out."

No time like the present to take on his first student, Michael thought. "Sure, I'll teach you."

The boy's face lit up. "Awesome."

"But I want something in return."

"Oh, oh, I knew it sounded too good to be true."

"Hear me out—I don't want money. I need your help."

"Oh, like how can I help you?" He was all ears as he listened to what Michael had to say.

"You know these parts well, don't you? You know the forest that runs alongside the lake?"

"Yeah, I was born here. How could I not know? I live on the edge of the water with Gran. For many years, we lived in a shanty until the shaman built us a better house. I'm a half-breed—Indians always know their land." His face lit up. "The elder shaman taught me how to track wildlife for food."

"Good. You also know about the ghost town and the people who live there, don't you?"

"I know just about everyone in the area. Except for the bad guys, they stay out of sight."

"Okay, what I need is a guide. Someone to be on the lookout for potential places a man could hide."

"Why?"

"Because I'm looking for someone who may be hurt—for all I know he may be dead, but I need to find him dead or alive."

"Who is he?"

"My father—he went missing after a car crash."

"Drake, the billionaire." Nash flexed his brows. "His car went over the cliff. He was in the news. So he's your father?"

"Yes, he may have survived the crash. Some culprits are after him, trying to kill him. I need to find him before its too late."

"I'd be glad to help. Just tell me when."

"Today. Do you mind if we start on your Karate lessons later?"

"No, I'm just happy you will teach me. I want to help you find your father."

"Okay, partner, thanks."

Michael grabbed the binoculars and searched the area across the lake. He wondered about the girl he'd seen the previous day. The thought of her red hair and gorgeous body wasn't something he could wipe from his mind. Why was she watching him? Could she be a spy? He panned over to the flat rock. Sure enough, there she was again.

She sat up and rubbed lotion on her body. He spotted her horse in the background tied to a limb. Innocent enough she owned a horse and a rifle; but did she work for the enemy? A female tripping him up was the last thing he needed.

"What are you looking at?" Nash asked with big curious eyes.

Michael handed Nash the binoculars. "Here, do you recognized that person. Ever see her around?"

Nash peered through the scope. He took a while to answer. "I'm not sure, but I think that's Annie Maguire."

"Well, who is she? Where does she come from?"

"She lives on a ranch about three miles from here."

"What kind of ranch?"

"Horse ranch, I think."

Michael frowned. "It's odd she'd be out here alone."

"Her kinfolk are probably not too far away. I heard stories any man who gets too close to her could get shot by one of the brothers or even by her father."

Michael grabbed the binoculars and gazed through the scope. Damned if she wasn't staring straight back at him with her own binoculars. "Well, would you look at that?"

"What is it?"

Michael handed the glasses back to the kid. "Hang on Nash boy— we're going for a little ride."

As the motor warmed, they changed into dry clothes. Nash helped Michael with the anchors and released the outboard tied to the houseboat. "We'll use the houseboat to navigate, but if need be we can always use an outboard."

Nash's eyes lit up with an inquisitive smile. "So what are you going to say to her?"

"I don't know yet—something like, why were you spying on me?"

"But, you were spying on her, weren't you?"

"Yes, but whose side are you on?"

"Yours, but she's just a girl. My gran always says treat girls with respect."

"Your gran is right, but you'll learn soon enough, some girls can be manipulative. They get what they want through other means."

"What other means?"

"Never mind, you'll learn in time."

Nash kept quiet as Michael maneuvered the houseboat across the lake and parked in front of the flat rock.

"Hello," Michael called out.

She sat up on one elbow. "Hello, who might you be?"

Michael was struck by her beauty. The few freckles across her nose gave her a natural, unaffected look, and he liked the way her thick auburn hair framed her face. But he remembered feeling that way once about Trisha and look how that turned out.

"My name is Michael Drake. I live across the lake." Michael wore his best smile. He hated to be vain, but women usually went for his dimples. "This is my friend Nash. Why were you spying on me?"

"What do you mean, spying? I've never seen you before in my life."

Michael and Nash gave each other a knowing look. "Okay, why are you watching me through your binoculars?"

She pushed her sunglasses up on her nose and laid back. "Why were you watching me through yours?"

"Good question," Nash whispered.

"Well, since we're on the subject," Michael said, not liking the obvious brush off, "did you see the burglars who raided my cabin yesterday?"

She sat up and removed her sunglasses. "I have better things to do with my time than stare across the lake at your place. But I often scan the surrounding area searching for wildlife... Now that you mention it, I did see two men yesterday afternoon. I couldn't make them out, but it appeared they wore dark clothing. If I had known they were burglars, I would have called the police."

"You had no way of knowing. Did you see what kind of vehicle they drove?"

"Yes, they were in a black van, like a big Cargo Ram."

"Jeez, she knows her vans," Nash whispered.

"Well, thank you for the helpful information," Michael said. "It's nice meeting you. Sorry, we got off to a rocky start. I didn't get your name."

She stood and reached for her bathing suit cover-up. "No problem. Annie Maguire is my name."

Michael held back a gasp as she slipped a yellow see-through poncho over her head, then hopped up on her horse with the ease of a bareback rider and took off. He got a warm feeling when she turned and waved before she disappeared into the forest.

€€€

The chill in the air brought goose bumps as Michael navigated the houseboat toward the west end of the valley. The glassy surface of the lake reflected images of burnt umber, oranges, and bright yellow. "Hold on to the wheel a minute," he told Nash. "I'll go get us a couple of windbreakers."

He went below and grabbed two jackets off hooks in the closet. The houseboat was well equipped with a kitchen, living area, two private bedrooms, and one and a half baths. Thanks to Bruno, the boat was now stocked with food. He grabbed a couple apples off the snack bar and hurried back upstairs.

He tossed Nash a jacket and threw him an apple. "You're doing such a good job navigating I think I'll make you captain of the ship."

They laughed and joked about who was the fastest swimmer as they cruised the lake at about ten knots. After a while, Michael took the wheel. "Since you know this area so well, tell me about potential hideouts? Anything come to mind?"

Nash hiked himself up on the edge of the bow and took a bite out of his apple. "There are some awesome gold mining tunnels. I've been in them, but it's scary. Once I had a friend trying to hide from some kids who were bullying him at school. He hid in a tunnel and got his foot caught between two big rocks. His leg slipped through, and he was stuck there for a long time."

"Was he injured?"

"Yes, it took hound dogs to find him. He went to the hospital with a broken leg, but he came out of it okay. His leg was in a cast for a while. After that, his parents schooled him at home."

"Not a bad idea with today's educational system."

"That's what Gran says."

"What did they do about the kids who bullied him?"

"I don't know for sure what the school did, but I heard they got in big trouble with their folks."

"Well, at least they received discipline for their actions. Can you gauge how far we are from the tunnels, now?"

"They're on the other side of the ghost town, so I'd say about two miles yet."

"Your gran may be worried. I'd better drop you off at home."

"Yeah, I wish I could go with you and help you search for your dad, but Gran will look for me right about now."

"It's too dangerous, anyway. Where is your place from here?"

He pointed. "Just around the bend. Don't forget tomorrow's cookout."

"I'll be there." Michael navigated close to the shoreline. "Tell your gran I'll bring some fine wine."

"She'll like that." Nash jumped out of the houseboat, turned and waved.

Michael waved back as he pulled away and headed home to dock the boat.

€€€

Michael sat in his Jeep studying the Three Lakes County map. He had a good idea where the tunnels were. One mine, located a quarter of a mile inland from the lake, was on the other side of the ghost town, just about where Nash said it would be. This one went down three levels below ground. He'd try there first.

Old Gold Miner's Road narrowed as he drew closer to Rogue's Hollow. He cut through the main drag of the once vibrant boomtown and kept one eye on the rearview mirror. It looked like any ghost town he'd ever imagined—empty. If criminals and ex-cons lived there, they kept behind closed doors. The bulge of the Beretta holstered on the inside of his jacket comforted him.

On the outskirts of town, he spotted a black van approaching from behind. The vehicle looked like the one Annie Maguire described parked in front of the cabin the day of the break-in.

The same men probably knew he drove a Jeep. He made a quick right turn onto a dirt road that he had marked on the map. Clouds of dust blocked his view from the rear. He pulled to the shoulder and waited. After a few seconds, the dust settled, and he saw no one on his tail.

A few more miles led straight to the mine. The tunnel was easy to spot with two ore carts and pickaxes by the opening. He parked behind a large boulder, then put on his backpack and grabbed his cane.

As he entered the mine, the smell of wet clay hung in the air like the badlands after a heavy rain. He shined his light in all directions then traveled deeper into the tunnel. No sign of human activity anywhere.

He called to his father, "Dad, this is Michael. Give me a signal." Over and over, he repeated the words to hollow walls—nothing. He traveled further down the shaft. If his dad had entered the tunnel injured, he couldn't have traveled far without leaving blood or some sign he'd been there. But his father was smart enough not to leave a trail for the wrong people. He shook the thought from his mind that his old man was probably dead at the bottom of the lake somewhere.

Then, a voice in his head leveled charges against him. *If he's dead it's your fault. You're responsible for your dad's misfortune. If you had protected him, he'd still be alive. Just like your friends in the helicopter, they died, while you lived.*

He leaned against the side of the cavern then fell to his knees. "Damn it; shut up!" He placed his hands over his ears as the deafening sound of rotor blades echoed in his brain. One by one, he saw their faces as the chopper whirled into the canyon. "Pete, Joe, Adam, John… Why didn't I die," he cried. "Why didn't I die with you?"

For the next hour, he hunkered down on the second level of the mine shaft. The only sound other than the turmoil in his head was the drip-drip-drip in a pool of water from the corner of the cave.

When lucidity returned to his mind, he stood, and the ground beneath his feet swayed. He could have sworn the mine shaft moved. Then he realized the tremors were in his own legs. He braced his hands against the wall of the cavern to steady himself until his strength returned.

€€€

The following day, Michael sped toward town like he was battling another war in Kandahar. He'd often wondered if some people weren't destined to live on the edge. Even at birth, his mother had big surprises for him. She died and left him with strangers who thought they knew something about parenthood. Ironically, the man who adopted him wasn't that much of a stranger—he was the guy who planted the seed in his mother's womb. He never told his father he knew. But what the hell, lovechild or not, none of that even mattered now.

The engine whined as he shifted to a lower gear and slowed behind an old car coughing out a cloud of fumes. Every expletive he knew lingered on the tip of his tongue, but he gripped the wheel and swallowed his anger—the last thing he needed was road rage. He eased around the vehicle.

Ten minutes later, he rolled into town and parked on the street. He sat for a moment to clear his head, then fumbled in his jacket pocket and found the address Detective Fox had given him. With his cane in hand, he covered the few blocks toward the center of Lakeport.

The Web Building towered above him eighteen stories. He double-checked the address—it looked like the right place. For a moment he hesitated. Did he want to do this? Did he want to spill his guts to a group of strangers in a therapy session? No. But far too often the enemy within played a losing game in his head, and somehow he had to fix it.

He forced himself to walk into the lobby, press the button and wait for the elevator. When the automatic doors opened, a familiar pair of eyes stared back at him. It had been a long time since he'd seen the high cheekbones, the full lips, and the curvy body. Another dude stood next to her. But, what did it matter? She was nothing more to him now than a bad memory.

He nodded politely. "Hello, Trisha."

A flick of anger shot through her eyes as she spoke. "Mikey, you look like hell. How's it hanging?"

He kept a straight face. Her laughter echoed through the air as they stepped off the elevator, and he stepped in. What a witch, he thought. How could he have ever been in love with her? A question he could not answer. The doors closed, and he punched the button to the third floor. He shook off nausea and tried to focus on the reason he was there.

Number 301 was easy to find across from the elevator. He opened the door and froze at the threshold. The group of people milled around the room drinking coffee. The urge to turn and run almost got the best of him. He opened and closed his fists. If he stayed, he'd have to discuss the flashbacks, and he hated talking about the war. Not only that, he wasn't sure he could trust Fox or Robin with his weaknesses.

As he stepped in, a trickle of sweat dripped down his temple. He spotted Fox in the far corner of the room talking to a woman. A feeling of being in the wrong place in time and space overpowered him. He had a strong desire to crawl away before anyone saw him. But here he stood, anchored to the floor.

Fox came over and gave him a slap on the back. "Hey, buddy, glad you made it."

Michael's throat tightened.

"How about a drink at The Pinnacle after the session? You look like you could use one. Besides, I want to talk to you about your father."

Michael managed a nod.

Fox cocked a brow. "Hey, Mike, you okay?"

Michael swallowed away the lump in his throat. "I'm fine."

"Look, you don't have to say a word tonight if you don't feel up to it. Everyone here has had similar experiences. Sometimes just listening to others helps."

Michael shot him a sideways glance. "Hey, I said I'm fine."

"Well, okay. Help yourself to coffee and snacks. We'll start in about five minutes."

Michael crossed the floor to the coffee urn and poured the hot liquid into his cup. He took a sip and made a face—it reminded him of his buddies and the war.

Fox brought the group to attention. "Would all you Devil Dogs take your places now?" A hush fell over the room as the group seated themselves in chairs that formed a circle. There appeared to be about twelve people. Michael stood rooted to one spot. Fox gazed over at him and pointed to an empty chair.

Barely limping, Michael walked over and took a seat.

Fox made eye contact with each individual as he spoke. "Recovery from post-traumatic stress disorder is a gradual, ongoing process. There is no quick fix. Healing doesn't happen overnight. Memories of the trauma never disappear completely. This can make life difficult. But there are many things you can do to cope and reduce your anxiety and fear."

Robin entered the room and wrote on a white board with a red marker.

1. Intrusive, upsetting memories of the event

2. Flashbacks that act or feel like the event is happening in the present

3. Nightmares

4. Feelings of intense distress when reminded of the trauma

5. Intense physical reactions to reminders of the event such as rapid breathing, nausea, muscle tension, sweating

Fox talked about each topic. "It's important to face and feel your memories and emotions."

As the evening wore on, Michael grew tense as he connected to each person; yet, all they had in common was post-traumatic stress disorder. He had always viewed his flashbacks as a sign of weakness.

Maybe not.

He left the room and stood outside the door, his thoughts on a rampage. Afghanistan, the war, the embers in the pit of his gut had never burned out. Here he was in another war zone, fighting a different kind of enemy. These miserable bastards were after blood—not too different from the terrorists. So much was at stake. He barely needed his cane. Now if he could get rid of the damn reoccurring memories and put the war behind him.

He walked back into the meeting and took a seat in the circle.

CHAPTER 15

FLAMES FROM THE FIRESIDE cast illusive shadows between Dillon and Nicole as they waited for Cody to join them at the Bear Mountain Inn.

Dillon sipped his scotch on the rocks and studied Nicole's far-away look. "So, how was your day? You seem bothered by something."

Nicole stared at her Martini a moment then gazed across the candlelit table at Dillon. "I met Michael today."

Dillon flexed his brows. "Did he visit you at the mansion?"

"Yes, he and Bruno were poolside having lunch."

"You joined them for lunch?"

"No, I visited their table for a few minutes." She took the olive out of her Martini and nibbled.

"You seem upset by it?"

Her eyes welled with tears. "It's just that he reminds me a lot of Perry—his nose, his eyes, even his chin."

"Hey, you're not going soft on me, are you? A short time ago you couldn't wait to do away with Perry." Nicole's sexual addiction and mood swings worried Dillon. Could he trust her with confidential information? "So what did you talk about today with Michael?"

"Oh, he just wanted to know when I last saw Perry."

"I hope you didn't tell him anything."

Nicole rolled her eyes. "What do you think, I'm stupid? Besides, there's not much to tell. No one knows whether Perry's dead or alive." She giggled and squirmed in her seat. "I told him he could call me mom. I was only joking, of course."

Dillon stared at her, failing to see the humor. "I don't get the Mom stuff."

"Well, after all, I am his stepmother." She chuckled—then paused as her eyes filled with tears. "I'm sorry. It's just that seeing Perry's son reminds me that I have a kid of my own somewhere."

"Oh? I didn't know. You never mentioned it."

She nodded. "No one knows about her. I named her Amelia -- Amy for short. She'd be twenty-one today." The glow of candlelight reflected in her teary eyes. She reached for her Martini and downed it. "My beautiful little girl was six months old when she was stolen from me." She took a tissue from her purse and dabbed her eyes. "Please, I need another drink."

Dillon recalled how she practically raped him in the restaurant the last time she drank too much. "Are you sure you can handle another Martini?"

"No problem, I can handle my booze. I always get this way every year on her birthday. My psychiatrist says it's normal."

Dillon flagged the cocktail waitress and ordered another round. "Why didn't you go to the police and report the kidnapping?"

"I was seventeen and scared." She removed a compact from her bag and clicked it open.

"You were young."

She nodded and gazed at herself in the small mirror, dabbing at her eyes. "Too young to know what I was doing."

They were quiet a moment as the waitress served their drinks. Dillon spoke with sensitivity. "What about your parents? Couldn't they help?"

"Parents?" Her face grew dark as she sipped her drink. "I had a stepfather who molested me and a mother who didn't care."

"I'm sorry, I didn't know. Tell me how the kidnapping came about?"

She took a labored breath and put her compact back in her bag. "I stole my boyfriend's motorcycle and drove to Lakeport. After I found a place to live, I discovered I was pregnant. The problem started with my neighbor in the adjoining apartment. Her name was Mildred. Throughout my pregnancy, Mildred called me over for tea and cookies."

"Mildred—Mildred who?"

"I don't know." Nicole shook her head. "I didn't get her last name."

"Okay, go on."

"I needed a friend. I told her everything. She said she was a midwife and had delivered many babies. I explained I didn't want the authorities involved, and I would pay her to deliver my baby."

"Why didn't you want the authorities involved, and where did you get the money?"

"Not only did I steal my boyfriend's motorcycle, I stole his money. I was afraid he'd find me. I was on the run, so I didn't go to the police."

"You could have gone to a shelter." Dillon knew of such places dealing with some of the downtrodden when he took his job as sheriff seriously.

"I didn't know about shelters. I made the mistake of telling this woman where I hid the cash. When my time came, she was there. After I delivered, she babysat for me. When Amy was six months old, she took the money I had hidden in the freezer. I came home from work one day and found her and my baby gone."

"What did she look like, this Mildred? Maybe I can track her down."

Nicole grabbed a tissue from her purse and dabbed at her tears. "That was over twenty years ago. Mildred would be about sixty today. She was plain looking and wore shoulder-length brown hair with bangs."

"I'll look into it."

Nicole's eyes flash over Dillon's head as Cody entered the restaurant and slid into the booth.. "Sorry, I'm late, damn traffic."

"You must be Cody?" Nicole's voice changed from a quivering victim to a seductive vamp.

"You've got to be the beautiful Nicole I've heard so much about."

Nicole smiled and leaned far enough over to show plenty of cleavage. "Would you boys excuse me a moment while I go powder my nose?"

"Of course," Cody said, "a woman's prerogative."

Dillon rose and stood outside the booth as Nicole wriggled free. She batted her eyes at Cody and Dillon wondered if her sexual urges were kicking in. He didn't care who she screwed as long as it wasn't his partner.

Dillon sat back down and observed Cody's eyes travel after Nicole. One wrong move and Cody could take over Nicole, the map, and the gold. He was sorry he ever took the guy on as a partner. He hated to resort to murder, but if he had to kill the bastard, he wouldn't hesitate.

"You dog you—she's hot." Cody laughed. "Very hot."

The waitress came and took Cody's drink order. Dillon jumped to another subject. "What did you find out from the bug we planted at Drake's cabin? Anything?"

"Yeah, I picked up on a one-sided phone conversation between Michael and some dude he called Bruno. Looks like the Marine found another hiding place for the map. He didn't say where."

"So we're back to square one." Dillon frowned. "Anything else?"

"We did such a number trashing the cabin it will take time to put the place back in order. I heard through our bug that Michael is using the houseboat as temporary lodging."

Dillon knocked back his scotch and eyed Cody. "He doesn't stray far from the cabin, does he?"

"No, and it makes me wonder if the map isn't close by. Hey, I've got an idea." Cody smiled.

"Oh, yeah, what?"

"How about we send Nicole? She could go over to the houseboat and crawl in bed with the jarhead. See if she can't sweet talk him into telling his secrets."

"Nah, I think the Marine's too smart for that."

"You can never tell. He just might be dying for sex with a woman like Nicole."

"Did I hear my name mentioned?"

Dillon jumped to his feet and Nicole slid in the booth. She looked from one to the other and laughed. "Come on guys, I know you were talking about me. What were you saying?"

Dillon shook his head at Cody, signaling him not to talk about Nicole ingratiating Michael. "We were just remarking what a beautiful woman you are."

Cody gazed at her voluptuous breasts. "Yes, indeed, ravishing."

"You boys are too kind." She sipped her Martini, leaned back in the booth and fluttered her lashes. "You know, this is just a thought. I'd like to help in some way. How about if I pay Michael a visit? I bet I could persuade him to give a clue about where the map is hidden."

Dillon wondered if she hadn't overheard their conversation. "I'd rather you stay away from Michael and let us handle things." Her emotional stability would not survive an act of playing up to Michael. One wrong move saying something stupid, and their whole plan could fall through. They needed to find the map, but not through Nicole.

"Now wait a minute," Cody said as he looked at Nicole with curiosity. "How would you do it? Do you have magic charm, or what?"

Dillon glared at Cody. "I don't want her involved."

Nicole gave Cody her most sultry look. "Oh, you might just be surprised about my magic charm."

Cody leaned into Dillon. "Why not let her try? What would a little flirtatious prying on her part hurt?"

Dillon fumed. "I told you, I don't want her involved. I have my reasons."

Cody shot a cold stare at Dillon. "And I told you right from the beginning the jarhead would be a problem. You should have listened and allowed me to kill the son-of-a-bitch like I wanted. Now he's got the map, and we're stuck with him. If Nicole can convince him to talk, then I say she should go for it."

"Hey, no need to kill anyone," Nicole said. "Not while I'm here. I'll stop by his place tomorrow night for a visit. Just give me a few hours with that hunk."

"No. How many ways must I say it? Stay away from Michael."

They studied their menus. Nicole downed her drink, eyes blazing with fury. "I'd like another Martini."

"You've had enough to drink. We will order dinner now." He hated treating her like a child. But if she acted like one, he had no choice.

The waitress brought Cody's drink and took their dinner orders.

Nicole hiccupped. "I know what I want, steak and lobster and another Martini, please."

Dillon eyed her with disgust. "Just bring the lady her dinner and a cup of coffee."

He and Cody ordered grilled salmon, and the three ate their meals in silence.

€€€

"Care to come up for an after-dinner drink?" Dillon tried to keep the edge out of his voice as he held the car door open for Nicole.

"No thank you. I'll just be on my way." She pulled her keys out of her purse, got out of the vehicle and walked toward her BMW parked in his carport.

He reached for her hand. "Wait darlin'. Give me your keys, and I'll back out your car."

She jerked away. "No, I'll handle it."

She was a deceitful bitch, but with the Drake name, she held the power. He had to think fast. He called after her. "Do you still want me to find your kid?"

She stopped, looked down at the blacktop then turned around, her eyes questioning. With an unsteady gait, she walked back and stood in front of him. "You would do that? You would help me find my little girl?"

He wrapped his arms around her. "Come on, let's go have a Cognac and talk about how we'll track down your daughter."

Inside, Dillon set a bottle of French Hennessey and two snifter glasses on the oak coffee table. "Let's sit here." He pointed to the white rug in front of the fireplace. Two logs were already in the hearth, and with a flare of a match on kindling, he set them ablaze. He punched in soft music then poured them each a Cognac.

They relaxed on the floor propped against large throw pillows and watched the fire. Dillon broke the silence. "Okay, tell me everything about this woman you say kidnapped your baby."

Nicole took a sip of her Cognac and stared at the flames crackling in the hearth. "Mildred told me she had been a midwife for ten years and delivered babies around Rogue's Hollow."

"Go on." Dillon sat up and stoked the fire as he listened.

"Ex-cons and murderers were her best clients. She said they paid her well. I often wondered if my baby girl got caught up in that ghost town with those awful people."

Dillon lifted his Cognac snifter to his lips as he studied Nicole. She almost seemed human when she talked about her kid. "Did Mildred give you any kind of clue? Were you ever suspicious of her intentions to kidnap your baby?"

"No, not at all. She mentioned that before her husband died, they tried to have a child, but she found out she couldn't get pregnant. I thought nothing of it at the time."

Dillon vaguely recalled a lone baby found in a car parked alongside the road in the general area of Rogue's Hollow. His pa and brothers, lawmen at the time, had said they were looking for the kid's parents. Later, they found a body of a woman coiled up in the bushes where the car was parked. She'd been shot. That could have been Mildred, he thought. "Did you ever try to find Mildred and your baby? Did you investigate?"

"After I went to work and could afford it, I hired a detective. He came up empty-handed and told me I'd be better off if I dropped it. He never said why."

"What was the detective's name?"

"Everett Black. A short time later, they found him dead in his apartment."

"Hmmm, interesting. Okay, you've given me a few leads. I'll dig into it right away."

Nicole sat up and poured herself another shot of Cognac. "Find my daughter, and I will forever be in your debt."

That's what I'm counting on, Dillon thought. Keep her coming back to him until he had his hands on the gold, then dump her. If the map had been willed to him at the beginning like it should have been, he wouldn't have these complications.

He smiled and clicked his snifter against hers. "Don't worry, I'll find your daughter."

€€€

Dillon wasted little time. The following day at the sheriff's office, he checked the police files on his computer. He searched for murdered women in early 1990, around the time Nicole's baby had been stolen.

Two murders, a young male shot in the chest linked to a string of carjacking crimes. The other, a woman with a bullet lodged in the back her head. She had no identification and was buried as Jane Doe. Both bodies were found in proximity along the shoulder of Old Gold Miner's Road—the road leading to Rogue's Hollow.

He searched the database at length for baby findings. One small article caught his eye. The information filled in the puzzle pieces of what his pa and brothers had said about a six-month-old baby girl found strapped in a car seat in an abandoned Chevy. The article withheld the name of the person who found the baby. What he found interesting was that the abandoned car had disappeared before the police could get to the scene and collect info regarding the owner of the vehicle. They never resolved the murder, and the case went cold. The woman shot in the head most likely—Mildred.

Dillon sat back in his swivel chair and toyed with the ends of his handlebar mustache. If he could track down the person who found the baby, maybe he'd get answers on the kid and where she lived today.

He picked up his landline and punched the buzzer for his secretary. "Molly, get me Detective Cooper, ASAP."

"Sure thing, boss."

Ten minutes later Ross Cooper walked through the door. "Yeah, Dillon, what can I do for you? I hope this is important, I'm kinda in the middle of something."

"Put everything on hold. I want you on a cold case right away."

"Okay, what's it about?"

Dillon filled Cooper in on the missing baby. "This case goes back to the early nineties. I don't care how you get the info. I want the name of the person who found that kid. Do you understand?"

"No problem, Sheriff. I think I know a few people who owe me favors."

CHAPTER 16

NIGHTFALL SETTLED as Michael climbed the steps to the top deck of the houseboat. He grabbed an icy Heineken out of the fridge and stretched out on the chaise lounge. A cool breeze whipped across his face as he sipped beer and stared up into the black sky filled with stars. He wondered about his father—would he ever see him again—dead or alive?

The Marine Corps had taught him you can't bury your head in the mud and expect results. Shit happens because you make it happen. Reliving the war in his head had thrown him off course. Maybe he'd try another therapy session next week just for the hell of it.

In the meantime, he'd do his best to find the thugs responsible for hurting his father. He could get real used to the old principle of an eye for an eye.

He reached for the key around his neck and stroked it between his fingers. The map was safe for now guarded within the boundaries of the algorithm he'd created. Even if they got their hands on the flash drive and plugged it into a computer, it would take a squad of geeks to figure out the formula. But was it all worth it? Was his father's life not more valuable than buried gold?

As he stared at the sky, stars twinkled back at him as if in response to his thoughts. Water lapped against the hull of the boat, killing the dull silence of the night. His eyes became heavy, and he slipped away.

Slight footsteps from the lower deck of the boat connected with the symbolic images he'd concocted in his dream. Weight pressed against his chest like a loaded barbell. His breath came in spurts. The sound grew closer, and his eyes snapped open.

Like a cobra ready to strike, he sat up and grabbed for his Beretta on the side table. The muscles in his face stiffened as he cocked the chamber and aimed at the stairwell. "Come on, you bastard, show yourself or I'll shoot and I never miss."

"Whoa, Michael, wait..." Moonlight reflected across her face and hair.

His brows arched in recognition, and he lowered the gun. "Nicole, what are you doing here?"

As she stepped onto the deck, her white billowy dress whipped in the breeze, exposing long bronzed legs and red bikini panties. She stood in front of him. "Do you always greet people with a gun pointed at their head?"

He placed the Beretta back on the side table and rose to his feet. "You're lucky I didn't blow your brains out. Have you heard of a phone? You know, it's a little gadget you put a number into, punch and send, and then put to your ear..."

She smiled and smoothed her windblown hair. "I'm sorry; I guess I should have called first."

"Yeah, you should have. I don't take kindly to walk-ins. Things are a little testy around here these days since the cabin was trashed." He figured she knew all about that episode.

Her eyes widened. "Oh, your cabin was trashed? Sorry to hear that. I just came by for a visit. We've got a lot in common you know, with Perry and all."

Michael wondered what she was trying to pull. They had as much in common as a black widow spider and a baby's butt. He didn't trust many people, especially his father's wife. He decided to use reverse tactics to find out her ploy. With his most charming smile, he pulled out a chair from the patio table. "Well, be my guest, Nicole. Sit here. How about a drink? I have nothing stronger than Heineken."

"Sounds good, I love beer." She sat down, her sheer, white dress rising up her thighs.

He grabbed an icy bottle from the fridge, opened it and started to pour into a mug.

"That's okay; I like to drink it straight from the bottle."

He handed her the beer. "Can I get you a jacket to throw over your shoulders? It's a bit chilly, how about a blanket to cover your legs?"

"Why, yes, I'd like a cozy jacket, please."

He grabbed the windbreakers he and Nash had worn earlier. He put one on and placed the other around her shoulders.

"Like father, like son." She giggled. "Perry used to pay attention to me just like this." Tears welled in her eyes. "Your father was so good to me."

He sat down and pulled his chair close to her. "So, tell me your theory on what happened to my father. Do you think he's still alive?"

She gazed out at the lake a moment then fluttered her lashes as she looked at him. "I don't know what to think. I'm really worried about him."

With those few words, he knew she was lying. He had studied deceptive behavior when he trained for Special Operations, one of his last assignments in the Marine Corps. First of all, liars tend to flutter their eyelashes. Also, a lying person is more likely to cover their mouth with their hand, almost as if to cover the lies they utter. He noted she did both when she spoke about his father.

Uncertain how it would all play out, he went along with her game hoping to catch her off guard. He could hardly believe they would send someone so transparent to play him. Perhaps greed for gold had dulled their wits.

As the evening progressed, he served her two more beers, and could see she was getting a buzz on with the third. He recalled his father's words on the plane trip home. *I'm sure Nicole had something to do with Ida's death.* Michael was never too fond of his stepmother, Ida, but no one deserved to be murdered even if they were comatose.

He leaned forward in his chair and eyed Nicole. Perhaps he could pry open her dark side. His tone was empathetic. "You must miss Perry."

"I do, I certainly do." Her lashes fluttered, and she lowered her head.

He patted her hand. "So tell me, how did you meet my father?"

She took a sip of beer and smiled. "We met when I applied for a job at The Rock. It was love at first sight. He hired me as hostess manager. Would you believe I moved up the ladder real fast and became the general manager?"

He believed it, knowing how in love his father had become with the woman. He would have given her a slice of the moon if he could have managed it. "That's quite a job, running a big seafood restaurant like The Rock."

"Oh, I had experience. I once helped run a busy truck stop café when I was sixteen." She looked at him and didn't waver. Michael realized the woman had more smarts than the bimbo act she portrayed.

"You started out early."

"Yeah, I did." She gazed out at the lake. "But that's another chapter in my life." She leaned her head back in the chair and closed her eyes. "You are so easy to talk to, Michael. I feel comfortable around you. Not like some of the other characters I've been with."

He wondered if she was referring to her sheriff friend. "Thank you, I'm glad you feel that way." Since she was so comfortable, maybe she wouldn't mind a few hard questions. "I've been meaning to ask you, Nicole... whatever happened to Ida? Did you know her before she passed away?"

She opened her eyes with a start and sat up straight. Her jaw tightened as she looked down at her hands folded in her lap. "I knew of Ida. She was after your father's money, you know... Why are you bringing her up now?"

Michael smiled. "Oh, no reason."

She finished the last of her third beer and sighed. "To tell you the truth, I was concerned for Ida the whole two years she was in that coma."

Yeah, I bet, Michael thought. So much so you smothered her to death with a pillow. His father's words echoed in his mind. *I found Nicole's diamond hair-barrette tangled in the bed sheets shortly after Ida was pronounced dead. It doesn't make sense because Nicole never visited Ida—she hated Ida.*

"So, what happened to Ida?"

"I don't know." She covered her mouth with her fingers and shook her head. "The nursing home called one day and said she died in a coma."

Michael smiled through his anger. "Can I get you another beer, Nicole?"

"I'd love one."

He grabbed a Heineken out of the fridge and brought it to her.

She stood up and ran her tongue over her bottom lip. "I hope there's no more talk about Ida. I'd much rather talk about you."

It took every effort to hold back his rage as he stared into the eyes of the woman responsible for the disappearance or death of his father.

He could not help but shudder at the touch of her fingertips under his half-open shirt. "I've been meaning to tell you what a great body you have." She stroked his chest then fondled the key around his neck.

He removed her hand and tucked the key and tags under his shirt.

She stood on unsteady feet and giggled. "Oh, now, you've got my curiosity up. I want to know more about the little ole key and tags around your neck."

She was too intoxicated to drive home, and he hoped too drunk to remember the key. She squealed as he picked her up and carried her down to the guest bedroom. He plopped her on the bed. "Get a couple hours sleep. When you wake up, you can go home."

She thrust out her bottom lip like a spoiled child who'd do anything to get what she wanted. "No, I don't want to sleep. I want to make love to you." She hurled her arms around him and threw him off balance. He fell on top of her. "Take off your clothes—no wait—I'll take them off for you. It's more exciting if I do it." She fumbled for the buttons on his shirt and his belt buckle.

He pulled away from her and jumped to his feet.

"Oh, shoot. Where are you going? Come back here. You're so sexy, just like your father." Her glassy eyes gazed up at him.

He stared at her and wondered how his father could have been so blinded by this woman. "Sober up. We'll talk later." He walked out and shut the bedroom door.

Around 2:00 am, Michael checked the bedroom and saw rumpled sheets and no Nicole. He had to give her credit. She knew how to play her cards with men—that's how she trapped his father. But he found her attempt to play the dumb blond unravel as the night wore on. He hoped her drunken state wiped away the memory of the key around his neck. Her surprise visit was all the more reason he needed to stay alert.

He slept for a few hours, then got up and put on a pot of coffee. While he waited for Nash to join him for Tai Chi, he scanned the dense forest across the lake for anyone who looked out of place. After Nicole's little visit, he wouldn't put anything past her or her cohorts.

The outlying area looked calm, but his old playground, the flat rock, had the company of his favorite redhead. He enlarged the zoom on the binocular scope and enjoyed watching her as she sashayed to the end of the rock and dove in. Her head, arms and body moved together like a living work of art.

By some standards, ogling her through the binoculars might be construed as spying or even stalking. Without a qualm, he enjoyed every stealthy moment observing the female anatomy of the lovely Miss Annie Maguire.

Then he saw the rip-current, about ten feet out from where she romped in the water—a little too close for comfort. His jaw tightened as he watched her flip over on her back and float toward the current.

Nash arrived and walked up to the boat railing next to Michael. "Hey, what's going on?"

"Got a little problem here—no time to explain." Michael grabbed a rescue tube from the side of the boat then handed Nash the binoculars and his cell phone. "Keep a close watch and be prepared to call 911."

Ignoring his weak leg, a swift dive drove him a quarter of the way to the center of the lake. When he came up for air, he swam freestyle front crawl, the fastest stroke he knew. He and his childhood buddies raced to the flat rock many times.

He got to her as she entered the rip-current. When she saw him, her eyes widened. Her arms thrashed wildly in an attempt to swim back to the rock. The more she fought against the current the further away she was driven.

Michael joined the torrent of water and moved with the current until he caught up with her—then he placed the ring buoy around her body. "Try to relax," he shouted. "Go with the flow of the current."

"No." She struggled against him and pushed to swim in the opposite direction toward the flat rock. "No," she screamed, "let me go."

He felt the powerful pull of the current as he wrapped his arms around her. "You can't fight it. Stay with me on this." He grabbed her chin and forced her to look into his eyes. "Go with the movement of the water and you'll be okay—it will eventually pass."

She pushed, shoved, and cried, but finally gave in.

Like a monster with its own itinerary, the rip carried them on a journey across the water. Heavy wind gusts strengthened the channel, driving them deeper towards the center of the lake. When the current lost power they found themselves on the opposite side, about a mile from the houseboat. Once they were free, they swam back, along the lakeside.

Sirens wailed in the distance as Michael helped Annie aboard the deck of the barge.

Nash greeted them and handed out towels. "How is she?"

"I think she's okay." Michael guided Annie into a chair and wrapped her in a large terry-towel. He examined her for shock. Her coloring was good, but her body shook from chill. He took her pulse rate and found it a little spiked but nothing out of the ordinary.

"Nash, dry clothes in my bedroom; can you get them, please? And, could you please hand me my cane?"

"Sure thing." Nash retrieved the cane then went below for dry clothes.

Michael turned full attention to Annie. "Pretty scary wasn't it?"

The medics and firemen arrived and took over. They checked Annie thoroughly. "She's fine," A big blond fireman who looked like a Swede spoke with authority. "Keep her warm."

"I'm okay. Just a little confused about what happened." She turned to Michael. "Thank you, for saving my life."

"You had me worried there for a minute. But we made it, didn't we." Michael brushed a few strands of hair from her face. "You're shivering, how about a cup of hot tea?"

"Yes, I'd like that."

The fireman squeezed Annie's hand. "If you need anything more, give us a call. In the future be on the lookout for rip currents; they are a source of danger in this area and cause more than one hundred deaths annually in the United States. The power of the current can drag you away from shore, and death by drowning usually comes following exhaustion while fighting the current." He smiled. "Looks like you're in good hands here."

"Thanks for all your help," Michael said to the medic and bid farewell.

Nash brought dry clothes and handed Annie a large, knit, pullover with long sleeves. "A little big, but it should keep you warm."

"Red, my favorite color." Annie chuckled and slipped the shirt on over her head.

They hurried downstairs and settled at the kitchen table. Michael made hot tea with lemon and honey and served homemade chocolate chip cookies that Bruno had brought over from the mansion. Nash couldn't keep his hands off them, and Annie ate her share.

"Tasty cookies." She took a sip of tea.

Michael gazed into the greenest eyes he'd ever seen. He couldn't believe how beautiful she was. But there was something about the structure of her face, or maybe it was in her smile that looked familiar to him. He'd seen her somewhere, and it gave him a queasy feeling, like the yin and yang of good and evil. He couldn't put his finger on it.

"You were spying on me, weren't you?" She smiled. "Otherwise how would you have known I faced a dangerous rip current?"

"Well, I wasn't really spying—"

"Nash chuckled. "He spies on you a lo—"

Michael nudged Nash under the table. "What Nash is trying to say is that I often survey the area and just happened to see you swimming in the lake."

Michael felt the depth of her smile, and it was hard to concentrate on her words. "Well, you saved my life. If it hadn't been for your… survey I surely would have drowned, and I can't thank you enough."

"I'm glad I was there for you."

"I have to head back now. My horse is tied to a tree, and my brothers worry about me."

"Let's get you on your way, then." Michael smiled and rose to his feet. "You stay and finish your tea with Nash while I man the ship across the lake."

€€€

Once on the other side of the lake, Nash stayed aboard while Michael helped Annie off the houseboat. The two of them circled around the huge flat rock toward Annie's horse.

As they approached Knight, Annie came to an abrupt stop. "I hear voices. I don't think we're alone."

Michael's adrenalin pumped as muffled sounds became louder. He felt for his Beretta under his jacket as two men on horseback broke through a small opening of thick oak trees.

"Are you sure this is the place?" One man said to the other.

"Yes. I followed her here once. This is where she swims and sunbathes."

Annie squeezed Michael's arm. "It's okay. They're my brothers. Let me handle them. They're upset."

Upset was a nice way of putting it, Michael thought. If icy stares could shoot bullets, he'd be frozen stiff.

"Annie, thank God we found you." The man got off his horse, cocked his rifle and aimed at Michael. "Who the hell are you?"

Michael started to speak "I'm—"

Annie stepped forward. "Now you wait a minute, Zack. For the last time, quit trying to run my life. At least give me a chance to explain."

"Start explaining." He eyed Annie but kept a close watch on Michael.

Jonas dismounted his horse, crossed over and stood next to Zack. "We've been searching all over the forest for you. You've been gone for hours. Where'd you find this guy? Did this guy hurt you?"

"You idiots, this guy, as you call him, saved my life. His name is Michael Drake. I'd have drowned in a rip current if he hadn't come along when he did. I may tell you about it sometime when you simmer down. Now get that gun out of his face."

Zack stared at Michael and lowered his rifle. "If you helped Annie like she said, then we're more than obliged to you. Please accept our apologies."

"I appreciate your concern for your sister," Michael said. "I couldn't comprehend why she came out here alone either. I don't blame you for being worried."

"Well, she's been trying to prove her independence." He looked over at Annie, then back at Michael. "I guess we are a little rough on her—just trying to keep her safe. Let us make it up to you. Have dinner with us out at our ranch. That's the least we can do to repay you. Besides, I want to hear how you saved Annie's life."

"It's unnecessary to repay me. I'm glad I was there when she needed me. But, I'd like to have dinner with you." He reached for a handshake. "I didn't get your names?"

"I'm Zack Maguire, and this is my brother Jonas." They all shook hands. "We own the Maguire Horse Ranch in Crystal Valley. How's tomorrow sound, around six? We'll have Maria and Jose cook-up steaks and Mexican food—that's their specialty and you wouldn't want to miss it."

Michael smiled at Annie. "I wouldn't miss it for the world."

CHAPTER 17

SHERIFF DILLON PROPPED his feet on the desktop and ogled his new Durango boots. "How do you like them?" he asked Molly as she whizzed into his office with his first cup of coffee.

"Cool, Sheriff, very cool." Her plump face glowed as she hummed a tune and set his coffee in front of him.

If only there were more Mollies in the world, he thought, as he watched her leave the room—perpetually on time, trustworthy and never frazzled. Not exactly a woman of the world, but always there to meet your needs.

He sighed. He had to figure out what to do about Nicole. She was such a bitch. But until he had his hands on the map, he needed to keep her happy.

In the side drawer of his desk, he dug around and found the box of Cuban cigars given to him from one of his snitches. There was nothing really to celebrate, he just loved the taste. He lit one and took a long, drag as he checked his notes about Nicole and her missing kid.

Twenty years ago, someone spotted a six-month-old baby in a 1967 Chevy, and like a sneaky bird of prey, snatched the kid right out of the car seat. The baby hadn't been seen or heard from since. Maybe it was Nicole's kid and maybe it wasn't.

The main question: who found the baby girl and withheld the name from the adoption records? He reasoned one of two things must have happened. Since the vehicle was in the vicinity of Rogue's Hollow, the tyke may have wound up in the old ghost town with the scum of the earth. Or... he drummed his fingers on the desk and watched cigar smoke swirl to the ceiling... Or what?

He took a sip of coffee and reached for the phone as it rang. "Yes, Molly?"

"Ross Cooper, boss."

"Thanks put him through. "Dillon puffed on his cigar as the detective came on the line."Yeah, what you got, Cooper? Anything on the kid?"

"Let me tell you, it wasn't easy." Cooper breathed heavy into the phone. "But I finally convinced that arrogant bastard in the records department that if he didn't give me what I wanted, I'd tell the world about his secret sex life, and believe me it ain't pretty."

Dillon stubbed out his cigar. "It always amazes me how you detectives dig up shit on people. But please, spare me—just give me what you've got on the kid."

"Okay. A baby girl, six months old at the time, was taken out of her travel seat from an old 1967 Chevy. Mind you, the year is 1990. The man's name who came along and rescued the baby was Zack Maguire. He and his two sons live on a horse ranch located about ten miles north of Lakeport."

"Yeah, I've heard of them." Dillon played with his mustache as he listened to Cooper.

"Well, according to the records, the Maguire's searched everywhere for the baby's parents. They couldn't find anyone with ties to the kid, so they adopted her through legal channels. And, by the way, the Chevy disappeared shortly after the baby was taken. I'm still tracking the car—old junk yards are my next stop."

"Good work, Cooper. When you find the missing car, let me know."

"Will do."

"Are you free to go with me out to the Maguire Ranch tomorrow morning? I need you there as a witness, just in case something goes wrong."

"I'm free, but I don't think the Maguire boys are going to like it much when they find out the adoption records have been compromised, exposing their daughter's personal life. From what I understand, they are not men to mess with—they have a gun arsenal and they're not afraid to use firepower."

"Okay, leave that to me. I'll break it to them gently. Surely they'd want to know the girl's mother."

"That may work. I just hope I get a bonus for all the trouble I went through to get this info for you."

"Don't worry—you'll get your reward. Just keep a lid on what you know. Did you find out her name?"

"Yeah… Annie Maguire."

€€€

Dillon took the rest of the day off, went home and made his special shrimp and crab Louie salad. Nicole was due around noon. When he answered the door chime, he expected to see her in her usual chic style.

Instead, one earring was missing and her face looked puffy. She raked her fingers through a mass of blonde tangles, made her way into the kitchen and sat down at the breakfast nook. Her first words, "I need a drink."

Give her what she demands, Dillon thought. When she's hammered, there's no peace. He mixed her a Martini and placed it in front of her. "How about something to eat like a seafood salad?"

"No. I'm okay. No lunch."

She downed the drink. Dillon filled her glass with more and made himself a Scotch on the rocks. "What happened? Why are you so upset? You look a mess."

"Michael…"

"What about Michael? Surely, you didn't…"

She nodded. "Yeah, I did. I went over to his boathouse. We had a friendly visit."

"I told you not to go over there."

"I know…" She stared out the open sliding door to the backyard. "I'd like to take a dip in the pool now and later lie in the sun for a while. Can we?"

"Tell me about Michael first. You went to his houseboat and then what? Did you sleep with him?" Not that he gave a damn—he worried she might have said something stupid.

She sipped her drink and shook her head. "No, we just talked."

"What about?"

"He kept asking me about Perry; if I knew what happened to him."

"You mean, he drilled you?"

"No, not really. Don't worry, I didn't let anything slip."

"What else?"

"He asked a lot of strange questions about Ida, Perry's second wife."

She stared at her Martini glass and swirled it on the tabletop as if she were in deep thought.

"What about Ida?"

"He wanted to know about her death."

"Well, you didn't have anything to do with Ida's death, did you?" Dillon arched his brows and twirled the ice around in his drink.

She looked at him and didn't answer. He saw murder written all over her face. She'd stop at nothing to get what she wanted. It occurred to him, as it had many times, to watch his own back around her.

"Can we go out by the pool now? I drank too much last night. I've got a hangover..."

"Not yet. What else did you and Michael talk about?"

"I got a little plastered drinking beer, and well... you know how I get sometimes."

Dillon was sure she was referring to her sexual appetite. "Tell me about it."

"After a few beers, I admit, I tried to seduce him."

Dillon looked at her disheveled hair and wrinkled clothes. "Yeah, I figured as much. So what happened?"

"First of all, I ran my fingers under his shirt, across his chest. He has a nice body if you know what I mean." She smiled, gazing at Dillon's muscular pecs.

"Then what?"

"Then the strangest thing happened. While I was feeling all tingly and wonderful, the son-of-a-bitch removed my hand like I was trespassing on sacred ground. But not before I realized I wasn't just fondling his hunky chest, but his dog tags and a key."

"So?" Dillon took a gulp of his drink.

"A key... Don't you get it? He was adamant about tucking the key back under his shirt. I may have been a bit intoxicated, but I think the key might open a bank vault."

"You mean like a key to a safe deposit box?"

"Exactly. The map might be hidden in one."

Dillon stared at her in awe. "Maybe your little jaunt over to Michael's is worth its weight in gold."

€€€

The following morning, Dillon drove through the gates of the Maguire Horse Ranch and sped down a mile long dirt road surrounded by green meadows and rich grazing land.

Detective Cooper sat next to him, his eyes glued to the horses in the pasture. "Awe, would you look at that field covered with green clover. I always wanted a horse... I remember when I was a kid, I—"

"Later, Cooper," Dillon spat out. "Right now, I need to concentrate on the situation at hand."

He came to a stop and parked his police vehicle in the circle drive in front of the sprawling ranch house. They got out of the car and approached the front porch.

A tall fellow with white hair stepped from behind the screen door and met them as they walked up the steps. Dillon liked the guy's handlebar mustache—it looked much like his own—at least they had something in common. But the eyes weren't smiling.

"Can I help you?"

"I hope so." Dillon put on his best smile as he and the detective showed their police badges. "This is Detective Ross Cooper, and I'm Sheriff Dillon Hobbs of Three Lakes County. We'd like to pose a few questions to Seth Maguire. Is he around?"

"I'm Seth Maguire. We seldom get the law out here. What's this all about?"

"We'd like to talk to you about Annie Maguire. We understand she's your adopted daughter."

A younger man opened the screen door and stepped out onto the porch. "What about Annie? Why are you nosing around about her?"

"That's okay, Zack," Seth said. "I'll handle this. Yes, Annie's my adopted daughter. What about it?"

"Sorry, but I wouldn't call it nosing around. Recently it has come to our attention that Annie was found by Seth Maguire in an old car when she was a baby—right around 1990. We'd like to—"

Dillon's smile froze as he heard the sound of a firearm cocked behind his back. He turned around to see a rifle pointed straight at him.

"Why would that be your concern, mister?" Jonas held the rifle steady.

Dillon became aware that Detective Cooper wasn't at his side. He made a quick scan of the area and spotted him petting a horse at a nearby corral. Damn gumshoe, he thought, as he tried to avoid looking down the barrel of the Winchester pointed straight at his heart. He focused instead on a face with a nasty scowl and tried to stay calm. "We may have found Annie's birth mother." He cleared his throat. "We thought you might like to know."

Jonas squinted at Dillon. "Those adoption records were sealed. How did you find—"

Dillon knew they'd ask, so he had a ready lie. "I found the information on my desk one morning—a mother's plea, searching for her missing daughter. I don't know how it got there."

"How do we know she's the actual birth mother of Annie?" Seth asked.

"We don't know for sure. What we do know is Annie was adopted by Seth Maguire right about the same time this mother's baby was kidnapped."

Zack doubled his fists as he leaned forward into Dillon's space. "Now wait a minute. You're not accusing us of kidnapping Annie, are you?"

"No, no," Dillon stepped back and waved off the idea, "No, we're not accusing you of anything, but we're looking into more details of the kidnapping."

"Twenty years too late," Jonas said still scowling.

"Lower your rifle, son. If they have information on Annie's birth mother, we'll look into it. If it turns out this woman's Annie's kin, then we'll break the news to Annie in our own way."

Jonas lowered his rifle. "I don't like it, Pa. They had no right to look at Annie's records."

"I know son. Let's wait and see what comes of it."

Dillon wiped the sweat off his brow, anxious to get the hell out of there. "Just give me a date and time, and I'll be back to collect Annie's DNA."

CHAPTER 18

MICHAEL SHOWERED and slipped into a pair of faded jeans and a navy-blue crewneck shirt. Tonight he would meet Heoma, Nash's grandmother. Her reputation as a Medicine Woman gave clout to the theory she owned supernatural powers. Michael scoffed at such drivel, but he held respect for the woman. Maybe Nash's intense belief in her swayed his judgment. Whatever, he carefully handpicked aged Cabernet Sauvignon and Merlot from the wine cellar in the cabin.

An early start before sunset put a catch in his step. He hurried onto the deck of the houseboat to start the engine and was surprised to see Detective Fox and his partner climb aboard. He hardly recognized Robin out of her police uniform, wearing tight blue jeans and a pink silk blouse.

"Ahoy," Fox called out. "Great looking houseboat."

"It's beautiful," Robin said, eyeing the surroundings.

"I like it, and may never go back to the cabin." Michael smiled politely. "Hey, I don't mean to be rude, but I've made plans. If you have news about my father, I'd like to hear it, otherwise—"

"Just stopped by for a second," Fox said. "We checked out the cabin to see if there were any changes. The place is still one big nasty mess."

Michael nodded. "Yeah, we've been waiting for you to give the word before we renovate. Did forensics find any clues?"

Fox shook his head and squinted against the afternoon sun. "No, but one thing puzzles me. Why did they leave the wine cellar untouched?"

"Yes, I wondered too," Robin said. "Not only is the wine cellar a perfect place to hide whatever they were looking for, but they could have had a jolly old time smashing wine bottles to smithereens. They destroyed the rest of the cabin why not the wine cellar?" She gazed at Michael and smiled.

Mesmerized by her sexy persona, his voice cracked, and he cleared his throat. "Well... I imagine because the trap door is hidden under a carpet, and they are dumb asses and didn't figure it out."

She threw back her head and laughed. "Makes sense." The smooth curve of her neck, the porcelain skin—the more he took in her beauty the more he felt a tug at his heart... or was it his groin?

She brought her sunglasses down from the top of her head, but not before her eyes roamed across his chest and tight abs. "We wanted you to know you can go ahead with your plan to renovate the cabin. The crime scene folks are finished with their investigation."

Damn, before she covered her eyes he could have sworn she hit on him. He tried not to look at her breasts pressing against the pink, silk material of her blouse and forced his gaze level with hers. "That's good to hear. I'll tell Bruno to get started. Our first plan is to put in a new security system with cameras."

He quickly walked over to the engine and started the blower, hoping it was enough of a hint for them to leave.

Fox followed and stood next to him. "Before we go, I've been meaning to ask. Do you plan on joining us at the next PTSD support group? The first and second times are always the hardest. It gets easier every week."

"I don't know. I'll think about it."

Robin came over and stood next to Fox. "We are there if you need us and we hope you come to the next meeting."

A breeze whipped at her long, dark hair. Her perfume of tangy citrus beckoned. Maybe if I tell them I'll be there, they'll leave. "Yes, I'll be at the meeting."

After they left, he couldn't help but wonder why he was so damned important to them. Did all vets with post-traumatic stress disorder get this special treatment? Or could something else be in the wind, like a great big pot of gold? He knew he was cynical—perhaps he inherited the trait from his father—but he couldn't get past the idea that it smelled like a setup.

€€€

He stood at the helm and ran the houseboat at about seven knots. The sun settled behind Mount Konocti and splashed a vivid palette of reds, purples and oranges across the sky. Perfect balmy weather for outdoor partying, Michael thought.

When he reached Nash's place, he pulled up close to the shore and dropped anchor. A slight sound in the water caught his attention. By now, darkness overtook the lake, and he strained to see into the black night.

After fighting terrorists in Afghanistan, night-eyes never left his side. He dug them out of his backpack and adjusted the vision. As he aimed the scope toward the center of the lake, he caught the tail end of what appeared to be a yacht with the name *The Shark* glowing in white letters on the stern. No lighting on the boat only added suspicion to what he already knew. They would never give up. He kept the vessel in his sight for as long as he could.

€€€

Michael judged the cabin had been built around the early 1900's. The large hand-hewn logs stood out in rugged but good condition. Nash had mentioned how poor he and his grandmother were, but nothing appeared poor about the construction of their cabin or the land that it was built on. The view of the lake had to be spectacular during daylight hours.

He stepped onto a well-lighted front porch and knocked on the door. Nash greeted him with a wide grin and ushered him into a living room filled with hearty laughter. Michael at once felt comfortable as Nash introduced him to the elder shaman sitting around the fireplace.

"They tell the same jokes over again," Nash said. "Each time it's funnier than the last, or so they say."

"Well," one pointed out, "the older you get the less you remember, and those turn out to be the best jokes."

That brought more laughter.

Then Nash grabbed Michael's hand and guided him into a spacious kitchen painted bright yellow. Two pretty ladies with red aprons and long braids bejeweled with turquoise beads smiled at Michael. Nash introduced them as his Aunt Hola and Aunt Nata. "They are twins, and what one says the other one means."

Michael looked from one to the other and saw they were identical. Nash bragged about their cooking. "The fruit and veggies come from their own garden. Just wait till you taste the desserts they whip up."

"Sounds amazing," Michael said as he gazed around the kitchen and spotted an old wood stove in the corner, similar to the one in his own cabin.

"Have either of you seen my gran?" Nash asked his aunts.

"She's helping with the cookout." Aunt Hola smiled and pointed toward the door.

"Okay, let's go find her." Nash led Michael toward the back yard. "Wait till you see what they're cooking."

As they stepped outside, Michael breathed in the tantalizing aroma of meat grilling on an open fire. Nash led him to several people sitting at tables and made introductions. "This is Michael, my Marine friend who's teaching me Martial Arts."

Another table touted various salads, vegetables, and desserts. Three men were in charge of two sets of open fire cooking. One for chicken and the other Michael wasn't sure of.

"I hope you like rattlesnake meat," Nash said with a straight face.

Michael swallowed. "Well, I don't know… I've heard it tastes a lot like chicken." He also heard it wasn't too safe to eat because it carried parasites.

Nash was quiet a moment, then burst out laughing. "Come on, we don't eat snake anymore, or bugs or any kind of stuff like that. I was teasing. What I meant to say is I hope you like beef tenderloin. The meat will melt in your mouth."

Nash introduced him to more friends and family and then led him to a striking woman with flawless skin and large penetrating eyes. Her black hair, braided with red and turquoise silk, hung down one side of her shoulder. She wore a simple white cotton dress complimented by colorful beads draped at the neck. No one had to tell him he was gazing into the lovely face of Heoma, Medicine Woman.

"Gran, this is Michael. You know, the Marine I've been telling you about. Michael, this is Heoma, my gran. Isn't she awesome?"

Heoma smiled and extended her hand to Michael. "Before I ever met you, I felt your spirit. Thank you for looking out for my grandson. He needs a good role model in his life, and you've become his best friend."

Michael took Heoma's hand and held it in his. "Nash talks about you often, and I'm glad to meet you at last."

Her eyes lit up as she spoke. "Come, join us at our table. I'll introduce you to Awan and a few of my closest friends."

As Michael followed Heoma and Nash to their table, he looked into the friendly faces of more shaman and their wives. Heoma introduced them one by one, and they each stood and shook his hand.

Then one face stood out more than any other. Something about the man's eyes and silver hair around his temples looked familiar. The oversized western style beige shirt covering his gaunt body couldn't hide his sophisticated charm and suaveness. The red and turquoise beads hanging at his neck gave him an authentic American Indian appearance. He seemed to fit right in with the Ohlone Shaman.

An awesome look-alike, Michael thought, as he studied the man's chiseled features. He appeared to be healing from abrasions on his face, and his left arm was in a sling. Then their eyes connected and he knew. The infamous Perry Drake had just walked back into his life—alive and well,.

He wanted to shout. 'Hey Dad, it's me, Michael.' He wanted to run up and grab him and shout, 'Dad, I found you at last.' But he kept silent and waited for a signal of recognition. None came.

"This is Awan," Heoma said. "In Apache the name means *somebody*. He is somebody, but we don't know who, so we call him Awan. The shaman found him over a week ago face down on the shore of the lake, nearly dead. The cuts on his face and abrasions to his body are still healing. We think he lost his memory due to a concussion."

Michael saw slight bruising around the left eye that had not completely healed. "Shouldn't he have medical attention?"

"We would send him to a hospital, but what more could they do for him than the healing powers of the Ohlone Shaman and myself. We healed his body. In time, his memory will return on its own. For now, we just enjoy him as he is."

Awan smiled at Heoma. "And who is this young man? I haven't seen him around."

Heoma reached out and patted Awan's shoulder then she felt his forehead as if checking for fever. "This is Michael Drake. He is Nash's friend. He's come to visit us."

Awan stood and shook hands with Michael. "Pleased to meet you."

Michael sat across the table from a face void of expression. He barely tasted his food as he stared at his father and tried to figure out what to do. The more he thought about it, the more he became convinced his dad was safer here than in a hospital or at the mansion.

He hated to think what might happen if word got out that Perry Drake was still alive. Nicole and her thugs put him in this condition, and if they had the chance, they'd finish him off. He'd wait for some alone time with Heoma and tell her the whole story.

Nash jumped up when the games began. "Hey, Michael, want to play a ball race? It's called Shinny."

"I think I'll sit this one out and visit with your gran."

"Okay, see you later—I'll help with the clean up when I come back." He ran over to a lighted area in the yard to play the game.

Awan got up, stretched and started to clear the table with his one good arm.

"Help yourself to more dessert, Awan," Heoma said. "There's plenty of bread pudding."

"No thanks, I'll go watch them play ball. I'll be back later to help with the dishes."

Heoma smiled at Michael. "How about you, more dessert?"

"Thanks, maybe later. Everything is so good. You are such fine people. It's a miracle how you found Awan and put him back together in one piece."

"Well, he's not in one piece, but in time he'll come around. He's a good man, and it will be interesting to learn of his past."

Michael swallowed back the lump growing in his throat. "I think I can help in that area. Heoma… there's something you need to know."

"Oh, and what is that, my lad? You look so serious. This whole evening you seemed bothered by something."

"Well, I must tell you in confidence, but it can't go any further than you."

"My dear boy, you have my word. My lips are sealed. Why are you so worried?"

"Heoma…" Michael sat next to her at the picnic table. He felt the same trust in Heoma that he'd had for his adoptive mother, Nora—it felt good to believe in someone again. "The man you call Awan is Perry Drake. He is my father..."

"Oh, my word, your father?"

"Yes, but for now, I don't want his identity to be known to anyone. The people who tried to kill him would go after him again if they knew he was here, alive. I've been searching for him—"

"So that's why you were nervous all evening. I can imagine how stunned you must have been to find your father here after all this time. It's sad to say, a father who doesn't even recognize you."

"Yes, but I'm thankful he's alive…" Michael swallowed back emotion.

Then Heoma's face grew dark. "Who are these people who tried to kill your father? Do you know their names?"

"I know two of them. My father is a wealthy man. He has assets the average guy wouldn't understand. He also has a wife who wants him dead, all for the sake of his money."

"And, who is this devil woman?"

"Her name is Nicole Drake. I'm certain Dillon Hobbs, the sheriff of Three Lakes County, is in on this with her. There may be more."

Heoma nodded—her eyes black pits. Her voice grew husky. "These people after your father are evil. Not to worry, dear boy. I'll take care of it."

He'd been a skeptic about magical spells that harness evil spirits to produce unnatural effects, but he'd take all the help he could get. "What do you plan on doing?"

She smiled as she rocked back in her seat. "I'll take care of it, that's all you need to know. Your father is welcome to stay here with us for as long as it takes. We've made him comfortable in a bungalow with two elder shamans." She pointed to a small building that looked like a storeroom. "They play cards, and he seems to fit right in. He doesn't know who he is yet, so he wouldn't know the difference, but I think he likes it here."

Heoma possesses nothing but a good heart, Michael thought, and put supernatural powers out of his mind. He grabbed a checkbook from his backpack, wrote a check for twenty thousand and handed it to Heoma. "This is a small token of thanks for all you've done for my father."

Heoma eyed the check. "I cannot accept this. We love Awan... your father." She gave the check back to Michael.

"Please, after this, refer to my father as Awan. No one but you must know he's my father." He folded his hand over hers with the check. "Money is no object with me, and you need this money. You deserve it. You take this." He smiled.

Her eyes welled with tears. "How can I thank you?"

"You've already thanked me by saving my father's life. I will bring you more money in a few days. I will also open an account for Nash's college fund."

They sat a few moments, each in their own thoughts. Then Awan came back and dug into the bread pudding. Both Michael and Heoma smiled at each other with a secret only they knew.

CHAPTER 19

MOLLY'S OVAL FACE lit up into a big smile as she delivered Sheriff Dillon his morning coffee. "Here's the latest report from Detective Jones," she said, setting the manila folder next to his mug. "Will that be all, Sheriff?"

Dillon removed his cigar and smiled. "Thanks, Molly. I'll have more coffee later." He shook his head in awe as he watched Molly leave the room; the woman sure reminded him of his mother.

He placed the cigar back between his teeth and leaned back in his swivel chair. He would never have survived the brutal bullying of his pa and brothers if it hadn't been for his sweet ma. They not only threatened his manliness with their constant taunts about his blond curls and dimples, but jeopardized his future as the sheriff of Three Lakes County.

Ma believed in him. Damn it, if his pa and brothers hadn't turned against him, hadn't willed the map to Perry Drake, life would be a hell of a lot easier.

He stubbed out his cigar in the large cluttered ashtray, took a sip of hot coffee and opened the manila folder marked *lost baby*. Cooper did a fine job on the cold case, he thought, as he studied the report.

Annie Maguire was Nicole Drake's daughter. Too many coincidences entered the scenario for it to be any other way.

According to the cold case file, Jane Doe's body lay face down in heavy brush with a slug lodged in the back of her skull—that had to be Nicole's babysitter, Mildred. He figured earlier that same day Mildred kidnapped Nicole's baby and planned a trip to Rogue's Hollow to practice midwifery. She didn't make it. Weather reports showed heavy rain. The old Chevy sat near Jane Doe's corpse with a flat tire on the muddy road headed toward the ghost town.

Dillon took another gulp of coffee and stared out the window. *Maybe Mildred knew too much. Maybe she'd seen something she shouldn't have seen and paid dearly with her life.*

He looked up as Molly poked her head through the door. "More coffee, Sheriff?"

"Yeah, fill her up, please."

Molly walked in with the coffee pot and refilled Dillon's cup. "Anything more, sheriff?"

"No thanks, Molly." Dillon smiled. Yep, she sure favored his ma in a whole lot of ways, and he liked the attention.

His swivel chair squeaked as he shifted in his seat and lit a new cigar. He placed Jones's report back in the manila folder. Tonight, over drinks, he'd question Cody to see if he recalled anything about Jane Doe. The incident happened twenty years ago when Cody was a kid of about nineteen. Cody and the underworld were no strangers. The guy had lived in a drug infested neighborhood and was arrested for selling crack. A drug-pushing punk like Cody just may recall the murder.

He'd like to tie it together in a nice package for Nicole with no loose ends. Then again, it occurred to him that Nicole might dump him once she had what she wanted. He'd tell the bitch to kiss his ass as soon as he had his hands on the gold. Until then, the more he strung her along, the better.

At least Annie's family insisted on DNA tests—this would give him the time he needed. Nicole's genetic information could be collected anytime without her knowledge. His friend in forensics owed him a favor. When he fetched Nicole's DNA, he'd send it in to be analyzed. He'd put off telling Nicole for as long as he could.

As his cell phone rang, he reached for it and squinted at the screen. "Damn it, Cody, I thought we agreed no phone calls on the cell—you never know if some asshole is listening in."

"Well, howdy to you too, Sheriff. I'm just calling to let you know I can't meet you at Big Red's tonight. Something's come up."

Dillon rose from his chair and barked into the phone like a pit bull. "We agreed to meet for our strategy session at least once a week. What could be more important?"

"How about we meet on my yacht? We can talk and strategize there, can't we?"

"Yacht?" Dillon's tone escalated. "I didn't know you owned a yacht."

"Well, there's a lot about me you don't know."

Dillon sat down; the heat on his face could melt an icicle. "Look, you screwed up once with the damn bomb—"

"And you'll never let me live it down."

"Who else is on the yacht? That's all we need—some joker listening to our conversation about the map."

"Not to worry, we'll find privacy. I have a date with a gorgeous brunette. Meet me at the Lakeport Marina tonight, and I'll introduce you to her. I'm having food catered in for later."

Dillon felt he'd been foxed. "I'm scheduled to meet Nicole at the Bear Mountain Inn at seven."

"Call her. I'm sure she'd love to have dinner on the yacht. Why not pick her up early—she can join in on our strategy session? She knows everything we know, doesn't she?"

"No, Nicole is unstable."

The main thing he wanted to discuss with Cody was the key to a possible lock-box. If they were going to get their hands on the gold, they had to find the map, and it didn't seem too farfetched that the key Nicole saw around Michael's neck could be the lynchpin. They needed to discuss this in their strategy session, alone.

He smelled a double-cross, but he'd go along with the change in plans to see where it led. If this jerk, who called himself a mouthpiece for the underworld, gave him too much grief, he'd yank their so-called partnership right out from under his fucking nose. He'd shoot the son-of-a-bitch if he had to. He could always think of a way to dump the body and make it look like self-defense.

€€€

The sheriff pulled up the collar of his black Barracuda jacket as gusts of wind whipped across the marina. The longer he stood on the cold dock listening to Cody talk about his luxury yacht, the more agitated he became.

"Notice the name printed in blue and gold," Cody said, pointing to the side of the vessel. "Ain't that classy?"

Dillon wanted to knock the smug glow off the bastard's face.

"Oh, don't you love it, Dillon?" Nicole giggled and jumped up and down on her red stiletto heels. "*The Shark*... I can't wait to see the inside."

Dillon grimaced and switched his cigar to the other side of his mouth. He surmised Cody wanted to impress Nicole, which wasn't hard to do, considering her passion for material things. But why? The quintessential narcissist playing the nice guy role had to be for one of two reasons—sex with Nicole or to get his hands on the Drake fortune—or both.

Nicole could slip into her compulsive behavior anytime and climb all over Cody for sex. Dillon's blueprint didn't include her cozying up to his partner, at least not until the pot of gold at the end of the rainbow came through for him. He needed to put a stop to it and keep Nicole reined in.

Dillon cut Cody a flat look. "This gorgeous brunette you mentioned on the phone, where is she?"

"Oh, she'll be along. Come on, I'll give you a tour of the yacht before she gets here, then we can all sit down for a drink."

Dillon wondered how Cody could afford such luxury, but then, the guy had connections to drug lords. He received huge kickbacks from pushers. Maybe he was the drug baron himself.

They climbed aboard and crossed to the center of the deck. Cody sauntered behind a circular bar. "I call this section The Sky Lounge because you can either sunbathe on the deck or star watch." He showcased a television. "For those who enjoy sports, the retractable 42-inch T.V. is available."

Dillon resented Cody's pompous demonstration and overzealous grin but kept silent.

"The bar is stocked with booze of your choice," Cody went on. "Whatever your heart desires, just name it."

"I'll have a double Martini," Nicole said, "with two olives."

Cody brayed, "Oh yes, plenty of drinks for our girl, right Dillon."

As the three stood at the bar, Dillon appeared calm on the surface, but telltale beads of sweat formed and trickled down his temples.

Nicole reminisced. "This reminds me so much of Perry's yacht. We used to party on nights likes this. Oh, I miss that lifestyle." She gazed at Cody with doe like eyes.

"Let's, see what we can do about that. Wait till you see the rest of *The Shark*, it will blow your mind."

He handed Dillon a cold beer and whipped up a Martini for Nicole. With drinks in hand, the three toured the yacht. Each room had its own uniqueness, and Cody expounded in great detail as he showed off his toy.

They returned to The Sky Lounge and settled at a custom teak table with an open view of the lake.

"Let's wait here for Robin," Cody said. "As soon as she arrives, I'll crank up the yacht and we'll take everyone for a cruise."

"Robin? Who's Robin?" Nicole pursed her lips and arched her brows.

"A nice surprise. She'll be here soon. You'll like her."

Cody pulled out a cushioned chair for Nicole and settled her in before Dillon had the chance. This gave Dillon more reason to believe the guy was up to something. He watched his partner devour Nicole's every move. It was obvious to Dillon it wouldn't take much for Cody to trigger Nicole's sexual impulses.

"When did you purchase the yacht?" Dillon asked, trying to draw Cody's attention away from Nicole.

Dillon's words drifted in the breeze on the open lake. Cody's eyes were all over Nicole. "Let me get you another Martini." He lifted the decanter of prepared gin and vermouth and poured the mixture into her glass then plopped in two oversized stuffed olives. "There you go, doll."

"You're a darling man, thank you. I love a guy who's attentive." She gave Dillon a smug glance.

Cody gazed over at Dillon. "I'm sorry, did you say something?"

Dillon glared across the table at the two of them. "Nothing important.

Nicole frowned. "Must you be so glum, Dillon."

Dillon leaned back in the seat, dragged on his cigar and stayed quiet. Now was not the time to start a squabble. Besides, what could you expect from a nympho and a two-bit crook?

"I know what, let's dance." Nicole wriggled to her feet, her red knit top dropping off one shoulder.

Cody flexed his brows. "Good idea, I'll turn up the music."

Dillon eyed them as they glided across the deck of the boat to a slow rumba. Nicole exaggerated her hip movement as Cody pulled her close to his body.

Dillon helped himself to another beer and stood at the railing with his back to the dancers. The muscle along his jaw line tightened. He'd like to grab Nicole by the arm and drag her off the yacht, but knowing her temperament, it would only make matters worse.

Stay focused on the map that leads to the gold.

He squinted toward the dock. The sun hadn't quite gone down. The silhouette of a woman with long wispy hair walked toward the yacht.

Could be Robin, Dillon thought.

But the woman turned around and walked the other way. As he watched the woman fade into the distance, it surprised him to see her turn around and walk back toward the yacht.

€€€

Her dark hair whipped in the breeze like chocolate swirls as she stepped on the deck of the yacht and cut across to the bar. Her curves were well rounded in white slacks and a yellow knit top. She parted her pink lips in a slight smile. "You must be Dillon. Uncle Cody mentioned you many times."

Uncle Cody? Well, isn't that special?

"Yes, I'm Dillon, and you must be Robin." He tried to be pleasant in hopes the sarcasm he felt didn't show in his voice. He wondered if *Uncle Cody* discussed the gold with her. What happened to honor among thieves? Their verbal agreement felt about as solid as the bomb the asshole planted in Perry's Safari.

"I got a little lost tracking down my uncle's new yacht," Robin said, as her eyes swept across the deck. "Looks like he's busy dancing; may I sit with you?"

Dillon pulled out a chair. "I'd be delighted. Would you like something from the bar?"

Her mouth broadened in a smile. "Thanks, I'd love a glass of Chardonnay."

Dillon stepped behind the bar and chose a bottle of wine. A flash of anger crossed his face as he glanced over at Cody and Nicole on the dance floor. Jealousy had no place in his heart, but he felt obsessed over his plan to use Nicole to his advantage.

He popped the cork on the bottle and poured wine into a goblet. "Nothing but the finest for the lady," he said, placing the glass on a napkin in front of Robin.

He sat across from the woman and studied her face. She didn't look like the type to be tangled in any illegal business. But in his experience, the squeaky clean could be the worst.

Cody and Nicole finished dancing and crossed the deck. Nicole eyed Robin like a female bobcat.

Cody took Robin's hand. "I see my beautiful niece has arrived."

"Yes, and beautiful she is." Dillon tapped his beer mug against Robin's wine glass in a toast. "Here's to new friendships and who knows what else?"

"Happy to see you two hitting it off," Cody said. "Why don't you dance while I lift the anchor and start up the engine?"

Dillon rose to his feet and held his arms out to Robin. "Care to dance?"

"Love to." The two strolled out on the open deck and began the Tango. The dancing lessons Dillon had taken in his youth led to dating some of the hottest girls in college. Robin followed his every move as if their two bodies were one.

Now and then Dillon glanced over at Nicole. Her bottom lip protruded like a baby's pout. This could only mean one thing. She's pissed.

Cody sailed the yacht about a half mile down the lake and dropped anchor. It was still light enough to enjoy a view of colorful autumn trees with a backdrop of snow-capped mountains. Cody served catered lobster tail and crab legs, with melted butter, artichokes, and twice baked potatoes.

Later, they cruised the lake, and everyone thanked Cody for the fine dinner. He smiled and leaned back in his chair. "Nothing but the best for my friends," he said gazing over at Dillon. "So what do you think of *The Shark* now?"

Dillon lit a cigar and kept a straight face. What was he supposed to say? Then it dawned on him. Cody's narcissism craved attention; not only craved it, demanded it. Perhaps the years in federal prison drained him of self-worth, causing him to cry out for a stamp of approval. Just maybe, Dillon thought, he could use this flaw to his own advantage.

He paused a moment before he answered, then plastered a smile on his face. "The finest yacht I've ever seen. The name of your yacht, the yacht itself, the food, your niece, everything, is... well, excellent. Bravo, for being an outstanding host on *The Shark*."

Cody cut Dillon a blank stare. "Well, thank you. Such praise I didn't expect."

"You deserve it." What a buffoon, Dillon thought.

The two women disappeared, leaving the men alone at the table. "So you are okay with our little change in plans?" Cody asked. "I figured we could meet at Big Red's anytime—maybe tomorrow or the next day." He raked his fingers through his thick, dark hair and laughed nervously. "No big deal, right?"

Yeah, asshole, no big deal; I had important news about where the map might be hidden. It killed him to fake a smile, but he curled his lips as best he could. "Sure, sure, no problem—I'm glad I met your niece. And, man oh man, that wonderful meal. My favorite, crab legs and lobster tail."

Cody leaned across the table and spoke. "Well, if you have something important to tell me, now's your chance. We're alone."

He answered in the same quiet tone, "Nah, nothing that can't wait. Maybe next week we can get together and hash things out." Dillon kept a straight face as he eyed his partner. He wouldn't tell the guy shit, not if his life depended on it.

CHAPTER 20

MICHAEL FELT A SENSE of peace. His father was alive and couldn't be in better hands. A soft breeze stirred the air as he sipped beer and stared at the stars. The houseboat rocked and water lapped against the hull. He relaxed on the chaise lounge, closed his eyes, and slid into a dream state.

Moments later, he snapped open his eyes. Whether real or imagined, something stirred in the night. After seven years of combat, not paying attention to his instincts could mean the difference between life and death. He didn't stop to analyze; he grabbed his night scope from his backpack. Except for the steady drone of crickets, and an occasional critter from the nearby woods, the surrounding area of the lake seemed peaceful.

Then, like a quiet hulk in the night, an outline of a boat appeared. The name of the vessel glowed on the side of the stern. *The Shark.* Twice in one night could only mean one thing—enemies in the mist.

€€€

The following day, Michael placed three bottles of aged wine in the back seat of his Jeep, along with a bouquet of long-stemmed roses.

The Maguire Horse Ranch was a straight shot through the center of the ghost town and into the rolling hills. It had been a long time since he'd seen horses grazing on green pastures. A refreshing trip to another world compared to the paranoia he felt lately in a town where he grew up.

It took a rip current and a gun barrel pointed at his gut to get close to Annie. Now that he'd met her, he found her back-woodsy family likable. Most of all, he enjoyed the attention they gave him for saving Annie's life. Better a hero at home than a dead one in the sands of Kabul. Maybe his dinner date tonight with Annie and her family meant the start of something good.

What he felt for Annie was more than a sexual conquest. He thought about Trisha and the wild passionate nights on Big John's yacht. Those were memories he'd never escape. Annie was in a class all of her own. Perhaps it was her inner beauty shining through as well as her red hair and sexy body that appealed to him.

He came to a fork in the road and squinted through the glare in the windshield at a sign with an arrow pointing south toward the horse ranch. He turned and sped along an endless dirt road. When he reached the house, he parked in the circular drive and sat for a moment looking around at the grounds.

The ranch had an old west feel to it, yet modernized with a freshly painted horse barn, complete with what appeared to be a tractor shed and ample horse pastures. The place had history, like a settler's homestead that alludes to romance of the rugged ranch life of the 19th Century. He was impressed by the grand view of the valley on the edge of a forested hillside.

His leg nearly pain free, Michael folded his cane and placed it inside his jacket pocket. With wine and flowers in his arms, he walked up the porch steps, rang the bell and waited—then knocked and waited some more. After a good three minutes, the door opened and Zack stood at the threshold. Michael saw Annie through the screen standing by a stairway. She dabbed her eyes with a tissue; he could tell she'd been crying.

He scratched the side of his head, not knowing what to think. "If this is a bad time, I can come back later."

"No, please, come in." Zack pushed open the screen door. "We were having a little family discussion. Sorry, you caught us off guard."

The second he walked into the house, the delicious aroma of Mexican food hit his nostrils. He handed Zack the bottles of wine, then turned to Annie and gave her the flowers. "For a beautiful lady."

Annie reached for the yellow, long-stemmed roses. "My favorite, how lovely, thank you. So sweet of you."

Michael smiled, but he couldn't help see a tear on her cheek. "I'm glad you like them."

Her eyes widened. "I love them. Excuse me a moment while I put them in water."

Michael hoped that whatever saddened her earlier would soon be washed away.

Zack turned to Michael and spoke in a low tone. "Thanks, Annie needed a lift. We're having an issue."

"It's none of my business, but if I can help in some way.

Zack's face tightened. "You saved Annie's life—you've already done so much. We hardly know you, but somehow I can tell you wouldn't do anything to hurt her."

"No, I wouldn't. And I'm glad to have your trust."

"Let's wait till after dinner. It's up to Annie if she wants to talk about it. Come with me, and I'll show you around the place. Jonas and Pa are out mending fences. They'll be along later."

Michael followed Zack into the large living area where a massive stone fireplace dominated the great room. "This is where we meet in the evenings to talk, read, play games, chess, or watch TV."

Sculptures of the rugged west, like bucking broncos, cowboys and Indians added to the southwestern rustic flair of the room. But, more than that, Michael couldn't take his eyes off the paintings. "Who's the artist?"

Zack smiled. "That would be our little Annie who's not so little anymore. She is quite the artist. And the sculptures are handed down by the ancestors."

"Talent certainly runs in the Maguire family."

"Ah… it would seem so, but there's one little detail." Zack cut across the room and straightened an oil painting hanging over the fireplace.

"What detail would that be?" Michael followed him eyeing, the framed portrait of a girl on a horse.

Zack turned to Michael and smiled. "Annie is adopted. She came into our world when she was six months old."

"Oh… I see."

"You seem taken back by this."

"No, it's just that… well, I was adopted." It felt odd for Michael to hear himself say the words out loud. He wondered why he felt compelled to do so now.

"Oh, then, you and Annie have a lot in common, don't you?"

"My situation is a long story with many twists and turns."

Zack rendered a hearty laugh. "Well, then, I'd say you and Annie have plenty in common. Her twists and turns could be made into a movie."

Michael chuckled. "At least we're not boring."

"No, certainly not." Zack's lips broadened into a smile.

They toured the rest the house and wound up in the kitchen. "Meet Maria, one of our cooks. Jose is around somewhere. They are creating their specialty today."

Michael sniffed the air. "Smells delicious."

Maria smiled at Michael. "Hola, help yourself to the guacamole and nachos." She pointed to a buffet table filled with dips and chips and finger food.

Jose waved from behind a small bar in the corner of the kitchen. He spoke above the blender. "Strawberry Margaritas coming up, pronto."

They crossed over to a screened porch area overlooking an emerald, green meadow. Michael spotted Annie placing the yellow roses in the center of an oblong table. Jose served bright red salty drinks in large crystal glasses at each place setting.

"Let's all sit down now while the drinks are good and icy," Annie said.

"What about your Pa and Jonas?" Michael asked. "Shouldn't we wait for them?"

Annie smiled. "It's okay. I just saw them walk in through the side door. Somehow, they always know when it's time to eat."

€€€

Seth sat at the head of the table and said a prayer. After, they all made a toast to Michael, thanking him for saving Annie's life.

"Let's eat and enjoy," Seth said, as Jose and Maria wheeled in the courses of Mexican food: Taco Salad with Guacamole, Mexican Rice,

Chicken Quesadillas, and Grilled Shrimp with Mango, Beef Enchiladas and Refried Beans.

"Is there no end to this food?" Michael wanted to know as he piled his plate high.

Annie eyed Michael from across the table. "Save room for dessert. We have apple enchiladas coming up, topped with vanilla ice cream."

Later, after dessert, they retired to the living room. Jonas lit a fire in the hearth and in a little while it crackled and popped.

Michael praised Annie. "I had no idea you were so talented. The painting over the fireplace looks like the same area where you swim every day at the lake. That's a portrait of you and your horse, Knight, isn't it?"

Annie smiled and nodded.

"Beautiful." Michael shook his head in awe.

"Tell me how it happened—how you saved Annie from the rip current." Zack asked.

"Well, I happened to be surveying the lake, as I usually do around that time of the morning and..." Michael saw the corners of Annie's lips extend into a smile. He knew that she knew he was surveying her and not the lake. He smiled back and winked, then explained how he swam across the lake and reached her in time before the current carried her away.

They sat for a few moments, each in their own thoughts. After a while, Zack turned to Annie and chuckled. "Bet I know something you don't know little sister."

"What's that? Know it all big-brother..." She leaned against a pillow on the floor next to the fireplace, her big eyes challenging Zack.

"Well, for your information, you're not the only one in this room who came into this world without warning."

Her fun-filled face dropped. "What in the world are you saying? Must we discuss this in front of our company?"

Zack shot a glance over at Michael. "That's just it. Michael's been down the same road."

Michael crossed the room and got comfortable on the floor next to Annie. "It's okay, I understand. It's no big deal. Let's change the subject if you want to."

Annie's eyes filled with tears. "It is a big deal. When the only family you've ever known tells you…" She reached for a tissue on the nearby side table and dabbed at her eyes.

"Tells you what, Annie?" Michael asked.

She turned her head and stared into the fire. "You might as well know. They say my birth mother found me. Apparently, I was kidnapped when I was a baby. My birth mother's been searching for me all these years. I always knew I was adopted—but kidnapped…"

Michael looked up at Annie's pa. "Is this true?"

Seth rose to his feet. "We don't know for sure."

"Where did you get the information?" Michael asked.

"Dillon Hobbs, the sheriff of Three Lakes County visited us yesterday."

Fireworks went off in Michael's head. "Did you say, Dillon Hobbs?"

"Yes, do you know him?"

"No, not really, what did he tell you about Annie's birth mother?"

"He said this woman's baby had been kidnapped right about the time we found Annie stranded in that old car alongside the road. Thing is, we had the adoptive records closed, but somehow they opened the file and got all the information. That's how they found us."

"Did you find out the woman's name who claims to be Annie's birth mother?"

"Not yet. The sheriff just said he'd be out next week to collect DNA from Annie. He seemed secretive... said something about the woman's wealth, and that she lives in a mansion in Lakeport."

Then Michael saw it. The shape of Annie's face, the expression in her eyes, the mouth and how her bottom lip jutted out when she showed disappointment. No wonder she looked familiar to him on the first day they had met. Why didn't he see it before? Except for her red hair, Annie could be Nicole Drake's double... or daughter.

CHAPTER 21

THE MOTOR PURRED as Annie shifted her Miata to a lower gear and sped toward Lakeport. The sports car was a surprise gift from her brothers on her twenty-first birthday. They adored her, protected her, taught her how to ride a horse, shoot a gun and gave her more than a sister could ever want in the way of love and protection. She adored them—she also loved her independence.

All of her life she wondered where she came from but was too afraid of what she might discover. Now she wanted answers; the name of her so-called birth mother for starters and her address.

No more fantasizing, making up stories in my head. I'll see with my own eyes the woman who delivered me into this world.

She would persuade the sheriff to tell her the full story. Was she kidnapped? She had a right to know. The DNA evidence could wait.

She drove to the unincorporated area of town and parked at the curb on a side street behind a patrol car. She hopped out of her Miata and hurried along an old broken-down sidewalk. A verse from school days came to her from out of nowhere... *step on a crack, break your mother's back...* Such madness, she thought, shaking the rhyme out of her head. *Stay focused.*

A half-block later, she pushed through a heavy glass entrance with black lettering that read: Sheriff Dillon Hobbs -- Three Lakes County.

After standing in front of the receptionist's desk for a few minutes, she realized the front office was as empty as the string of chairs lined against the wall. The only sound came from faint voices behind a door at the south end of the room. The large round clock on the wall read 8:10 a.m. She sat in a hardback chair and waited.

The voices behind the door grew loud and argumentative. When she heard the word *kidnapped*, she rose to her feet.

Well, surely they weren't talking about me.

She sat back down.

Or, maybe they were.

She stood and walked toward the voices. At a closer vantage point, she saw the door was open about half an inch.

She watched the entrance for people coming into the office and grabbed a periodical off the magazine rack; pretending to thumb through it, she listened to the conversation.

Her eyes grew big, then bigger. Their words were loud and clear.

"I told you, I would try my best to find your daughter. But the way you acted the other night on Cody's yacht... well, I'm reaching the point where I don't want to help you with anything."

"What do you mean? Are you jealous of Cody?"

"No, I'm not jealous, but we had a deal—a partnership—remember? We'd find the gold and split it along with the Drake fortune. Cody only merits a small percentage of the gold."

"So, you stopped searching for my daughter because of Cody?"

"I don't trust him. I'm sorry I partnered with him. And, I am beginning to lose trust in you. Besides, do you really think you're a fit mother?"

Nicole's voice rose with a catch in her throat. "What a lousy thing to say."

Annie could barely contain herself as she listened to the words she didn't want to hear. She swallowed back tears and centered in on the conversation.

"Keep your voice down. If I found your daughter, what kind of example would you set?"

"Who are you—the protective uncle? You're a fine one to judge. You, the big shot dirty sheriff."

"Don't switch things back to me. You know what I mean. You're drunk half the time and out of your mind for sex. Why don't you let it be and forget you ever had a daughter?"

"You bastard. My kid was kidnapped, and you promised to find her."

"Well, I don't like the way you're falling all over Cody—you, with your sex addiction. How do I know you aren't sleeping with that shyster, telling him everything? I have to know I can trust you."

"Look, we didn't kill Perry for Cody, did we?" Her voice raged on. "We murdered the asshole for ourselves, so we could be together, right? So we could share the gold—the wealth. Come on, baby. You can trust me."

"I don't know… I'd like to trust you, but it's not easy," his voice softened. "One thing that concerns me is the dud bomb Cody planted in Perry's car. For all we know Perry may not be dead."

"Oh, he's dead all right. His body would have turned up by now. Yeah, he's fish meat at the bottom of the lake. I'm seeing my attorney next week to push forward the Drake money into my name and mine alone."

"What about the key you saw around Michael's neck?"

"What about it?"

"I want that key. I feel it will lead us straight to the gold. You didn't tell Cody about the key, did you?"

"No, no way."

"Well, we can always kill the jarhead and get the key. In some ways, you could say he's led us straight to the gold." They both laughed.

Annie placed a hand over her mouth to stifle a sob.

"Did you hear that? Someone's listening at the door."

Cold blooded murderers. Get out now.

Annie sprang toward the exit and caught her foot on the edge of a chair. She stumbled and braced her hands on the floor before landing face down. A rush of adrenalin surged through her bloodstream as she scrambled to her feet for the door. Her new birthday boots felt like heavy weights but once outside, she picked up speed and fled like a deer running from prey.

She turned right and spotted the parking lot straight ahead. Hot tears rained down her cheeks as she darted around one parked car after another.

When she saw a large sports utility vehicle, she slipped between its hulk and a late model sedan. Seconds later she hunkered down between the two cars. Her heart raced as she held her head in her hands.

Murderers... This is no time to panic. Think what to do.

Something her pa told her flashed through her mind. *If you run into a wall, don't give up. Figure out how to climb the wall, go through it, or work around it.*

Her head snapped up at the sound of footsteps and voices. She eyed the SUV. All she needed was a place to hide until the danger passed. She tried the door handle. No luck. She tried the other vehicle.

Thank goodness for small-town folks trusting enough to never lock their car doors.

She eased into the sedan's passenger side and crouched down in the seat. Her heart pumped against her ribs as footsteps stopped on the other side of the SUV. The voices were faint, but the sheriff's tone carried a throaty pitch.

"Was it a man or a woman?" he asked.

"I think female. I saw the back of her head. Whoever it was, I saw lots of hair and its red."

"At least we know what color her hair is. You go that way, I'll head this way."

Annie heard the click-clack of heels on the pavement. She couldn't see, but the sound faded to the right.

She peeked through the glass windshield enough to see the shadow of the sheriff a few feet away and then watched him take off in the other direction.

She remembered parking on the street and walking along the broken sidewalk past the parking lot. Her car had to be a straight shot, maybe forty feet ahead parked at the curb. She held her position inside the sedan for about ten minutes and then bolted for her Miata.

€€€

With one eye on the road and the other on the rear view mirror, she raced out of town like Big Daddy Gartlits on a quarter-mile drag strip. Things would get much worse if she didn't get to Michael right away. He knew more than he had let on at Sunday dinner. How much she didn't know, but she intended to find out. First, she had to warn him about the threats to his life.

She stopped at the junction and made a right turn. Michael's cabin was about twelve miles up the hill. It was close to noon—hopefully he and Nash were finished with their morning exercise.

She smiled to herself as visions of Michael's sexy anatomy flashed through her mind. She liked how his muscles rippled over his body when he practiced Tai Chi.

He wasn't the only one who surveyed the lake. She'd been watching him for days through her binoculars.

She parked next to Michael's Jeep and walked the short path to the houseboat at the water's edge. The soles of her boots clunked as she trekked up the incline to the deck and went aboard.

"Ahoy, anybody home?" she yelled.

No answer.

She climbed the ladder to the top deck hoping to find Michael and Nash exercising.

Empty. She wanted to cry. She needed to talk to him.

Lowering herself down to the main deck, she gazed around one more time. Maybe if she sat and waited a few minutes he'd show up. Then she thought better of it. Her pa and brothers would be worried by now.

As she turned to leave, a voice called out. "Who's there? State your name, or I'll blow your fucking head off."

Oh my God.

She raised her hands over her head like she'd seen the bad guys do in movies. "It's Annie. Annie Maguire. I'm sorry. I didn't mean to cause a problem."

"Annie?"

Michael walked out from behind the sliding glass doors of his bedroom, a towel wrapped around his neck. He was shirtless, wearing a pair of faded jeans.

Annie eyed his glistening chest from what appeared to be a recent shower. She wanted to laugh and cry at the same time. "I didn't know if I came to your boat I'd face a gun barrel. Are you going to shoot me?"

Lowering his gun, he stepped up close to her, eyes ablaze. "I'm sorry. I heard heavy footsteps out here on the deck." He gazed down at Annie's boots. "I get triggered… it happens when I least… it's post traumatic…" He ran his fingers through his dark, wet hair. "Never mind."

Her eyes welled with tears. "It's okay, I understand.

"What are you doing here?"

"So much has happened this morning, it's hard to know where to start. I'm glad you're here. Can we talk?"

"Of course." Michael took the towel from around his neck and dried his hair. "Mind if we sit on the top deck of the boat?"

"Fine. Do you always carry a gun around with you?" Annie eyed the weapon in his hand.

"Yes, I do. I suppose out of habit from the war. One can never be too careful." They climbed the ladder. Michael placed the gun on the umbrella table and pulled out a chair for Annie. "Sit here. How about something to drink?"

"Water, please." She sat and felt at ease in his presence.

He reached for a Heineken in the fridge, brought Annie ice water with lemon, and sat next to her. "So what happened? What's got you upset?"

"I had to warn you. They're planning to kill you."

"Wait a minute. Slow down." He squinted at her. "Who's they— who said they would kill me? Start from the beginning."

Annie swallowed a big gulp of water, leaned back in the chair and eyed Michael with suspicion. "I'll be honest with you. Will you be honest with me?"

Michael stared at her as if he were insulted. "I'm not sure I follow. We haven't known each other that long, but I've always been honest with you."

Annie's voice had an edge to it. "No, you haven't. Let's put it this way. Maybe you didn't tell me everything. For starters, my birth mother, you know her don't you?"

Michael stared at her for a moment. "We don't know for sure who your birth mother is, at least I don't."

"I went to see Sheriff Dillon Hobbs this morning. I learned a lot."

"I thought you would wait for the DNA results."

"I got curious. I wanted to know if I'm a kidnap victim. So I went to see the sheriff for answers."

"What did you find out?"

"Nothing on the kidnapping, but I found out my birth mother is married to Perry Drake, your father." Annie held his gaze before speaking again. Her heart palpitated. "You didn't tell me."

Michael peered at her with drooping eyelids. "The sheriff told you this?"

"No, I didn't get the chance to see the sheriff. I overheard him talking to my birth mother, Nicole. That is her name, isn't it?"

Michael's brows drew together, and he nodded. "Yes, that's her name."

"I got there early. The office was empty. By a fluke, the sheriff's door was open a crack. So I listened."

"If she turns out to be your birth mother, I'm sorry you had to learn about her that way. But what's this got to do with someone trying to kill me?"

"She's a murderer, Michael. They admitted killing your father. They laughed about it. Now, they're coming after you."

"Did they say why?"

"Something about a key that will lead to a fortune in gold."

Michael took a long guzzle of beer before he spoke. "You might as well know they've been after the gold for some time now. They trashed the cabin looking for the map. Now they are on to the key. So what else did you overhear?"

Annie eyed the key around Michael's neck. "That's about the time they heard me, and I had to leave in a hurry. Is this the key they want?" She reached out and held it in her hand.

"Yes, that's the one." He held her hand and squeezed it tenderly. "Thank you for the warning. So, you say they heard you? Did they see you?"

"Yes, they came after me. I heard them say they saw the back of my head. They know my hair is red."

Michael gazed at her hair. "It may be a good idea for you to change your hair color until you're out of danger. They'll be looking for a redhead."

Annie ran her hand through her auburn locks and tucked a few strands behind her ear. She grimaced. "I can always wear a wig."

"Let's worry about that later. I'll follow you home."

CHAPTER 22

MICHAEL PARKED HIS Jeep in the circular drive next to Annie's red Miata. The chill in the air hinted at the first bite of autumn. A golden brown carpet of leaves crunched underfoot as they walked the short distance to the house.

The family met them on the front porch. Seth shook Michael's hand and brushed a kiss across his daughter's forehead. "We worried this morning when you didn't show up for breakfast."

"I'm sorry, Pa. I had things I had to do on my own. I—"

"Let's talk inside." Seth squinted at the dark clouds overhead. "Looks like rain. I'll build us a fire."

"I'll help," Michael said.

The smell of burning firewood, along with freshly brewed coffee wafted through the air as they gathered around the hearth in the living room. Jonas pointed to a buffet table. "Coffee refills here. Help yourself to chocolate cake. There's ice cream's in the fridge."

Annie sat on the floor in front of the fireplace. "I've had a trying morning. Do you mind if I sit and relax? I don't want to eat or talk right now." She turned and gazed at the flames.

Seth frowned at his daughter. "I was hoping you could tell us why you disappeared before breakfast this morning. What's got you so upset? If this has something to do with your birth mother, I can't understand why you aren't happy at the prospect of finding her."

Michael broke in... "Annie came by to see me at the houseboat this morning. She's distressed at what she found out about her birth mother."

Jonas gave Michael a questioning look. "If you know what happened, please tell us."

Michael's eyes connected with Annie's; she nodded, giving him the go-ahead. All three Maguire men stared at Michael for answers. "All right, but this may come as a shock to you. The mother Annie has dreamed about all of her life is... well..." How could he tell them about Annie's mother? "Let's put it this way, she—"

"That's okay, Michael. Let me tell them." Annie leaned back in her chair and let out a bitter laugh. "My mother is far worse than the wicked witch in any fairytale." She rose to her feet and stood in the middle of the room. Her voice sprang to a high pitch as if the intensity might dull the pain in her heart.

"In fact, there's no nice way to sugarcoat it. When you think of my birth mother, think of a mama wolf spider. Once born, her babies congregate on her belly ready to be fed. If she decides her babies are more delicious than adorable, they may wind up her next big meal. I'm pointing out to you that my mother is—"

"My God, Annie." Seth walked over to his daughter. "I've never heard you talk this way."

"I know Pa, but..." She stared at her hands. "I've lived in a fantasy world far too long." Her voice lowered to a whisper. "My mother is a murderer."

Seth wrinkled his face in disbelief. "But, how... how do you know this?"

"Because I overheard her and the sheriff discussing details surrounding how they murdered Perry Drake. The worst part is Perry Drake happens to be Michael's father." She gazed over at Michael. "My birth mother and Sheriff Dillon Hobbs are partners in crime. They conspired to murder Michael's father and now they're going after Michael."

"But why?" Seth looked toward Michael.

"I think you should start from the beginning," Michael told her. "Tell them where you were this morning and why."

She sat down, took a deep breath and exhaled slowly. "All of my life I'd heard stories from the family how Pa rescued me when I was a baby. How he found me kicking and screaming in that car seat in an old Chevy parked on the road headed in the direction of Rogue's Hollow..." She paused a moment and looked at each family member then brushed away tears.

"So, I went to see the sheriff for answers. What I came away with was a nasty brush with death." She explained the details of what she had overheard as she listened at the door in Sheriff Dillon's office.

"You were in real danger, little sister," Zack said. "You barely escaped. Are you sure they didn't see you?"

"They saw the back of my head."

"These people won't stop until they get what they want," Michael said. "They know whoever eavesdropped at the door overheard too much. They are after the gold and they will maim or murder anyone who gets in their way. As a precaution, I strongly advise Annie to change the color of her hair before the sheriff comes out here to collect her DNA?"

"That's tomorrow afternoon," Jonas said.

Zack rose from his chair and walked over to Annie. "Tell me what color you need and I'll go to town and pick it up right now."

Annie got a tablet and scribbled the hair color info onto a piece of paper and handed it to her brother. "It's best if you go to a beauty supply store. First, look for a blond wig. If you can't find one, tell the sales person you want color and instructions for a honey blond." Annie smiled. "I might as well go all the way."

Michael eyed Annie's beautiful auburn hair. "Good, I'm glad we've got the hair color change in the works. Good idea on the blond wig. If not, don't worry, your color will grow back."

"Just curious," Jonas said. "What about Annie's birth father?"

Michael pondered the question for a moment. "Well, whoever he is, he's someone Nicole knew before she arrived in Lakeport. Maybe later we can track him down."

€€€

After Michael left the ranch, he drove to the bank and moved the flash drive to a second security box. He left the old key around his neck and placed the new one on a chain, along with car keys. If they killed him, they'd snatch the wrong key, never suspecting the switch. He doubted any of them had enough brains to figure out the algorithm he'd created on the flash drive. But that didn't mean they couldn't hire someone to crack the encryption.

With the map safe for the time being, he drove to the mansion to tell Jo and Bruno the good news about his father.

€€€

Images of car bombs and shattered glass flashed across Michael's mind as he sat with Bruno and Aunt Jo at a table overlooking the Lakeport Marina. The glassed-in room on the mezzanine floor of the mansion reminded him of a place in Kandahar during a jihad suicide attack.

Things got fuzzy as intrusive images entered Michael mind. The smell of death seized the air.

Damn! Here it comes...

Michael saw a ceiling of black storm clouds contrasting with the bright overhead chandeliers that hung throughout the Drake Room. Rain rippled on the water around the yachts in the marina. He stiffened. Images blurred.

Do something fast, man…

He spotted sliced lemon on the edge of a water glass. The counselor's words burned in his brain. *Control the emotional trigger.* He reached for the lemon wedge, chomped down and allowed the sour juice to permeate through his mouth.

A feeling of calm took hold of his mind and body. He'd neutralized the flashback. Violent images subsided. Whiffs of burning flesh lessened and Bruno poured tea from Drake's fine china.

He smiled inwardly. *I almost took a side trip to hell and no one even suspected.*

"I thought we'd sit in The Drake Room for a change," Bruno said. "The staff quarters are so bloody dull this time of day. I figured we needed a bit of a pick-me-up on a rainy day. Besides, I'm sure this room isn't bugged." The corners of his mouth creased into what might be considered a smile.

"Always one step ahead, aren't you, Bruno?" Michael grinned.

"I have to be—with your father gone it's a real bummer. I'm having a hard time dealing with his disappearance… or death as it may be."

Jo picked up her cup and took a sip of tea. "So what do you bring us, nephew? Any news on Perry?"

Michael wanted to tell them Perry was alive. They deserved to know. He gave Bruno a questioning stare. "I have news, but…" he looked around the dining area. "How can I be sure this room isn't bugged? With Nicole living on the third floor, what prevents her or one of her cronies from planting wiretaps?"

"Oh, I have my ways of making sure it's clean," Bruno said. "Talk freely, we're okay here."

Michael chuckled. "That's right, I almost forgot, you are a direct descendant of 007."

"Laugh all you want. But, you must admit, my gimmicks work. I kept track of you during your wild days of rebellion, didn't I?"

Michael grimaced, playfully admitting defeat. "That you did. That you did. In fact, I may want to borrow one of those handy tracking devices you used to hide under the hood of my car. Have any more of those lying around?"

Bruno's bushy brows elevated. "You bloody better believe I do."

Jo smiled, her eyes intent on her nephew. "Okay, now that we can talk freely, tell us the news."

Michael reached across the table and patted Aunt Jo's hand. "Couple things have come up. But, what I'm about to tell you must not be repeated out of this room." He looked from Bruno to Jo. "Do I have your word?"

Their eyes reflected they understood the seriousness of the matter.

"Carry on, old chap," Bruno said. "We get it."

"First of all, you'll be happy to know that Perry is alive." He sat back in his chair and waited for the news to sink in.

"Oh…" Jo let out a small cry. Her eyes welled with tears. She placed her hand on her heart and breathed in deeply. "Did I hear you right? Perry is alive?"

Michael nodded and smiled. "Yes, Aunt Jo, your brother is alive."

"Oh… I do like the sound of those words. Thank God." Her eyes looked overhead to the skyline ceiling.

Bruno quickly brushed away a tear that had formed in one eye. "That's jolly good news. I really missed that old bloke. Where's he hiding out?"

"There's something you need to know. He almost lost his life."

"Is he in a hospital?" Jo asked, drying her eyes with a tissue.

"No. But he's safe. No one must know he's alive until I take care of the ones who did this to him."

Bruno leaned toward Michael. "When can we see him?"

"I'm sorry. You can't see him, yet. We want to keep his real identity a secret."

"But, where is he?" Jo asked.

"He's staying with a group of Ohlone Indians. They found him near death along the water's edge. The Ohlone's nursed him back to health. He's okay now, but he has no memory due to a concussion. He doesn't recognize me. But he's safe—that's the main thing."

Bruno poured more tea. "This calls for a celebration." He dialed the kitchen and ordered Old English Cookies. "Goes perfect with tea—fresh made this morning. Stay for dinner, and I'll have Cook make your favorite—Shrimp Scampi."

"How can I refuse?" He studied each of their faces. Jo, with her nourishing smile—Bruno, with his dry humor. It felt good to be with the only family he'd ever known.

Then, the smile on Aunt Jo's face faded. Her pupils enlarged into black spheres. For a minute Michael thought he'd said something wrong. He recognized the look—he was a teenage kid caught with naughty magazines under his bed. Then he realized she was looking beyond his head, toward the staircase on the mezzanine.

"What is it, what's wrong?" Michael turned in his chair and followed Jo's gaze.

"Looks like we may have company—it's the queen of the third floor with her giant bodyguard."

Nicole stood at the door in six-inch stilettos, perfectly poised and sure of herself. Her breasts protruded against a white knit sweater like twin peaks. Big Ben hulked next to her glaring. Michael glared back.

Bruno glowered under his white brows. "Damn, it takes everything I've got to contain myself around that woman."

Michael smiled at Bruno, teasingly. "Why Bruno, I didn't know you were attracted to that type."

"No, you bloody know what I mean, you bugger."

Jo tapped the table with her long polished nails. "Okay, you guys, they're moving on."

Michael watched as they disappeared up the staircase. He turned to Jo. "I wanted to talk to you about Nicole."

"Okay, I'm listening"

"First of all, how's Snoops doing these days?"

"Snoops is doing what Snoops does best—snoop." Aunt Jo curled her lips into a tenuous grin.

"What's the latest on Nicole, anything?"

"Well, yes. Snoops managed to place some type of device on Nicole's phone so we know who she calls. That's the latest."

"That's helpful." Michael looked over at Bruno and wondered if he wasn't supplying Snoops with clever gimmicks. Or better yet, maybe Bruno was the infamous Snoops.

"Don't look at me." Bruno shook his head. "I'm just the butler."

"As I was saying," Jo went on. "Did you know Nicole has connections to the Sheriff of Three Lakes County—a sheriff by the name of Dillon Hobbs?"

"Yes," Michael said. "It's one of the things Perry was so upset about. He was sure Nicole was having an affair with the sheriff."

Jo went on. "She's made a lot of calls to this sheriff. But here's the kicker. Snoops tracked several calls made to a Cody Roark. He's a high roller ex-con who lives on the outskirts of Rogue's Hollow."

Michael studied his aunt. "I've never heard it put quite like that—a high roller, ex-con?"

"Yes, the description fits. We learned that he received his law degree in prison. Somehow he got the charges dropped so he could practice law in California. He defends some of the most dangerous criminals in Rogue's Hollow. He has a history of drug smuggling—."

"So," Bruno broke in, "we know in some bogus way our little darling up on the third floor is connected to these blokes."

Michael ran his fingers through his hair. "You say his name is Cody Roark?"

"Tell him about the calls to Desiree," Bruno said.

"I was just getting to that." Jo nodded. "We found several calls made to a Desiree Hunter. The location is a small town in central California. We believe this is Nicole's mother."

"What's the name of the town?"

"It's a farm town called Kings, about ten miles out of Fresno."

Michael nodded. "That's helpful to know. Nicole worked at a truck stop café some twenty years ago—probably between here and Fresno. She was a runaway."

"How do you know this?" Bruno asked.

Michael drew his brows together. "Well, the little darling visited my houseboat one night. If she was after information, I beat her at her own game. Too much beer and she gets real talkative. She filled me in on some of her early life before she arrived in Lakeport and married Perry."

"Why is any of this important?" Jo asked.

"She had a child—a baby girl when she was a teenager. That girl is now grown. Her name is Annie. She's a friend of mine."

"Aha… Annie is your new girlfriend, right?" Bruno said, his eyes twinkling.

Michael shook his head. "I don't know, too early to tell."

Jo smiled. "I'll get Snoops right on it."

CHAPTER 23

THE DRONE OF the wipers thumped rhythmically across the windshield as Dillon made a right turn leading to the Maguire horse ranch. Every muddy pothole on the narrow road felt like a jolt from hell.

Molly clasped her chubby fingers around the handgrip above the doorframe and stared wide-eyed at the road. "How much further?"

"Just a couple miles." Dillon squinted through the rain-splotched windshield and chomped down on a cold cigar.

Molly sighed. "Not sure what you want me to do, but anything to make up for being late yesterday morning."

Dillon's pulse rose. Yeah, damn it. If she hadn't been late, someone at the door wouldn't have overheard Nicole's admission to murder. Nicole and her big mouth—how many times had he warned her not to visit him at sheriff's office?

Molly turned toward him, her voice firm. "Well, you know I'm here for you whenever you need me."

He wondered how she'd react if he told her he was part of a conspiracy to kill Perry Drake. He had the feeling she'd react like his mother—he could do no wrong. "Right now I just need you to be a witness as I swab for DNA."

"Is this person wanted for a crime?"

"No. It's only to prove identification." He was in no mood to talk and hoped she'd shut up.

By the time he pulled up to the ranch house and parked, the rain had turned into chunks of hail. "We'll stay in the truck until this storm passes," he told her.

They sat in silence for the next five minutes while hail pounded the police car. When the hail turned back to rain, he saw a figure of a man through the screened-in patio. "Okay, let's make a run for it."

With their heads down against the torrent, they reached the porch and ran up the steps. The door flew open and Seth peered at them. "I take it you're here for Annie's DNA?"

"Yes, I'm Sheriff Dillon Hobbs, and this is my assistant, Molly." Dillon put on his best smile. "If I remember right, you're Seth, Annie's father, right?" Dillon extended his hand.

After an obvious snub, Dillon dropped his arm to his side. He tried not to think too hard on why he felt about as welcome as a snake's belly is to a rat. "Sorry we're a little late, but the rain—"

"Wait here." Seth shut the door leaving them stand outside under the covered porch.

"Not too friendly, is he?" Molly said.

"So I noticed."

Within minutes, a blonde beauty held the door open. "Come in. I'm Annie. We can do the test on the screened patio."

Dillon tried to cover his shock as he stepped through the entrance and met a clone of the infamous Nicole Drake. "Hello, I'm Sheriff Dillon Hobbs. This won't take long."

"We've been expecting you."

Molly handed Dillon his briefcase. He snapped it open and took out the packet with the DNA swab.

Annie sat in a wicker chair and opened her mouth as Dillon swabbed the inside. His hands shook as he placed the swab into a sterile container. "Okay, that's all there is to it."

She stood and flipped her blonde hair behind one ear.

Even her body language speaks Nicole.

"How soon will you know if I'm a match to this woman?"

"Sometimes it takes a while. When I receive the results, I'll send you an official letter by mail."

She nodded, without making eye contact. When she did, she quickly looked away.

Something stinks, he thought. He'd been a cop and a police detective far too long not to see the signs. Her father wouldn't even shake hands. People usually show respect to an officer of the law. Not that he cared, but it was a sign. Could they know more than they were letting on?

€€€

Dillon dropped Molly off at the sheriff's office and met Nicole for lunch at The Mexican Sombrero. Mariachi singers crooned love songs as they sipped icy Margaritas in salt-rimmed glasses.

Nicole licked salt from her full pink lips and gazed around at the motif hanging on the walls of the restaurant. "This is my kind of place. Paintings of bullfighters and paso-doble dancers give me genuine feelings of Old Mexico."

Dillon stared at her, still amazed at the resemblance between her and Annie—same full lips, same snapping green eyes. If he didn't know better he'd say they were twins. With Nicole's recent cosmetic surgery, she didn't look a day older than her twenty-one year old daughter.

It was as if Nicole sensed his thoughts. "So, what is the latest on the search for my baby girl—anything yet?"

He'd found Nicole's daughter, but he'd be damned if he'd tell her. The DNA test was a mere formality. "I've found a few leads, but nothing substantial. I'll let you know."

"Figures." She tilted her glass to her lips and took a swallow.

"What do you mean?"

"I mean, it figures you aren't doing much of anything to find her. You're still mad at me. Well, I can assure you, I'm not sleeping with Cody if that's your problem."

"Who's worried about it? Cody has nothing to do with this. I'm doing my best to locate your daughter. My detective is working his ass off to nail her whereabouts. But tell me this... I'm curious. What are you going to do if I find your girl?"

She looked at him with a blank stare then lowered her gaze to the surface of the table. "That's a silly question. I may be a lot of bad things, but..." She reached into her purse for a tissue and dabbed at her eyes.

Dillon wondered if this was another phony act. Where were the tears? It was hard to tell with her. She was such an expert manipulator.

She put the tissue back in her purse and then downed her drink. "Right now, I want another Margarita." She scooted next to him and grabbed him in the crotch.

Dillon glared at her. "So you don't know what you'd do, do you? And please get your hand off my dick; I told you I don't like to do that in public places."

She removed her hand and wriggled back across the table from him. "You're sure one frigid man when you want to be."

"Answer my question. What's the first thing you'll do when you meet your daughter?"

"Well shit, I'll probably hug her. Can we change the subject? Please, order me another drink."

Dillon admitted he was a real bastard—using Nicole for his own gain had always been his plan of action. As soon as he got his hands on the map, he'd leave the bitch. Bad as he was, somehow he couldn't find it in his heart to put a psychotic, sex addicted murderer, like the one sitting across from him, on the back of an innocent girl. He didn't see the advantage in it.

He signaled the waiter.

A skinny man, wearing a red Guadalajara shirt and a large sombrero, hurried to their booth. "Are you ready to order, señor?"

"Bring us a couple more Margaritas please, and we'll look at the menus."

The mariachi band waltzed over singing in full harmony. Nicole made several song requests and tipped the musicians a couple hundred dollars each. The waiter brought drinks and menus.

Dillon studied the list of Mexican entrees. "Do you know what you want to order?"

"No, I don't. Please order for me."

Dillon signaled the waiter and ordered the Steak Ranchero Dinner with Cheese Enchiladas.

Nicole looked across the room and laughed. "Oh, look who just walked in."

Dillon turned to see Cody stroll toward their booth. He wasn't a tall man but well proportioned. His blue jeans and a green polo shirt fit him like a male model. Arrogant bastard, Dillon thought, he even moves like the cock-of-the-walk.

"Hey, you two, am I interrupting?"

Nicole giggled. "No, of course not." She scooted over a few inches to make room and patted the leather seat with her manicured fingertips. "What a coincidence running into you here. The mariachi band is fabulous and the Margaritas out of this world."

Dillon stared at Cody with an expressionless face. "Yeah sure, sit down. We were having a private meeting, but no problem."

The singers strolled on to the next table as Cody slipped into the booth and waved his hand around as he spoke. He sat so close to Nicole, his arm brushed against the side of her breast. "It's no coincidence I found you here. I spotted Nicole's red BMW parked in front of the restaurant. I have something important to tell you both that will send you over the moon."

"Oh... I'm all ears," Dillon said. "Where's my space suit?"

Nicole turned and smiled at Cody. "I'm eager to hear what you have to say."

Cody held Dillon's blank stare. "Brace yourself. It's a biggie."

The skinny waiter with the big sombrero came over and took Cody's order. "I'll have what they're having, only make my drink salt free." He pressed his hand to his heart dramatically. "Gotta watch the blood pressure."

Dillon formed a knit in his brow. "All right, tell us what you've got."

Nicole frowned. "For God's sake, Dillon, give him a chance. At least wait till his drink gets here."

His salt-free margarita arrived, bearing two maraschino cherries and a chunk of lime. He lifted his arm, casually sweeping his elbow against Nicole's breast. He took a gulp of his drink and swallowed slowly, a slight smile stealing across his lips.

Dillon's voice had an edge to it. He wanted to punch his lights out for hitting on Nicole but thought better of it. "Okay. The spotlight is on you. What's the news?"

Cody looked across the table at Dillon. "It's twofold."

Dillon cut him a doubtful smirk. "What do you mean *twofold*?"

"There're two parts to our good fortune, that's what I mean. First of all, Robin, my niece, who you got the chance to meet yesterday on my yacht... is a cop." He took a sip of his margarita and paused for a moment as if to wait for their reaction.

He got one. Dillon's mouth fell open. "Jesus, did I hear you right? A cop?"

Cody laughed. "Yes, you heard right, but don't get nervous. She's on our side. I practically raised the kid myself before I went to prison. Then when I got out, she was all grown up. But get this... she never forgot her roots."

Nicole eyed Cody, tentatively. "So what does this all mean?"

"It means, she's agreed to help. Since she's a cop, she knows what's going on with the jarhead. She knows he has post trauma war syndrome—"

"You mean, Post Traumatic Stress Disorder. My older brother suffered with it after Vietnam," Dillon said.

"Yeah, whatever. My point is, Robin knows Michael's weakness, and she's willing to coerce him into handing over the map."

"How's she going to do that?" Nicole asked. "He's no dummy."

"No, that's just it—he's highly intelligent. That's why we need Robin. She was also a Marine. Believe me, she's tough."

Dillon narrowed his eyes. "So, you said it was twofold. What's the second part to your scheme?"

"The second part is all about Perry." Cody patted Nicole's hand.

"Perry?" Nicole's eyes grew big. "What about Perry? You mean they found his body?"

"Perry is alive. I found him, or I should say my boys did."

Dillon tapped the table with the palm of his hand. The knit in his brow grew bigger. "No one outside the three of us is supposed to be in on this deal. Not Robin. Not anyone. What do you mean your boys found him?"

"Well, fuck!" Cody waved his hand through the air. "It'd be nice to receive a little appreciation for finding the bastard."

Dillon wanted to plow his fist through his partner's pompous face. "Look, you son-of-a-bitch, we agreed on the two of us, plus Nicole. Who do you think you are? First your niece, now you're bringing your goons?"

"Relax, man. They know nothing about the map or the gold. They work for me, and I pay them. They are loyal. They know what happens to them if they're not."

"So, where is Perry?" Nicole asked.

"He's hiding out with a tribe of Indians along the water's edge on the east side of Lakeport."

"Well, I'll be damned," Nicole said. "All this time he's alive."

"Right. Can we all agree that finding him alive is very much to our advantage?"

"Didn't we want the guy dead?" Dillon snapped. "Maybe he'd be dead if the damn bomb you planted hadn't been a dud—"

"Yeah, yeah, yeah. We've been over that at least a hundred times. So what else is new?"

Dillon cut a sharp look across the table. "It wasn't a little mistake. You screwed up."

"Well, things change." Cody ran his hand across the top of his thick hair. "Maybe I can make it up to you."

Dillon stared into Cody's cold eyes. "Dare I ask how?"

"Leverage, my man—if we have to, we'll kidnap the bastard and use him as leverage."

CHAPTER 24

NICOLE TURNED THE key in the lock and strode through the door of her luxury suite. Her six-inch stilettos were the first to go. Then she peeled off her white angora sweater and tossed it in the corner of the living room. By the time she entered her walk-in closet she had stripped down to bra and panties and grabbed her favorite see-through kimono off its hanger.

She choked out a giddy laugh then a sob caught in her throat.

My God, I need a drink.

She slipped into her robe and crossed over to the mini-bar in the front room. Her hands trembled as she placed cubes of ice into a metal cocktail shaker, poured in vermouth and gave it a couple of swirls. A crescendo of nervous tension built in her mind like the musical score of *The Phantom of the Opera*.

Perry's still alive, still alive, still alive…

She grabbed a bottle of gin out of the fridge, poured three shots into the container and swirled the mixture.

Damn it, why? I pictured him dead at the bottom of the lake, and all the while he's alive, living with a tribe of Indians.

She poured part of the mixture into a chilled, stemmed Martini glass, plopped in two olives then took the lot with her to the daybed.

"I didn't really want him dead, but…"

Her Raggedy Ann dolls spoke to her with their dead button eyes. *"Yes, you did. Admit it. You're guilty as hell."*

She placed her Martini on the side table next to the metal shaker and wrapped her arms around her dolls.

What could I do? He grew old.

Ever since she could remember, the feel of her rag dolls pressed against her heart comforted her. Thoughts of all she'd been through, how hard she'd worked to gain the status of Mrs. Perry Drake flashed across her mind.

If I hadn't been molested by my stepfather and ignored by my sex-craven mother, I'd have never run away from home, never gotten pregnant. I wouldn't have married Perry or lived in this mansion overlooking Lakeport. For a kid without a high school diploma, I've done all right.

"Yeah, sure," one of her dolls piped up, *"you even murdered poor Ida."*

"Murder? No. She was comatose. I just placed a pillow over her face to help her along."

She pushed her dolls aside, sat up straight and reached for her Martini. The icy gin soothed her parched throat. She downed it and poured more from the shaker.

In three hours she'd meet Cody at Le Patio Restaurant. She could hardly wait to see him again. Since Dillon hated French food, no chance she'd run into him there.

Nicole squeezed her rag dolls one last time and cut across the room to the bathroom. She placed her Martini on the side ledge of the Jacuzzi tub and turned on the jets. Humming a tune, she disrobed and waited for the whirlpool to provide the perfect combination of water and air. Then slid in, sat back and felt the pure pleasure of bubbles explode over her body.

With her eyes closed, she fantasized sex with Cody. Her psychiatrist said she'd hurt the healing process of her sexual addiction disorder if she indulged in fantasies. She giggled and opened her eyes just long enough to take a sip of her Martini.

What does the shrink know?

For a lengthy time, she relaxed in a dream state. Then her eyes snapped open. Footsteps echoed across the hardwood floor. Her secretary always knocked first or rang the chime.

Perry has a key... Maybe he's returned.

She listened a moment and thought she heard the outer door open and close.

Her heart pounded against her ribs as she climbed out of the tub, grabbed a towel from the drawer and tiptoed into the living room. The air held a pungent odor, like a strong herb she couldn't place. The eerie silence brought goose bumps to her wet skin.

An object propped on the daybed grabbed her attention. With the towel wrapped around her, she crossed the room and stared down at an Indian arrowhead nailed to a note centered between the two ragdolls. Her mind raced to comprehend its meaning. Should she even touch it?

Trembling, she reached for the note and read the words written in red script.

As blood runs gold

Blood runs cold

Soon you die

€€€

Nicole sat in a booth next to Cody at the French restaurant. Her voice cracked as she spoke. "I was scared. What... who could have done such a thing? I'm careful to keep my door locked at all times. No one has a key except my secretary... and Perry"

Cody took Nicole's hand. "This is obviously an attempt to frighten you."

"But who? How did this weirdo get into my suite to plant this threat?" She lifted her drink to her pale lips.

"Try to stay calm. Did you bring the note and the arrowhead with you?"

She grabbed them out of her bag. "Here, I'm too scared to look at it again."

He put his glasses on and read the note aloud. Then lifted off his specs and gazed at Nicole. "The arrowhead looks authentic, just like the one I received."

"Oh my God, you received one too?"

He glanced around the room as if to counter watchful eyes, then reached inside the breast pocket of his sports jacket and retrieved a plastic bag. The edges around his lips were tight as he placed the bag in front of Nicole and watched her pull out another Indian arrowhead with a note.

Her eyes widened. "The arrowhead is almost identical." She read out loud: "*As blood runs gold - blood runs cold - soon you die.*" Her voice trembled. "They're out for blood, aren't they?"

"Remain calm." Cody shoved the items back into the plastic bag and placed them in his jacket pocket.

"How can I stay calm? Didn't you say Perry's living with a tribe of Indians? This is his doing—I know it is. How serious are you about kidnapping him?"

"So far we've done nothing. As I told you, we may use him as leverage later if we need to."

"What will your people do to him?"

"Do you really want to know?"

"No. But do you plan on killing him?"

"Let's put it this way, he'll become our strategic advantage."

"When you are finished using him, I think you'd better kill him. If he knows I'm part of this scheme the bastard will come after me. I know he will."

Cody patted her hand. "Relax. Everything's going to be fine. Come on, let's dance. Free your mind from worry. Leave Perry to me."

"Where does Dillon fit into all this?"

Cody smiled and didn't answer.

They did a slow dance, and Nicole soon forgot about everything except Cody pressing against her. Passion worked through flesh and bones.

Nicole whispered into Cody's ear. "Let's do it in public… can we? There's hardly a soul on the patio."

Cody led her in a slow two-step across the dance floor out to the patio. One couple sat on the other side of a large plant.

Nicole went wild as Cody sat in a chair and placed her on his lap facing him in a straddle position. She gyrated back and forth until Cody had to quiet her moans and screams. "Be still, baby, we could get thrown in jail for this."

CHAPTER 25

TAI CHI HAD paid off in more ways than one. Michael's mind and inner balance felt calm; his gate nearly perfect. Just in case the old injury flared up again, he tucked a cane on the inside pocket of his jacket.

As he entered the PTSD meeting room, Detective Fox welcomed him at the door with a pat on the back. "What? No cane?" He smiled. "I'm proud of you. Glad you could make it to the group. The first two times are the toughest."

Michael forced a smile. He still hated spilling his guts to a bunch of strangers.

Fox cut him an understanding look. "Hey, I get it. We're in the good old USA, thousands of miles away from the battlefield, but don't tell that to the guy who relives this shit every day. Believe me, I know what you face. That's why I'm here. I need you as much as you need me. Now grab some hot mud, it'll bring back memories. We'll get started in about ten minutes."

"Thanks." Michael forced another smile. By now he viewed Fox, not just as the detective working on his father's case, but as a friend. "I have to admit, I'm glad you're here."

Fox nodded. "Okay, good to know. Let's have a drink at the Pinnacle after the meeting. I'd like to have a talk about your father."

"Fine, meet you at Pinnacle."

He wasn't about to tell Fox his father was still alive until his doubts about Robin cleared up.

Michael cut across the floor and joined a group of people at the coffee urn. As he reached for a paper cup, he felt a slight bump on his arm.

A sweet voice cooed, "So sorry."

Michael's lips parted in a smile. "No problem."

Her brows lifted in surprise. "Hey, Michael, nice to see you here tonight."

"Great to see you, too, Robin." He blinked and tried to focus on her face. Even dressed in a police uniform with her hair slicked back into a bun she couldn't hide her feminine qualities. Although Annie was his number one lady these days, he couldn't ignore Robin's beauty. Paradoxically, his attraction to her was a mix between sexual impulse and mistrust. The very danger she represented seemed to make her that much sexier.

"I thought we may have scared you off," she said.

He turned the handle on the urn and coffee spewed into his cup. "Not at all. I've used some of the methods I learned at the last meeting. They worked pretty well." He drew the cup to his lips and took a sip.

"Glad we helped. What method did you use?"

His face grew solemn as he recalled the near incident at the mansion. "It's kind of a fuzzy memory, but I think I controlled the trigger."

"Aha, perhaps you can bring that up in the group tonight." She pulled her brows together. "Well, excuse me, I see Fox—looks like he needs help setting up chairs for the group. Catch you later."

There it was again, the duplicity in her eyes; like she meant one thing while saying something else. Then again, maybe she was as innocent as a baby's smile, and he was over analyzing because of his own trust issues.

By the time he crossed the floor, they had finished arranging chairs. He grabbed something to read off a bookrack and took a seat. As he flipped through pages of the magazine, his thoughts drifted to his father. His goals would have to take a detour; his Dojo put on hold—but that was okay. He'd find the bastards responsible for his father's murder attempt and bring them to justice. At least the Ohlone Indians protected the old man. The important thing now was to control the damn flashbacks—then get on with his life.

His eye caught something in the magazine that stopped him cold. He squinted and brought the page closer. The caption under the picture read, "Cody Roark proudly waves to friends as he shows off his new yacht. He names his pride and joy, *The Shark.*"

He stared at the picture. *The Shark* had appeared on the stern of the yacht that had cruised by the houseboat the night before. Snoops had found Cody Roark's name in Nicole's phone list. Aunt Jo called him a high-roller ex-con who earned a law degree in prison. Things were beginning to add up. He tore the article out of the magazine and slipped it into his jacket pocket.

Fox's commanding voice brought him back to the present. "Listen up. All you devil dogs find chairs, the meeting has officially started."

Twelve men and two women took seats in the circle of chairs. Robin entered and made a list of topics for discussion on the portable board.

Fox headed off the meeting. "Let's go around the circle now. Give your name, rank and how long you've served the Marine Corps."

They introduced themselves, much the same as at the last meeting. Michael even surprised himself this time. He told the group how he stifled an oncoming flashback with the simple use of a lemon wedge. "I think I controlled the trigger."

"Tell us how it happened," Fox said.

Michael explained his experience at the mansion. "I traveled back in time to a place in Kandahar. A place I escaped during a suicide bomb attack. At the time of the flashback, the lemon wedge stood out on the edge of a water glass. I grabbed it and sucked on the sour juice. Believe it or not, this little distraction was enough to take my mind off the memory of the incident."

The group applauded. More stories from others followed. One man said, "I don't know what the triggered mine, but it hit me hard. I was strolling along the beach one evening. I felt peaceful and relaxed. Then I went home to bed. Suddenly, I panicked. I bolted out of bed thinking I was on the edge of death. I paced the floor till I dropped and sleep finally came."

Another man rose to his feet. "My wounds are just as real as the ones that bleed. I have all my limbs. My physical body's in good condition. No… my wounds are the invisible kind. I bear my wounds in my soul. I'm not ashamed to say I struggle daily."

For Michael, things got tougher when Robin asked the group, "What do you think haunts you the most about your war experience?"

The sudden whirling sound of chopper blades echoed in Michael's head. Then he heard someone call his name. "Michael, tell us what's happening to you right now?" Fox stood before him in a blur.

Michael's breathing came in spurts. "The chopper crashed. We're on the ground. I can't get to them. I'm in pain—my leg…"

"Can't get to who, Michael—who do you see?"

"My buddies, I can't get to them. I can't move my leg…"

"Where are they?"

"Oh, no, no, no…" Another wall of gunfire exploded in his head. "My buddies… I should be with them. They need my help."

"Do you feel guilty that you lived, and they died?" Fox's tone was strong but soothing.

Beads of sweat dripped down Michael's temple as he rubbed the back of his head and opened his eyes. "I can't stop thinking about it. I crawled to them. I still see myself holding Pete. He died in my arms on the battlefield. They all died on the battlefield. I see their blood spatter." He looked at his hands.

"Getting it out will help. You're almost home free when you can talk about it."

Fox walked to the center of the group. "Home free—is there such a thing? Coming home from battle seemed to be one of the easiest things in the world to do. Didn't it?" He looked at each of their faces. "You could just get on a plane and head home. How ironic. Now, after spending hours, weeks and months, maybe even years getting the help you need by talking to a group about your inner wounds, you are now only beginning to understand how to come home."

€€€

As the elevator made a swift trip up to the Pinnacle on the eighteenth floor, Michael tried to form a to-do list in his mind. He didn't want to schmooze with Fox, but since he promised to meet him for drinks, he decided to have one beer then split.

Now that Cody Roark had come into the picture, doubts about spies in the mist had vanished. No question about it—Roark tailed his houseboat the night Michael docked in front of Heoma's place. First thing on the list—check his father's safety and give Heoma a heads up about Roark. Supernatural powers or not, Heoma and the shaman were no match for these bastards.

He ambled into the busy cocktail lounge and lingered at the entrance until his eyes grew accustomed to the dark. Then he saw Fox signal from a small table at the window. He cut through the crowd and took a seat across from him.

Fox's leathery face, which normally conveyed a tough-guy look, mellowed when he spotted Michael. "Hey, glad you made it. You did all right tonight. It's not easy opening up to a room full of strangers. We've all been there; and I like that thing you did with the lemon wedge."

Michael didn't want to discuss war trauma—he'd had his fill of therapy for one evening. But he had to admit, he felt better after spilling his guts. He tried to be congenial. "Yeah, I even surprised myself."

The cocktail waitress scooted over to their table.

"Drinks are on me," Fox said, as he downed the last of his beer. "I'll have another Bud, how about you?"

"Thanks, I only have time for one drink." He looked up at the server. "Heineken, please."

Fox eyed Michael thoughtfully. "Hey, Robin will be along shortly. Sure you don't have time for at least two beers?"

Michael's jaw tightened. "I have a lot of things to do."

Fox nodded. "Okay, I can respect that. But while I have you here, tell me… have you heard anything new about Perry?"

Damn, the subject of his father again. If he broke the news, he'd have to reveal details about the old man's condition, along with the location. Fox's status as homicide detective didn't give him the right to know everything.

The cocktail waitress served their drinks. Michael took a long gulp of beer and threw the whole thing back at Fox. "Hey, you're the detective, why haven't you uncovered the body?"

"We've done all we can do to locate your father, dead or alive. Your dad's whereabouts is a big mystery." He leaned back in his chair and then leaned forward the way cops do when they want to make a point. "You know, it's against the law to hold back evidence? My gut tells me you know more than you're letting on."

Michael gave Fox a long, reflective look. A bond had formed between the two of them. He sensed he could trust the man—maybe he even needed the man. He had to trust someone, and it might as well be Fox. "If I tell you what I know, I want your solemn word it stays between us. You tell no one, not even Robin."

Fox cut Michael a dubious glare. "Why not Robin? She's my partner. There isn't too much we don't share."

"I'm sure there isn't. That's what I'm afraid of."

"What do you have against Robin? She's a cop. She's a Marine. She's one of us."

"I trust very few people. I'm at risk trusting you. I ask this because it may be a matter of life and death for someone."

"Could that someone be your father?"

Michael didn't answer the question. "In case something happens to me, someone should know the truth. It might as well be you. But I must have your word you will keep the information to yourself until I give the okay to reveal it."

"Whatever you tell me stays between us. I don't like it, but you have my word."

Michael looked around the crowded barroom. "This isn't the right place to discuss the matter. Meet me at my houseboat tomorrow morning around ten." Michael leaned back in his chair and heaved a sigh. He hoped he was doing the right thing.

Fox nodded, his eyes traveling over the top of Michael's head. "Robin just walked in."

Michael furrowed his brow. "I repeat, don't discuss this with Robin."

"I gave my word, didn't I?"

Robin whisked her chocolate-brown hair behind her shoulder and slid into the booth next to Fox. "Hello, guys. Sorry, I'm late. I had to change clothes. The police uniform is stuffy and hot." She lifted her face and smiled across the table at Michael. He tried not to read anything into her blue eyes.

So why do I think she's trying to seduce me?

"We were just about ready to order another round of drinks." Fox looked at Michael. "Weren't we?" It was more of a command than a question.

Michael couldn't think of a graceful way out of it. "I guess I can stay for one more beer."

"I'll have a vodka tonic," Robin said.

Fox signaled the server and ordered the drinks.

Robin adjusted her silky sheer top and smiled at Michael. "So glad you made it up to the Pinnacle, tonight. Get a load of that view." Her eyes wandered over his torso as she gestured toward Lake Crystal through the huge glass window.

He had to admit, the moon danced mysterious images across the water. A sudden picture appeared in his mind of Robin's nude body lying on the shore holding her arms out to him. He kicked himself. *Stop reading sex into everything.*

The drinks arrived, and Michael reached for his wallet.

"No, I've got this," Fox said, waving his hand at Michael.

"Hey, man, you got the last round, I insist." Michael pulled out two twenties.

"No way, my turn," Robin said, drawing a fifty out of her purse. "Don't try to talk me out of it."

"Can't argue with a woman when her mind's made up." Fox looked at Robin and grinned. "Put your money away, Mike."

They all laughed and made a toast to trauma war victims. Michael couldn't understand why he saw the good side of Robin, who seemed to care deeply for the fallen hero. Yet, something caused him to distrust her. Then he caught her staring at the place on his chest where the key hung under his shirt—and he knew.

€€€

As Michael rode the elevator down to street level, he punched Heoma's number into his cell phone. She answered on the first ring.

"Heoma, glad I caught you. How's everything going? Is my dad all right?"

"Michael, things are good. Your father is doing well. He hasn't regained his memory, but he's cheerful and eating well."

Michael breathed a sigh of relief. "I'll be over tomorrow. I have something important to talk to you about. I also want to give you some money and get the trust fund started for Nash."

He heard her choke back emotion before she spoke. "Michael... I can't thank you enough."

"I'd buy you the moon for all your help. I'll see you tomorrow."

Michael pushed open the heavy glass door of the building and stepped outside into a downpour. He turned the collar up on his leather jacket and walked a few hundred feet to his Jeep parked around the corner.

He needed to pee, and the sound of the rain made it worse. He kicked himself for not going at the Pinnacle when he had the chance. As he started to get into his Jeep, he noticed a sign across the street that read, Pete's Pool Hall. He made a run for it.

The minute he walked through the door the blast of foul air nearly forced him out the way he came in. *Too bad I'm not a heathen or I would have peed on the street.*

With his head down, he bolted past the small crowded dance floor. He had one thing in mind—find the head, take a leak, and get the hell out.

At the far end of the saloon, the sound of billiard balls crashed and split apart. He spotted a sign on the back wall that read, "Men's Room". He charged past the bar, into the billiard room, and hotfooted around the pool tables. A nasty looking dude with a lopsided jaw jumped in front of him blocking his way.

The man's lips lined up with his jaw in a twisted smile. "Hey, mister, watch where you're going, it's not nice to bump a guy's elbow when he's about ready to take a pool shot."

Michael gave him a blank stare. "Beg your pardon, sir, but I bumped no one's elbow. Mind letting me by?"

The guy eyed Michael up and down. "Well, look at them fancy fatigue pants. Ain't that a crock of shit?" He grabbed a bottle of beer perched on the side of the pool table and lifted it to his lips.

"Look, man, I've got no beef with you; I'm just trying to get to the head. Step aside."

"Oh, is that a fact?" He chugged down beer then let out a loud burp. "Well, maybe you ain't goin' nowhere until you say you're sorry for bumping my elbow."

Michael had to pee so bad he might say anything. The guy was obviously hammered. Maybe it was the Marine in him, but he'd be damned if he'd apologize for something he didn't do. "I told you, I didn't bump your elbow. Now let me pass."

"You hear that, Joe?" He looked across the pool table.

The man on the other side hollered back. "What's the problem, Sammy? That guy giving you a hard time?"

Alarm signals went off in Michael's brain. He was suddenly in a large, empty field with no cover, begging to get shot. The signals got louder. He faced his enemies—three of them—one on this side of the pool table and two on the opposite side. Common sense dictated three against one was not good odds. Survival instincts said he could probably take them on but was it worth it?

"I had a perfect angle on the ball until this asshole bumped my elbow." He chalked his cue stick and glared at Michael.

Another guy walked up behind Michael, his drunken verbiage spit in Michael's ear. "Say you're sorry. As a matter of fact, get down on your knees and apologize."

Now the odds were stacking up. The words of the great Theodore Roosevelt passed through his mind. *Don't hit at all if it is honorably possible, but never hit softly.*

The other man's face on the other side of the pool table came into focus. "What's the matter jarhead, can't speak?" Michael remembered the shitty grin behind the handlebar mustache—the sheriff of Three Lakes County—the guy responsible for nearly killing his father, not to mention sleeping with his father's wife.

The adversary whined again, "He needs to apologize for bumping my elbow and screwing up my shot. I had a lot of money bet on this game."

"I would gladly apologize, but I'll say it one more time, I didn't bump your elbow. Now step aside or…"

"Or you'll what?" Michael felt the tip of the knife on his ribcage as the guy with the speech defect spit more words into his ear. "Move to the back wall, take a right down the hall and out the door to the alley. Do it now."

CHAPTER 26

MICHAEL'S ASSAILANTS TRAILED close behind in the dark alley. One wrong move and Michael knew the guy with the Bowie would plow the blade through his thorax.

The whole thing might have been laughable—all he wanted to do was take a leak. But this was far more than a few drunken good old boys taking it to the back alley. This was about a map that leads to buried gold. This was about a dirty sheriff who must have spotted him the minute he walked through the door of the pool hall. If he wanted to live, he'd better make every move count.

The muddy ground sloshed underfoot as the man with the knife nudged him forward. His voice had an evil twang as he lisped his words; like he'd love to slice into a nice, juicy Marine just for the hell of it. "Keep walking," he said, "or I'll cut you into bite size pieces and throw you to the rats."

Michael did as he was told as he waited to make his move. Timing. It all had to do with timing.

Red and blue reflections from a neon sign flickered on what looked like a garbage bin. He walked with caution as he inched toward the reflections. His brain centered on the knife holder's movements.

"Okay, jarhead, that's far enough."

Michael stopped next to the garbage crib. The man switched the knife from the center of Michael's back to his throat.

Someone in the back shadows flashed a light in their direction. "Not yet, Bernie. Wait till the sheriff gets here to see how far he wants to take this thing."

Michael felt the pressure of the blade cut into his skin.

"Say what, Sammy, I can't hear you."

"I said don't do anything foolish till the sheriff gets here."

The man with the knife relaxed his grip just enough for Michael to control the knife. With a strong seize of the assailant's arm, Michael wrenched forward and then thrust backward with a butt to the guy's head.

The knife sailed through the air. Michael had a small advantage and plowed a fist into the man's groin. He followed with a savage leg kick to his kidney; the man fell to the ground and didn't move. The blade of the knife picked up a glint from the neon reflection and Michael kicked it underneath the trash bin.

One down three to go.

Even with little vision, the red and blue light flickers on the trash bins gave Michael a sense of counterbalance in the darkness.

But when three silhouettes moved toward him, he didn't expect his leg to give out. One man said to the other, "Grab the son-of-a-bitch."

In seconds, the two clods were throwing punches at him. With no time to think, his instincts kicked in. He took advantage of the attacker closest to him and palm-heeled his nose, thrusting him into the second attacker. They scurried on top of one another.

While they tried to get their bearings in the darkness, Michael hobbled as fast as he could toward the street.

They ran after him

There was no way out. He took a horse stance and faced them. To avoid using his leg, he blocked his opponent's attack with his fists— then pounded with rapid-fire left-right punches to the sternum and solar plexus. He used his fists again and again, moving into the attackers as he punched.

His bum leg was on fire as he tried to use his other leg. The dark alley worked to his advantage. One man plowed directly into Michael's soft kick.

"My nose—you broke my nose, you bastard!"

"Then stay the hell away from me," Michael said, giving him one final punch in the jaw with his fist. The man flew backward and Michael heard a loud splash in a mud hole.

The other two men ran toward the back entrance of the pool hall and disappeared.

Michael couldn't hold it another second. He unzipped, and let it go, right where he stood.

What a relief.

He heard a moan and peered down at a figure sprawled on the ground. The moon peeked out from the clouds and gave just enough light for Michael to spot a handlebar mustache. He laughed, taking sheer pleasure in knowing his urine had made its mark on none other than the Sheriff of Three Lakes County.

He zipped up his pants and couldn't help the elated feeling that spread throughout his entire mind and body. This had been one hell of a night. As the old saying goes, all's well that ends well. Then the scent of tangy citrus perfume hit his nostrils and everything went black.

€€€

Michael's head throbbed like a ticking bomb ready to blow. Drops of water struck his face as lightning and thunder threatened more rain. Someone threw a blanket over his body. He tried to make sense of the jumbled talk going on around him. One voice kept repeating, "Can you hear me, Michael? Can you open your eyes?"

His eyelids were two slits glued shut. The more he tried to open them the more his head hurt.

"He's coming around," the man said.

A familiar voice broke in, "Come on, Michael, wake up."

Someone wiped his face with a towel. He forced his eyes apart and stared at a man with a stethoscope. "Who the hell are you?" he mumbled.

"Rest easy, my name's Rob. I'm a paramedic. You've got a nasty bump on your head."

Fox leaned in, his brows pinched together. "Hang in there, buddy."

Rob called out. "Get that stretcher over here!"

Two husky EMT's wearing rain gear scooped him off the ground and placed him on the stretcher.

The rain came down hard as blinking lights painted a red blur in the alley. His reasoning kicked in. "Are you taking me to the hospital?"

"Yes, to the hospital." Rob touched his arm reassuringly as he walked alongside the stretcher.

"I'm fine. I don't need a hospital." He tried to raise his body off the stretcher as they carried him to the ambulance. Rob pushed him back down.

Fox, walked along on the other side of the stretcher. "I'll meet you at the hospital."

εεε

The hospital ER ordered Michael a CT SCAN and gave him a sedative. After his tests, he slept for a few hours.

When he opened his eyes, Detective Fox sat next to his bed with deep worry lines in his weathered face. "How do you feel?"

"I don't know. I've had better days."

"We're waiting for the results of your x-rays. Someone really clobbered you over the head."

Michael touched his head and groaned. "Yeah, tell me about it?"

Fox scooted his chair closer to Michael and spoke in a low tone. "Care to tell me how you wound up in that alley?"

Michael reached for a glass on the tray and took a swig of cold water. He chewed ice, the nip soothing his dry mouth. He tried to make sense of what happened. "It's complicated."

Fox wrinkled his brow. "Yeah, I gathered that. We found your dog tags and chain in the mud next to your unconscious body. Does that have anything to do with the complications?"

Michael nodded. "Yes, and apparently they got what they were after." He gazed at Fox thoughtfully. "I'll tell you everything from the beginning."

"I wish you would."

"How did you find me?"

"Kitchen help at the pool hall stumbled over your body and called the police. The officers knew I worked on your father's case and radioed me."

The doctor and nurse hustled into the room. His temperature was taken while the doctor gave Michael the results of his x-ray. "You suffered a head trauma with no visible signs of brain injury. You are lucky. You can go home today but take it easy. Any signs of weakness, persistent headache, memory loss, or unusual behavior, contact me right away."

Michael wanted to laugh. Unusual behavior? If only you knew.

"Thanks, Doc."

The nurse fluffed his pillow and smiled. "Your lunch will be ready in about an hour. After you eat your meal, you can get dressed and go home."

When they were alone, Michael gazed at Fox and knew the detective wanted answers. He closed his eyes for a moment and forced his mind to recall what took place at the pool hall.

Fox leaned back in his chair. "If you don't feel up to talking now, we can discuss the matter later. But I'd like to find who did this to you. The sooner I get on their ass the better."

"I agree. I'll give you the crux of what happened and why. But, again, I must have your word this stays between us."

"Once again, you have my word."

Michael rose up on one arm and started to speak, then noticed the door stood ajar a couple inches. "Shut the door, will you please."

Fox stepped over to the door, gave a quick look out into the corridor, then closed it and sat back down. "Okay, go ahead."

"I'll begin with last night. The whole damn thing started because I had to take a leak. After I left you at the Pinnacle, I stopped by that cesspool they call a pool hall. Little did I know my desire for a quick trip to the can would lead to…"

For the next half-hour, Michael unloaded the facts, right up to the time they found him unconscious in the alley.

Worry lines deepened on Fox's face. "So these goons, after screwing up your father's life with a near kill, are now after your blood; somehow they figured out you carry the key to the map that will lead them to the gold. Is that it?"

"Right."

Fox got up and walked around the room. He gazed out the window for a moment as if he were searching for someone then sat back down. "Okay, the names you've given me are Sheriff Dillon Hobbs and Cody Roark. Nicole Drake is your father's wife, and she's a big part of the conspiracy?"

"Yes. She teamed up with the men responsible for nearly killing my father."

Fox leaned into Michael. "You know, I told you a few weeks back, these men will kill, maim, torture, to get their hands on that gold. Remember?"

"Yeah, I remember."

"Well, I'm glad you've come to your senses and spilled your guts because that's exactly what's happening, and you need backup."

"Look, I don't need any I told you so bullshit." Michael laid his head back on the pillow and flinched. "You're lucky I trusted you enough to tell you anything at all."

"Save it, big, bad Marine. You're lucky I'm on your side. You're damn lucky I don't arrest you for obstructing justice."

"All right, I see your point. But save the crap for later. We need to come up with a plan to wipe out these bastards."

"I'm glad you're using the 'we' factor."

The door opened, and they both looked up to see Robin walk into the room. She wore her police uniform, and her face expressed a valley of concern. In her arms, she carried a colorful flower bouquet.

"Michael, I just heard you were injured. I'm so sorry. What happened, you poor thing?"

"Someone clobbered him from behind. We're waiting for his release papers," Fox said.

She set the flowers down on the side table and spoke like a true blue blood. "Michael, we'll find the lowlife who did this to you. I promise you that."

The hospital smell of body fluids and disinfectant couldn't cover up the scent of tangy citrus perfume that engulfed her aura. The same scent used by the person who knocked him cold in the alley. As he stared into the pretty face of his abductor, her character started to make sense to him now.

"Thanks for your support, Robin. It's good to know I have people in my corner, watching my back." He watched her eyes to see if her lashes fluttered at his play on words. In fact, by god, they did—a true sign of a bold-faced liar.

Too bad such a beautiful woman would have to rot in prison. He had to give her credit—she put on a damn good act. He smiled and couldn't wait to see her face when she turned the key to the bank security box and found it full of funny money.

She received a call on her police talkie and stepped aside. "I'll take care of this, Fox, you stay with Michael. I have to answer this call now."

"Thanks for the flowers," Michael said.

"I'll check back with you later." She flew out the door.

Michael breathed a sigh of relief. "Is she gone?"

"Yes, and I'm glad to see you seem to trust her more, now."

Michael laughed. "That was an act. I'm not sure how she's hidden her dark side from you all this time. I hate to tell you this, but she's part of the conspiracy."

Fox frowned. "You'd better show me some proof before you make those kinds of accusations against my partner."

Michael groaned. The thought of the tangy citrus scent she wore made his stomach turn. "What if I told you she's wearing the same perfume today as the joker who knocked me out wore last night? I kid you not—she's part of the cabal."

Fox's lips tightened. "What do you propose she's conspiring?"

"She's with the other three and will do anything in her power to get her hands on the gold. What do you know about her past, anyway?"

"I know plenty about her. We've been partners for a year. She's a damn good cop." Fox exhaled a frustrated breath. "I won't believe she's dirty until I have more to go on. But I'll go along with you for now. I'd like to put a plan in motion."

"What do you propose?"

"Not sure. Maybe have you wear a wire. If she's part of the problem we'll trap her."

"Tell you what. I'll skip lunch. I hate hospital food, anyway. Let's go to the houseboat. We can go over our plans then I'll take you with me to see my father."

CHAPTER 27

DILLON SQUINTED AT the purplish-red face that stared back at him in the mirror. The swelling that covered one side of his face and part of his mouth looked like the puffed up edge of a rotten apple. Blood from his split lip had seeped into his mustache and dried. He figured the ER would ask too many questions, so he did the best he could with first aid and dabbed on more peroxide. The more he thought about it the angrier he got.

He stuffed his pee stained khaki pants and cotton shirt into the washing machine, poured in plenty of detergent and turned on the washer.

If Robin hadn't come along when she did, I'd still be swimming in a pool of urine.

His uniforms were still at the cleaners, so he slipped into blue jeans, cotton shirt and then pinned on his sheriff's badge. He placed a pair of oversized sunglasses over his eyes—then slipped into his brown suede jacket, plopped on his Stetson and headed out.

Ten minutes later, he pushed through the glass door of the sheriff's building and made a quick exit toward his private office.

He bolted past the reception desk. "Good morning, Sheriff. Where're you going in such a rush?" Molly called out.

He kept walking. When he reached his office door, he turned and grumbled across the room, "I need coffee."

"No problem boss, coffee coming right up."

Inside, he took off his hat, left on his glasses and settled into his swivel chair. He tried to get comfortable, but every move pinched his groin where the jarhead whacked him in the balls.

If it's the last thing I do, I'll make that bastard pay.

He grabbed his yellow lined tablet and stared at his list of priorities. There had been several robberies in the area, which needed attention. Most of his mail was from angry citizens wanting justice. He snorted at the irony—law and order was the last thing on his mind. It had been a long time since he'd taken his job seriously. So much for the Hobbs legacy of crime and punishment; he wanted to laugh out loud, but his body pained him too much.

He welcomed the slight knock on his office door—it meant coffee. He yelled, "Come in."

Along with the morning mail, Molly trotted in and set his steaming mug in front of him, black and full to the brim.

"This was hand delivered." She placed an eight by ten blue envelope to the side, along with the mail.

"Who hand delivered it?"

"I didn't get the name. About ten minutes ago. Interesting looking lady of around sixty; black hair with an Indian headband."

"Well, I guess we'll know soon enough when I open it. Dillon reached for his coffee and tried to take a sip. The touch of the hot liquid to his lips burned like a blowtorch. He blotted his sore mouth with a tissue."

"Sheriff, about your face…"

"Damn," he mumbled, staring at the blood on the tissue.

Dillon was silent a moment as he dabbed more blood from his lips. "Yeah, what about my face?"

"You look like some poor old dog hit by a diesel truck. And look at that blood on your lips and mustache. What in God's name happened to you?"

Dillon glared at her and didn't answer.

"Okay, you'd rather not talk about it."

He glowered. "You're right. I'd rather not talk about it."

"I get it…" Molly turned to leave. "I won't mention it again."

When the door clicked shut, Dillon reached for his cigar box and tried to light up, then changed his mind. His mouth and lips were too damn sore for anything.

No coffee—No cigars. All because of that asshole Marine.

He drummed his fingers on the desk and wondered if he should call Cody or Nicole or wait for one of them to contact him. He decided to wait till noon.

The humiliation of getting beaten to a pulp and then peed on had better pay off.

He finished opening most of the mail and reached for the blue envelope. There was no return address. The bold black handwriting didn't look familiar. The sticker on the front depicted an apache arrowhead dripping blood drops down one side.

He unsealed the envelope and several photographs slid out. They appeared dark and out of focus. Dillon removed his sunglasses, and his vision cleared; he took a moment to get a handle on what he was looking at.

He let out a groan and came out of his chair. Cody and Nicole— one raunchy photo after another—showing the two having sex. He could see the city lights in the background of one photo. People were sitting on a patio having dinner while Nicole straddled Cody in the shadows on a chaise lounge. The disgusting smile on her face said it all.

He'd suspected it all along. Not that he cared. But she promised they were a team—partners in crime—lovers, working toward an end-game. How could she? With all people, Cody Roark.

He felt a slight bulge in the envelope and turned it upside-down. A DVD fell on the desk. The note attached had a picture of an arrowhead dripping blood down one side of the page.

The note read:

As blood runs gold

Blood runs cold

Soon you die

A shiver coursed through his veins as he crossed the room and placed the DVD into the player.

The video showed a row of boats docked on the marina; then the scene panned over to a yacht with the name *The Shark* written on the stern.

He wanted to yank the CD out of the player as Nicole and Cody boarded the boat. But he needed to learn everything he could about why his two partners found it in their thieving hearts to double cross him.

As much as he wanted to deny it, he had to admit that whoever sent him the photos and the DVD also sent him a death omen. The sheriff had lived in Three Lake's County all of his life and knew, or knew of, most of the Indian tribes. He knew better than to tangle with their medicine men. They had their own methods and still practiced the old ways. Rumor had it that some of the shaman elders practiced black magic. They were warrior shaman and overcame evil by battling might versus might, leaving the loser with major mental injuries… or death. Not the kind of games he wanted to play.

The next shot showed Cody and Nicole make their way across the deck of the yacht into the bedroom.

Inside, the two sat propped against pillows on a king-size bed, clinking wine glasses as they made a toast to their newfound relationship.

Then Nicole's wild, kinky side showed its ugly face—Dillon knew her outcry for more sex by heart. It took everything he had to watch the video.

After the interlude, Dillon listened to their pillow talk.

Nicole breathed heavily as she reached over for her goblet and took a sip of wine. "You know, it would do my heart good to kick Dillon to the curb. He's such an asshole."

Dillon thought about all the hard work he'd done tracking down Annie for the ungrateful slut. He'd been right about her all along. The best decision he'd ever made was not telling Nicole he'd found her daughter.

But her words struck a nerve. He'd been kicked in the face, kicked in the balls, ungraciously peed upon, and now kicked to the curb by his own lover. He hung his head and stared at the tile floor like an abused puppy.

Cody only added to his grief. "I know what you mean, sweet thing. He's a broke dick, and you deserve better."

Dillon raised his eyes and scowled at the screen. *What does he know about my dick?*

"Cody, you are one hunk of a man. Dillon's interest has only been my money and the gold. I've known that all along."

"I know baby. You don't have to worry about money with me. My bank account easily matches yours."

It became clear to Dillon his partnership with Cody had been a fraud from the beginning. Not only did Nicole take pleasure in dumping him, but Roark bailed on their agreement so he could get his hands on the gold, including Nicole and the Drake fortune.

I'd be the biggest fool on planet earth if I ever let that happen.

He eyed the monitor as Nicole broke into laughter. "Help me contain myself." She placed her wine glass down on the side table. "Can't you picture Dillon's face if he saw us together now?"

Cody laughed. "Yeah, he'd turn different shades of purple."

The irony, Dillon thought, as he flinched his purplish face.

Cody rose up on one arm and caressed Nicole's nude body. "Dillon's a thing of the past, baby. I'd much rather talk about you and me..." he paused a moment and chuckled, "...and the key."

Dillon's mind raced. *Yeah, I bet you would. Let's just see if the little two-timer keeps her mouth shut about the key.*

"What key?" Nicole asked with a knowing grin.

Cody reached over for his wine and took a sip. "You know; the key that'll lead us to millions in gold?"

"Oh, that key. Well, you know, I promised Dillon I wouldn't tell a soul, especially you."

Cody fondled Nicole's breasts then kissed her nipples, first one, and then the other. "Come on baby, tell me about the key," he said between kisses.

"Oh my god, Cody, stop. Do you know how much that turns me on?"

"Yes, I know, sweet thing..."

Cody pulled away from Nicole leaving her beg for more.

I'll be damned. He's using her sexual addiction to get her to talk.

"It's on the chain," Nicole uttered breathlessly as she straddled Cody.

"What chain?"

"The one around Michael's neck…" Her voice trailed off, and the DVD came to a stop.

Dillon stared at the blank screen in disbelief. Now he knew why the call had come in from Robin at the pool hall. Robin knew he played billiards every Monday night, like clockwork. She had been following Michael and phoned to say he was on his way into the pool hall. *"Coax him to the back alley,"* she had said. *"I'll take care of the rest."*

The whole scenario became crystal clear. Sweet, Uncle Cody had clued Robin in about the key, thanks to Nicole's pillow talk.

Dillon surmised the camera bug must have been planted on Roark's yacht as recent as last week. Which meant Nicole's blabbing about the key took place a couple of days ago. This would have given Robin enough time to follow Michael and set him up for the fall. Out of sheer coincidence, the jarhead chose a quick trip to the pool hall to take a leak.

Dillon's face had puffed up and ripened to a purple, reddish orange. He tried to cough, but every muscle in his body ached. He stared at the blank screen, but his mind worked overtime as a plan began to form in his head.

CHAPTER 28

NICOLE AND CODY sat across from one another in the Sky Lounge on *The Shark*. It was day three of their rendezvous. They drank champagne and snacked on chips and artichoke dip.

In the distance, from where they anchored the yacht, lavender fringed orchids grew wild along the water's edge. A few hundred feet straight up the mountain from there, the barrel of the sniper's rifle reflected ever so slightly and could easily be mistaken for the patters in the rock formation.

Nicole drew in a deep breath. "Cody, the view is beautiful, and the last two days have been magical."

Cody smiled and cupped his hand over hers, drawing her slim fingers to his lips. "Yes, baby, we've had the time of our lives, haven't we?"

Nicole's eyes were aglow. Her love for Cody had grown stronger by the moment. This was as good, maybe even better than her relationship with Perry before he grew too old. "I'm so happy we found each other."

Cody's brow wrinkled, the smile never leaving his lips. "But what do you think of Dillon? He hasn't called for three days. I expected at least an inquiry from him by now."

"I hope he never calls." Nicole lifted her glass of champagne to her lips.

"But, don't you think it's odd? The guy's a washed-up sheriff, but he's no fool. I'm sure he knows we're together. You'd think he'd call and say something about it."

For the first time in days, the smile on Nicole's lips froze, her eyes filled with fear. "Should we be worried? You don't suppose he'd do something crazy, do you?"

"No, probably not. But something's up with the guy, or we'd have heard from him by now."

Nicole thought for a minute about her daughter. It depressed her to think that her little girl was still out there somewhere, no thanks to Dillon who had promised to find her.

The lying bastard didn't even try.

She gave Cody an ominous stare. "Do me a favor. Please don't mention Dillon's name to me again."

"Okay, I won't. I'm sorry. Anyway, I have a surprise for you that I know will make you happy." He reached into the pocket of his sports jacket.

"My darling, I love surprises. What is it?" Nicole followed his hand with her eyes, a smile touched her lips.

Cody placed a small golden box on the table in front of her. "I've been waiting for the right moment to give this to you—just a little something that will change our lives forever."

Nicole stared at the box trimmed in gold leaf. "Oh… you shouldn't have."

"Wait till you see what's inside the box before you say another word." Cody's lips parted in a smile.

Nicole lifted the lid and peeked in. Her eyes grew wide as she studied the content. She shifted her gaze to meet Cody's. "Is this what I think it is?"

Cody nodded. "Yes, my love. It's the key to our future."

"You mean *the key*."

"Yes, baby. I mean *the key*."

Nicole reached in and lifted the gem from its resting place. She held it up like she was exhibiting the key to King Tut's Tomb—then she carefully placed it back in its small golden bed.

She looked up at Cody, her eyes full of questions. "But how—"

"When we docked on the marina for supplies earlier, Robin came by while you slept and dropped off the key. Aren't you happy?"

"Yes, I had no idea." Nicole's laugh had a shaky edge. "I'm stunned. I'm so surprised."

"I figured since you are the one and only Mrs. Perry Drake, you won't have a problem getting into the bank's security box for the map. So, for now, keep the box in your purse, and first thing tomorrow morning we'll be off and running to the bank."

Nicole smiled and placed the treasure in her large tote bag. "Now, there's no reason to kidnap Perry, is there? Not that I care whether he lives or dies."

"We'll put Perry on hold for now. One never knows. We may need him later as a bargaining chip. We know he's alive and where he's staying. Why on earth he's living with Indians is beyond me."

"Yes, I wonder about his choice of living arrangements, too. He's nothing like the Perry Drake I once knew."

Cody cupped Nicole's face in his large hands, his lips curled into a big smile. "How about I open us up a new bottle of champagne, and we can make a toast to our good fortune."

Nicole kissed him full on the lips, then threw her head back and laughed. "Marvelous idea."

She watched her new love as he rose from his chair and crossed the deck over to the circular bar. Tingles raced through her body as she thought of the last three nights making love with him.

My dream man... he satisfies my every titillating need.

So sweet, she thought, as she watched him hold up a bottle of champagne for her approval. "How about a little Dom Perignon all chilled and ready to drink; does that suit your fancy, baby?"

"Yes, my love. Perfect."

He crossed the deck toward her, two glasses and a bottle in hand.

Love that sexy swagger. I'm turned on just watching him walk.

Cody set the two champagne glasses on the table, popped the cork of the Dom and poured the sparkling liquid into the goblets.

Nicole stood and clasped the champagne glass in her hand as Cody proposed a toast. "Here's to the key that will open the door to millions in gold."

Nicole raised her glass, her eyes glazed and watery. Excitement swept through her body. "Here, here," she uttered.

They each took a sip of champagne and then Cody lifted his glass in the air for a second toast. "Here's to our new found love. May we always..."

The bullet made a sharp crack as it travelled through the crisp, fall air faster than the speed of sound.

In stunned silence, Nicole watched her lover's champagne glass tumble from his grip and crash to the floor.

Blood and brain spatter covered her hands, arms, and blouse as she looked down at Cody's blank eyes staring up at her.

For the longest time her eyes fixed on the man of her dreams—the man who lit up the room—the man who lit up her life with his chiseled features and charismatic presence. The man, who right before her very eyes, buckled to the floor like his knees were made of straw. She shook her head. *No, this can't happen. This makes no sense at all...*

She opened her mouth and no sound came out. When her voice finally connected to her brain, she screamed. She screamed so loud and for so long that a distant bald eagle wrapped its wings around its young.

CHAPTER 29

MICHAEL AND DETECTIVE Fox sat on the top deck of the houseboat locked in conversation. The afternoon sun warmed the air as Michael opened his laptop and looked across the table at Fox. "You don't have to search too far in cyberspace to find dirt on a person."

Fox wrinkled his brow and took a sip of his drink. "I'd like to relax here all day in the sun and drink your beer while you goof off on your laptop. But weren't we on our way over to see your father?"

"That we were, but I can assure you, I'm not goofing off. There's something more you need to know about your partner." He was certain Fox was squeaky clean, but for the sake of argument, he prodded on about Robin. "And I can tell by the look on your face you will not like it."

Fox glanced at the laptop. "Why would I? Just the thought of my partner as a dirty cop makes me cringe. I'm trying to stay open minded to what you have to say, but it isn't easy."

"Well, stay open to this. I just dug up some of her background."

Fox showed little expression as Michael read the caption from the on-line newspaper article.

"Robin Taylor wishes good cheer to her Uncle Cody at his birthday bash aboard his new yacht, *The Shark*."

Michael paused a moment and waited for a reaction from Fox. None came. "Did you know Cody Roark was her uncle?"

Fox shook his head. "No, I didn't know."

Michael struggled to find the right words. He didn't want to insult his friend. "As lead homicide detective in this neck of the woods, you're aware Cody Roark is one of the biggest drug lords around the area?"

Fox spoke in a flat tone. "Yes, I know who he is."

Michael continued. "The article tells how Uncle Cody raised Robin from the time she was a toddler after her folks died in an airplane crash. Here, read it yourself." Michael pushed the laptop in front of Fox so he could view the monitor.

Fox grimaced and squeezed his brows together as he read the article, then shoved the laptop back to Michael. "This doesn't prove she's a dirty cop."

"No, you're right, it doesn't. But you didn't know this about her, did you? Why did she conceal her background from you?"

Fox stared at his hands then looked at Michael. "Maybe she's a private person and wants no one to know about her roots."

"What's it going to take to convince you?"

Fox looked out at the lake for a moment, as if he were searching for answers then shifted his gaze back to Michael. "An intelligence officer in the Marine Corps is put through a horrendous grind of specialized training. Robin went through that training and turned into one of the finest counterintelligence officers I've known. I cannot believe she'd stoop to conspiracy with a group of low life criminals, not even for millions in gold. I don't care if Roark is her uncle. She's got too much to lose."

Michael leaned forward. "Maybe there's a side of her you're not aware of. Why would she strike me over the head and steal the key from around my neck?"

"You say she did. But you didn't actually see who hit you from behind."

"No, it was Robin. I'll never forget the smell of her perfume."

Fox leaned back in his chair. "Then there must be another explanation."

Michael smiled, took a gulp of beer and eyed Fox. "Okay... let's suppose I've been playing the devil's advocate, trying to draw you out. If she's everything you say maybe there's an explanation. Have you ever considered she may work undercover?"

"No, we've always been upfront with one another. She'd tell me if she worked on anything outside of our police work. What are you getting at?"

"Well, I think it's possible she's on a secret mission. Let's keep an open mind. If she's dirty, we'll find out soon enough."

Michael strolled over to the fridge, grabbed two more bottles of beer, popped them open and handed one to Fox. "There's something else you need to know before we go see my father."

"Oh, what's that?"

"It's about the key."

Fox narrowed his eyes. "Okay, I'm listening."

Michael sat down and took a gulp of beer. "In case something happens to me, someone I trust needs to know. I trust you for some damn reason."

Fox smiled and nursed his beer. "It's about time. Just remember, you're not in this thing alone."

"First of all, the key Robin went to all the trouble to steal is a fake. If she's the culprit, she whacked me over the head for nothing." Michael rubbed the back of his head and winced. "Whoever opens the security box at the bank with that key is in for a big surprise. They'll find a drawer full of funny money." Michael's eyes lit up with a smile.

Fox leaned in and arched his brows.

Michael lifted his beer in a toast. "Here's to the look of surprise on your face."

"I'm more than surprised. I'm amazed you've handled this alone up until now."

"True, I've had to stay one step ahead of the bastards." Michael reached into the zippered pocket of his leather jacket and pulled out a set of keys on a chain. "This is the real key." He dangled it in the air.

Fox's eyes flickered as he looked at the key. "So what does all this mean?"

"It means this key opens another security box at the bank—this key holds the map to the buried gold."

"Well, I'll be damned." Fox leaned back in his chair.

"But... only if you can read the map's algorithm; I destroyed the original map after I converted the old language into encrypted code and copied the data onto a flash drive."

Fox nodded. "I see... but, in case something happens to you, how—"

"I'll set it up with Bruno. That's all you need to know for now."

Fox's cell rang. "Hang on a second. I've got to take this call." Fox briefly spoke into the phone then stood. "That was headquarters. The Lake Police called in a shooting—incidentally, it just happens to be on Cody Roark's yacht."

Michael jumped to his feet. "I'll go with you. What's the location?"

"The yacht's afloat between here and the Lakeport Marina."

"Let's take the motorboat."

Ten minutes later, Michael and Detective Fox boarded the luxury yacht known as, *The Shark*. The local police and the medical examiner had already arrived. The police directed them to the upper level where the victim was located.

The body lie face up in a pool of blood with an expression of shock frozen in his eyes. Fox's face was grim as he stepped under the crime scene tape and bent down for a closer look at the body. "A clean hit right between the eyes." He glanced over at Michael. "Looks like the work of an expert marksman."

"The sharpshooter probably fired from up there." Michael pointed toward the fissures in the nearby mountain directly ahead.

Fox squinted up at the rocks. "Could very well be... I wonder if anyone's identified the body yet."

One of the investigators gathering blood evidence looked up from his work. "So far, what we know is the victim's name is Cody Roark, the owner of the yacht."

"Who called it in?" Fox asked.

"A fisherman upstream heard a woman scream and called the police."

"Do you know if the woman is here on the yacht?" Fox asked.

The investigator gazed across the deck at a lone female standing at the boat's railing. "We think that's her over there. She's not saying much, seems traumatized."

"Who is she?"

"She won't give her name. Just clutches her bag close to her chest and stares out at the lake."

The woman had her back to Michael, but he recognized the stance. How could he forget the night she snuck onto his houseboat and tried to seduce him? "That's my father's wife, Nicole Drake." He told Fox.

"Well, aren't we lucky?" Fox took a thoughtful moment. "Go talk to her. See what you can find out. Get her out of that open area. She's a sitting duck."

"I doubt if she'll say much to me."

"Try."

Michael crossed over to where she stood. It took everything he had to stay calm and not bear his teeth at the murderous bitch. "Hello, Nicole."

She jerked her head around and gave him a pained expression. Black mascara ran down her puffy face. "Michael? What are you doing here?"

"I might ask the same of you? How about we talk inside so we're not the next target?"

She looked across the deck at Roark's body then gazed out at the lake, her chin trembling. "I like it just fine here." She squeezed her tote bag closer to her chest.

"What happened, Nicole? Care to talk about it?"

She shook her head, her eyes glazed. "Go away. Leave me alone."

Fox joined the conversation. "Hey, let's find a better place to talk." He gazed up at the rocky mountain terrain, his beat-up face showing concern. "If the shooter were going take another shot, he'd probably have done it by now. But taking chances isn't too wise."

Nicole gazed up at the rocks, wide-eyed. Her voice quivered. "Who could have done such a thing? All we wanted was to be together."

"One never knows, does one?" Michael's lips curled upward, but his eyes weren't smiling.

Nicole glared at him then shifted her gaze to Fox. "Who are you?"

"I'm Homicide Detective, John Fox, with the Lakeport Police Department." He showed Nicole his badge.

"I hope you find the bastard who did this." She shivered and clutched her bag as if someone would snatch it out of her arms. "I'm cold."

"You must be exhausted, Mrs. Drake. Let's sit inside and see if we can't take the chill off, maybe whip up some coffee or hot coffee. I'd like to ask you a few questions. Do you mind?"

"Do I have a choice?" She reluctantly walked with them to a small enclosed snack lounge on the lower level. "I'd like to get off this damn boat as soon as possible."

Michael put on a pot of coffee while Fox and Nicole found a place to sit. Within a few minutes, he placed cream and sugar on the table and poured hot coffee into large mugs. "Couldn't find makings for hot chocolate, but this should warm you up." He sat across from Fox.

Nicole pulled a tissue out of her bag and dabbed at her face. Her voice broke as she spoke and her eyes darted nervously. "It's freezing in here. I want to go home. Can't you see I'm in mourning? A good friend of mine just got murdered."

"When the yacht docks at the marina I'll have Luis drive you home," Fox spoke across the table to her in a firm tone. "Just sit tight and drink your coffee. It will warm you."

She pushed her cup away. "I'd rather have a Martini…"

Fox pulled his notepad and pencil from his jacket pocket. His eyes were cold. "Mrs. Drake, were you with Cody Roark when he was shot?"

A sob caught in her throat. "Yes, I was…"

"Tell me what you remember."

She closed her eyes and leaned her head back against the chair. "Cody had just poured the champagne. He was making a toast, and then I heard a shot and he... poor Cody fell to the floor." She opened her eyes as tears spilled down her cheeks. "I... I couldn't believe it. One minute he's smiling, happy... the next, he's..."

"I'm sorry." Fox paused a moment and took a gulp of coffee then continued. "How long did you know Mr. Roark?"

"Not long. A few weeks." She stared blankly into her steaming coffee.

Fox scribbled something in his notepad then continued questioning. "Do you have any idea who may have wanted Cody Roark dead?"

Her eyelashes fluttered and she looked away. "I wouldn't know."

"Do you know any of his friends?"

"No."

Michael cleared his throat and broke in. "For someone who claims to be in mourning, you don't seem to know too much about your friend's life."

Nicole gazed blankly at Michael then looked above his head at the wall and didn't answer. She finally reached for her coffee and took a sip.

They sat in silence. Michael noticed Nicole's periodic glances at the dog tags hanging around his neck. She was easy to read. Was she toting the missing key in her bag?

Fox went on. "Tell me, Mrs. Drake, why were you on the yacht with Cody Roark? I noticed champagne and caviar. Were you celebrating?"

"No, we were..." She bit her bottom lip and struggled to find the words. "We were... on a date."

Michael could barely hold back his contempt for the woman. He covered it with phony laughter and nearly choked on his coffee.

Nicole's nostrils flared. "What do you find so damn funny? I can date. It's not as though your father were alive."

Michael controlled himself, leaned back in his chair and stared at her. The irony was that this woman would never find it in her heart to tell the truth.

Fox's face tightened. He couldn't hide the irritation in his voice. "I'd like to continue with a few more questions."

"Fine, fine, have it your way." Nicole pursed her lips. "Ask away."

Then angry voices grabbed their attention. A female cop stood in the doorway. "That's a private meeting. You can't go in there."

"Step aside. I'll go any damn place I want. I'm the Sheriff of Three Lakes County!"

Nicole remained seated as Michael and the detective rose from the table and walked over to the disruption.

"What's going on?" Fox asked.

"Tell your fucking squad to back off. I have every right to be here."

"You have no right to cause a scene and make demands," Fox said. "What's your problem? There's a murder investigation going on here. Who let you aboard this yacht?"

"First of all, I don't have a problem. When I received a call about a murder aboard this yacht, I rented a motor boat. I showed my sheriff's badge and came aboard. This is my jurisdiction."

Fox clinched his jaw. "You're way off base here. I'm with the Lakeport Police, Homicide division, and I'm in charge here. This is my murder case. Now back off."

Dillon directed his words toward Michael. "What's he doing here? He has no business on the premises of this crime scene."

"He does, if I say he does," Fox said.

Michael stood face to face with the enemy. He kept his cool as he recalled his father talk about the Sheriff of Three Lake's County screwing his young wife. Ironically, two of the people responsible for his father's attempted murder were in this room. The third—probably the dead man on the upper level of the yacht. He had to admit, the sheriff's face looked pretty bad—but the brawl in the alley was a temporary fix. He'd either find the proof he needed to put them both behind bars or watch them self-destruct.

Nicole walked over, her chin high as she eyed the sheriff and pointed at him. "Who's this guy?"

Someone you know quite well, Michael thought. They were both fine actors. Not a flicker of recognition between the two.

"Never mind," Nicole said. "He looks like a cop with a bashed up face, and I've had my fill of cops for one day. Now, will someone please get me off this boat and take me home?"

"It shouldn't be long now," Michael said, as he felt the yacht start to move.

Fox gave Nicole an agitated look. "I'm not through questioning you. Be prepared. I'll take you down to headquarters and question you there if need be."

"I'd be glad to take her home…" Sheriff Hobbs said.

Fox got close to the sheriff's face. "You're really beginning to piss me off. Like I said, I'll have one of the officers take her home. Not that it's any of your business how she gets home. Keep this up and I'll arrest you for impeding a murder investigation."

The sheriff glared and kept quiet.

"All right, let's be prepared for departure when the boat docks at the marina," Fox said. "Start walking ahead."

Sheriff Hobbs and Nicole walked in a single file toward the exit while Michael and the detective followed close behind.

Michael gazed up at the rocks where he surmised the sniper had taken the shot at Roark. He wondered if the local police or the SWAT team had stormed the terrain for the gunman. He didn't have to wait long for an answer. His life flashed before his eyes as he saw a reflection of the gun barrel—a nanosecond later the bullet skimmed the hairs on his scalp as it whizzed by his head and met its mark.

Fox's voice grabbed the air. "Everyone hug the deck. That son-of-a-bitch doesn't miss."

CHAPTER 30

SHERIFF DILLON'S HEAD spun around in shocked surprise--
then his legs caved and he went down.

Fox, on hands and knees, made his way over to Michael. "Are you
okay? For a few seconds there, I wondered if you were back in the
war."

"I'm okay. Looks like war right here on the home front."

Nicole had pressed her body flat against the deck and crawled a
few feet ahead toward the sheriff.

"What in the hell is she doing?" Michael asked.

"I don't know. I think she's placing the sheriff's head in her lap."

Michael moved closer and saw a flicker of life in the fallen man's
eyes. Blood from his head wound seeped onto Nicole's yellow skirt.
Her eyes were wide and shiny as she turned toward Michael. "He's
alive. Do something. You can't let him die! I can't lose him too."

Sirens howled in the background as Fox gave Michael a large
handkerchief to press against the wound.

Sheriff Dillon's lips moved as he labored to breathe. His words
slurred and he stared into Nicole's eyes. "I... I found her."

Nicole shook her head. "Be still, help is on the way. You're okay… you're going to live."

"No time. You have to know." He coughed and licked his lips. "I… your daughter… I found your daughter. Her name is… Annie."

"Oh, my god, you found my little girl?" Tears streamed down Nicole's cheeks as she embraced him.

"Yes, I found her… go see Molly… she knows wher..." His eyes closed.

The paramedics arrived and examined him.

"Alive?" Michael asked.

"Barely. He may have a chance if we get him to the hospital, fast." Two paramedics had the stretcher ready and carted him away.

Fox appointed Detective Luis to take over the investigation on the yacht. "Make sure the forensic specialists gather all the evidence. Get SWAT up there on the rocks and see if you can get a handle on the sniper. Let me know as soon as you find out anything. Call a squad car and have him meet me out front."

"Will do, boss!"

Nicole was quiet as she walked between the two men. Michael didn't trust the woman. As far as he was concerned prison was too good for her. Yet, he had just witnessed a human side of her. He wondered what Annie would do. Would she testify against her own mother?

"Can I go home now?" Nicole rubbed the back of her neck. "I'm exhausted."

Fox raised his brows thoughtfully. "Considering what has just happened, yes. I'll have an officer drive you home. But stay put."

"I will. All I want right now is sleep. I feel like a shipwreck. I need my rest. Did you hear what the sheriff said? He found my daughter. I need to be at my best for my baby girl."

Michael cut her a lowly stare. He wondered what Nicole would do if she knew her baby girl had heard every word she'd uttered about the killing of his old man.

Fox put a call into one of the officers to pick up Nicole and drive her home. He gave her specific instructions to prepare for more questioning for the following day.

After they saw Nicole on her way, Michael and the detective settled into a squad car with Fox behind the wheel. Michael buckled his seat belt and turned to his friend. "Nicole needs to be prosecuted— the sooner the better. As you know, she and her cohorts caused the near death of my father."

Fox tilted his head to the side and watched for oncoming traffic. "Without evidence, you'll play hell trying to convict her or the sheriff if he lives."

"There is a witness."

"Oh? Who might that be?"

"Nicole's birth daughter overheard Nicole and the sheriff discussing how they had set up my father with a car bomb. For all they know, my father's dead.

"I didn't know about a witness." Fox tightened his jaw as he stepped on the accelerator and passed a large dump truck. "Why are you just getting around to telling me about this now?"

"I learned about it a few days ago. I wasn't sure I could trust you. And I sure as hell didn't trust your partner, Robin." Michael frowned. "Speaking of Robin…"

"What about her?"

"Where is she? She's your partner. Why wasn't she at the scene of the shooting?"

Fox stared straight ahead, tightlipped. "Good question. She's may be at the office. That's where I'm headed after I drop you off."

"I find it odd she didn't call you."

Fox nodded. "I'm sure she had good reason."

Fox dropped Michael off curbside, across from the pool hall. "I'm glad your Jeep is still in one piece."

"Yeah, me too."

"I'll call you later." Fox stepped on the gas and shot away in a flurry.

Michael's gut instinct told him there was more to the female cop who called herself Robin. It was obvious the detective was on his way to find out where in hell she'd been for the past three hours.

€€€

The splash of red, orange and purple colors glistening on the lake predicted it was near sundown. Michael had just enough time before dark to gather a few belongings, lock up the houseboat and move back into the cabin. The renovation was complete, and he'd be surrounded by solid walls.

Maybe he was a target, and maybe he wasn't, but it was too risky to take the chance walking around in the open on the houseboat. Perhaps in Afghanistan there'd have been honor in dying for your country. But, he'd be damned if he'd get his brains blown out at home by some whacko sniper.

He gathered up clean clothes, then grabbed pizzas from the freezer and raided the fridge for cold beer. He would call Bruno and have him stock the cabin with food tomorrow.

With his arms loaded with bags of groceries and clothes, he stepped off the houseboat. The evening had settled into dusk and the sky was already dotted with stars. Thanks to Bruno, the pathway was scattered with small solar lights leading up to the door of the cabin.

The first sign of trouble was the familiar scent of tangy citrus perfume wafting through the night air. The second sign was the sound of a firearm cocked and pressed against his skull.

"Listen, and listen good, or you're dead," she said, her tone cold and sharp, like she wouldn't hesitate to shoot. "I want the key."

"What key?" Michael felt the cold steel of the pistol press harder against his head.

"Don't play games with me, Marine. I told you to listen. First, I want the key. Then, I want the computer password to the map's encrypted code. Now, start walking toward the cabin. One wrong move and you're dead."

"If I'm dead, you'll never get the password."

"Good point, but I'm acquainted with the underground. I know hackers hungry for money. Keep walking."

He recognized Robin's voice. "I have the feeling you will kill me anyway. So, out of curiosity, mind telling me how you know about the encrypted code?"

She snorted a dirty laugh. "Oh, that's easy. I had one of my men plant a bug on the upper deck of your houseboat where you usually sit. You told me everything I needed to know today in your little chat with Fox."

"Oh, you know where I usually sit? Well, aren't you the smart girl. If you think you can decipher the formula, you are welcome to it." It was Michael's turn to laugh.

"Quit stalling, asshole. Move." She pressed the gun into his back and pushed.

Nasty lady.

Fortunately, just in case his leg buckled, his cane was folded on the inside pocket of his jacket and easily extended by the push of a button. It was also handy to trip someone holding a gun in your back.

If he could throw her off-guard enough and get her rattled, he just might overtake her. The Beretta was tucked against his ribs, but he hated to kill her. He needed her alive to prove to Fox she was dirty.

"Assuming you're the sniper, what I can't figure out is why you knocked off your own blood relative, poor Uncle Cody."

"Try growing up with a sex abusing uncle and you'll find out what Post Traumatic Stress Disorder is really all about. Of course, I'm the sniper. Good old Uncle Cody was target practice. I was just getting warmed up."

"So it's not about the millions in gold." Michael stopped walking when he reached the cabin. "It's about revenge, isn't it? And the sheriff?"

"The sheriff knew too much. Enough talk. Place your bags on the ground, slowly. Remember, I'm as much a Marine as you and know all the same moves. So don't try anything. This Glock is pointed dead center at your head."

Fear gripped the edges of Michael's mind as he stared at Robin's reflection in the large picture window of the cabin. The gun pointed a few inches from his head filled him with cautious rage. What did he come home for—to wind up some crazy woman's vendetta?

His leg muscles tightened, his body wanted to run, but he was rooted to one spot. He would try to soften her. "Since your killing spree is all about retaliation toward your uncle—what will you do when you transfer the gold to money? Hide out on a beautiful island in the South Pacific for the rest of your life?"

"Not that it's any of your business, but I might do that after I donate a good portion of the money to the Post Traumatic Stress Disorder Foundation for veterans and rape victims." The strain in her voice was obvious. "Don't screw with me. I know the map is stored on a flash drive in a lock-box at your bank. The key to the bank's box is on the same chain as your car keys. I also know you're packing a piece. Walk up the stairs, set your bags down on the porch and slowly get your gun out and toss it."

He needed to be damn careful he didn't set her off. What else could he do but appease her? His only option was to ignore her demands and speak to her vulnerabilities. "I can imagine how you suffered as a child, Robin. My God, you were only five when your parents were killed, and your uncle took you in. I would think you joined the Marine Corps just to escape that bastard."

"As if you care." She couldn't hide the crack in her voice. "Wh... why do you think I became such a good PTSD counselor? From the war? Of course not. Most of my life I spent warding off demons dear old Uncle Cody strapped me with long before I joined the Marine Corps."

Michael did a good job diverting her thoughts, but he didn't like the image of the gun muzzle aimed at his head. Was he making matters worse? With her hair-trigger state of mind, it wouldn't take much for her to blow his brains out. All he could do was try.

He recalled some of her early history he'd read online. "You had a high ranking post in Afghanistan, didn't you? If I'm not mistaken, at one time you were part of a special operations motorcycle gang."

"Ah... yes. What can I say?" She laughed shamelessly. "Since the start of the war, the Taliban rode motorcycles to attack U.S. forces. They knew the most practical, low stress, low impact way to get around the battlefield and maneuver. Our team fought fire with fire. We were known as Afghanistan's lethal dirt bike gang; we called ourselves The USA Warlocks." She snorted. "We were the Taliban's worst nightmare. I wiped out dozens of those rapist bastards and enjoyed killing every one of them."

"I applaud you for it."

When she spoke again her voice barely rose above a whisper. "Don't give me your bullshit, Michael. You don't understand the impact of sexual abuse anymore than the Taliban when they rape and beat women. I saw the way you were undressing me with your eyes."

How could she equate me up with the Taliban? She must hate all men.

"Only because you're a beautiful woman; no bullshit intended. I'm not saying I understand completely what you were up against as a child. But wiping out some of the Taliban like you did is a good thing, and I salute you for it."

He wasn't sure, but he thought he heard a soft sob caught in her throat. "I don't need your pity or your understanding. Walk up those porch steps." She nudged him again with the snout of the gun.

Somehow he had to throw her off guard and get the gun. "I still use a walking stick when I climb stairs, you know." It sounded lame, but he had to try. "Mind if I get my folding cane out of my jacket pocket?"

"Is this your idea of a joke? You want me to believe you still use a cane after your kick-ass boxing exhibition last night in the alley? I watched you before I conked you over the head. As I recall, you kicked the shit out of several men."

"No, it's true. Especially after last night I weakened my leg. In fact, I actually re-injured the wound." His throat tightened. If he could get his hands on the cane he was sure he could overpower her. He carried a Devil's Walking Stick, made from the Hercules plant. He'd never used it as a weapon, but no time like the present to try it out on this monstrous woman. "The doc told me to stay clear of stairs for a while or anything strenuous."

"Funny, I didn't see you limping tonight in the least. All right; not that I feel sorry for you. I'm going to shoot you anyway, in the end. In the meantime, set your bags down and get the cane out of your pocket. No sudden moves. Remember, I've got the advantage. The gun is aimed straight at your head."

"No problem, all I want is my cane." You dumb wench, Michael thought, as he placed the bags on the ground in front of him, then stood straight. "The cane is in my left-side jacket pocket."

"Go ahead and get it; like I said easy does it—no sudden moves."

He reached in with his right hand, gripped the cane and pulled it from his inside pocket. Then he placed his thumb over the top button and pressed. The stick instantly expanded. He took a deep breath for a moment and leaned on the cane as if he were relieved from pain. Then he shifted his weight and swiftly whipped the stick around striking the calves of her legs. Her gun fired into the air as she tumbled off her feet and collided with the ground. Instantly, he straddled her, wrenched the gun out of her hand and tossed it away.

He sat on top of her and pinned both arms down. "Now, you listen, you cold-blooded bitch. Not all men are out to rape you like your uncle. So get off your crusade to kill every man you meet."

"How about this, you bastard." She spit in his face, rose her butt off the ground and hooked her legs around his neck. "How's that feel?" She laughed as she squeezed her thighs together in a scissor lock.

The pressure cut off his air. Everything went dark, and for a moment he felt death was imminent. She was damn strong, but not strong enough. It took all his brawn to topple her over into a swift summersault, raise his body up and then slam her bones into the ground.

She released the scissor lock, her flesh limp. Was she playing dead? He didn't know, but he'd be damned if he'd take any chances. With both her arms pinned over her head, he checked the pulse in her neck and found a slight beat.

Relieved he hadn't killed her; he straddled her and held her in that position for a good minute. He would carry her into the cabin and tie her up. He wondered if anyone would believe what he'd just experienced with this hellcat.

Then he heard the whir of chopper blades. The spotlight shined down and lit up the whole lakefront. Sirens howled; then three patrol cars came to an abrupt stop in front of the cabin.

CHAPTER 31

MICHAEL RELEASED HIS hold on Robin and jumped to his feet. He wondered how he would explain the whole crazy scenario. Going up against a cop was bad enough—but a female cop? Who would believe him?

Detectives Fox and Silva and three uniformed officers stormed onto the scene with their guns drawn. They were not in a "protect and serve" mode. One cop nabbed Michael's Beretta while the other placed him in handcuffs.

"That's okay," Fox said. "Take the cuffs off for now. He's a friend of mine."

The cop reluctantly freed him.

Michael rubbed his wrists. "Thanks, I know how this must look, but I can explain."

A paramedic rushed over to examine Robin. She moaned and tried to sit up. He gently pushed her down. "She's coming around. She may have a couple of broken ribs."

Robin opened her eyes and glared at Michael as the EMT's carried her on a stretcher to the ambulance waiting in the driveway. He glared back. He had nothing to hide, so why did he feel like he'd stepped into a big sinkhole? Robin would have blown his brains out if he hadn't taken control of the matter.

Fox looked at Michael as if he were waiting for an admission of guilt. Under the dim lights Fox's scruffy skin gave him a lizard-like appearance. When he flexed his brows it was almost scary. "Care to explain what happened here?"

Michael set his jaw and maintained eye contact. "Robin held a gun to my head. She wanted the key to the bank's security box. She was after the map."

Fox looked over at the other detective. "Didn't look that way to me; did it to you, Luis?"

"Not at all."

"From what we saw," Fox went on, "you were the aggressor. When we approached the scene you were straddling Robin. In fact, according to the medic, you broke a couple of her ribs."

Luis weighed in with a nod.

He looked from one detective to the other and wondered if he needed a lawyer. If Fox said kiss my ass, no doubt Luis would agree to it. "I was defending myself. You may not want to believe this, Fox, but Robin is the sniper. She shot her uncle. She shot the sheriff, and she all most killed me."

Fox stared at Michael in disbelief."Can't be, can't be."

"Why would I lie?" Michael puffed out a big sigh and frowned. "You didn't want to believe she knocked me out last night in that alley, either. Are you hooked on her, or what?"

"You'd better watch your mouth. You don't know how close I am to arresting you."

"Okay, but before you read me my rights, tell me this… How did you even know there was trouble in Dodge? Who called you? I sure as hell didn't. For all I know you're in on this with Robin. For all I know this is a setup."

Fox narrowed his eyes. "I resent that. First you accuse Robin of being a dirty cop and now me? For your information, the call came in from your butler. He told us there was a big problem out here."

"Really..." Michael scoffed. "Big problem? How would my butler know anything that goes on out here?"

"You tell me. He called and said there was a hostage situation at the lake cabin. I know how you distrust Robin, so—"

"So you assumed I was the bad guy." Michael shook his head in disgust. "You're an ass."

"Cut the crap. I'm not assuming anything. I'm giving you a chance to explain yourself."

"Doesn't matter what I tell you. When it comes to Robin, you're blind. She's a cold-blooded killer, guilty of multiple murders. She would have killed me if I hadn't outwitted her."

"Looks like you did more than outwit her."

Luis threw in another nod.

The abrupt squeal of breaks in the driveway drew everyone's attention. A car door slammed and a lone man rushed to the scene. "I got here as fast as I could. Damn, bloody traffic. But not to worry; it's all on the video tape."

"Tape? What's on tape? Explain yourself." Fox scowled. "First of all, who the hell are you?"

"I'm Bruno Higgins, the butler at the Drake mansion. I'd be glad to explain." Bruno licked his lips and smiled with a quirked eyebrow. "The new security camera caught every bloody move. From the moment that hellish woman aimed the gun at Michael's head, to the moment he threw her to the ground—it's all on tape." Bruno turned to Michael. "I'm glad you insisted we install the security cameras. That was spot on. The woman, who ever she is, could have killed you. By the way, congratulations, that was quite a trick you pulled with your walking stick, my lad."

CHAPTER 32

THREE MONTHS LATER...

The rich aroma of barbecued ribs wafted through the crisp night air as friends and family gathered in Heoma's backyard. The festivities eclipsed all others in the celebration of Heoma and Perry's engagement and the opening of Michael's new Dojo.

Michael grabbed a couple beers out of the ice chest and handed one to Detective Fox. They sat at a large redwood table exchanging views on where to donate a portion of the money from the gold.

"The fortune is now in a special Drake account," Michael said. "The Wounded Warrior Project and the Post Traumatic Stress Disorder Foundation of America are the two charities we've donated to so far. Your thoughts?" He popped off the lid and took a swig of beer.

"Good choices, but let's not forget rape victims. They suffer post traumatic stress the same as war veterans do. You just don't hear that much about it. They are the silent sufferers."

Michael saw the pain in Fox's eyes every time Robin's name came up. ""Like Robin, you mean. I haven't forgotten and I will gladly direct a portion of the money to The Rape Crisis Center."

Fox nodded. "Good."

"Have you heard anything more on where Robin might be?" Michael asked.

Fox's jaw tightened. "No, I haven't. I tried my best to visit her when she was in jail, and she refused to talk to me. That's the last contact I had with her."

Michael reached for a chip and dipped it in guacamole. "Strange how she escaped," he said between munches. "Are you sure she didn't have a little help from her friend, the prison guard?"

"Could very well be—they were close friends when Robin was on the police force. In fact, they were best buddies, inseparable. We've questioned Patty on several occasions. Her answer was always the same. She claims she helped her mom with yard work that day, her day off; her mom confirms it. This doesn't mean she didn't have a hand in Robin's disappearance. We just can't prove it." Fox downed his beer and reached for another. "For all I know, Robin may be out of the country by now."

Michael recalled Heoma's power with evil spirits. Roark and Sheriff Dillon got their due through Robin's sharpshooting—but, did something else guide the ship? Black magic, perhaps? Michael scoffed at the thought.

"Robin murdered one man and left the other with a major head trauma," Michael said. "And from what I understand, the bullet is still lodged in the sheriff's brain—not that the bastards didn't deserve it— but you can bet they won't go easy on Robin if they catch up to her."

Fox grimaced and lowered his gaze. "Hey man, I've said it before; I'm sorry I doubted you. She could have killed you." Fox shook his head. "I must have been blind not to see the signs. She's a dangerous person and to think I trusted her. She'll no doubt spend the rest of her life in prison if, and it's a big if, they ever catch up to her."

"She may be on the lam but sooner or later they'll find her." Michael shook his head. "I understand how much Robin meant to you."

"Have you thought any more about joining the Castle Rock P. D?" Fox asked. "You wouldn't make a half-bad partner. I need someone I can trust. I also need help with the PTSD meetings. You'd be an ideal candidate."

"I'll give it some thought now that my Dojo is up and running. Nash is my star Karate pupil. When I place him in charge I may come aboard."

They sat for a few moments, each in their own thoughts. Michael took a gulp of beer and gazed at his father and Heoma sitting at the adjoining table. They were in love—a beautiful couple. Perry looked tan, handsome and ten years younger sitting beside his gorgeous fiancé. He wondered if his father would ever regain his memory.

"At least Nicole is behind bars," Fox broke the silence.

Michael grabbed a handful of peanuts and popped them into his mouth. "Yeah, and the good thing is Annie didn't have to testify against her birth mother. Thank God for the DVD you confiscated from the sheriff's office. There was enough on that video to put them all away for life."

"I wonder if we'll ever find out who placed the hidden camera in the bedroom of Roark's yacht. It doesn't make sense."

It made perfect sense to Michael. He knew exactly who planted the hidden device. Heoma's words echoed in his head: *"These people who are after your father are evil."* He remembered her eyes became black pits—almost witch-like. *"Not to worry, dear boy. I'll take care of it."* Some things are best left unsaid, Michael reasoned.

"What about you and Annie?" Fox asked. "I thought the two of you were, well… kind of… in love."

Michael nodded. "We are… very much so."

"Well, where the hell is she then?" Fox playfully looked around. "Why isn't she at your side?"

Michael sighed. "We're taking it slow. She's studying art at college. She'll be home on spring break. Maybe a few years down the road we'll hookup. I don't think I'm ready for marriage yet anyway."

Luis and two other cops came over and sat across from Fox. This was Michael's cue to leave. Luis had never forgiven him for the brawl in the alley. He claimed he still suffered pain in his neck and shoulders from the headlock. Michael would rather leave the table than be glared at for the entire evening by this idiot detective.

"Hey, talk to you later, buddy," he told Fox. "I'll give some thought to joining the force."

Michael squeezed between Nash and Bruno at their table. Heoma gave Michael a welcoming smile, and he received a casual nod from Awan. It felt odd sitting across from his father, calling him "Awan" like a stranger. Now and then, he caught his father glance in his direction.

Michael listened to the conversation going on around him. Aunt Jo, who sat on the other side of Bruno, laughed from her gut. "Tell us again Bruno. Tell us how Michael whipped his cane out and whacked the female cop to the ground."

Bruno chuckled. "That beastly woman, thank God we put security cameras up when we did or Michael might be in jail. The minute I saw her hold the gun to Michael's head, I called the police, jumped in my car and headed straight for the lake cabin. Traffic was a bloody bitch. I stopped at one intersection after another watching the drama play-out on my smart phone—fortunately, I had an app for that."

The whole table broke out in laughter and cheers.

"Then what?" Aunt Jo asked. "Tell us what you saw when Michael used his fold-up cane,"

Michael felt invisible, like the scenario Bruno described had happened to someone else. Everyone remained quiet as Bruno carried on with the story…

"Well, as they walked toward the cabin, the woman pushed Michael ahead of her with the nose of the gun in his back. When Michael faced the cabin, she aimed the pistol directly at his head. I thought she would pull the trigger any moment—and there I sat, helpless at the bloody red light."

Bruno cleared his throat and took a sip of beer, obviously enjoying the limelight.

"Did you know Michael carried a fold-up cane with him?" Heoma wanted to know.

"No, I didn't. But wait, I'm coming to the best part."

They all hunched forward hanging onto Bruno's every word. He paused and looked at their faces then went on. "Unfortunately, I didn't have sound on the video, but I saw their mouths move. So I knew they were talking to each other. Then Michael reached into his pocket and pulled out his cane. He must have sweet-talked her into it."

Everyone laughed and looked over at Michael then turned their attention back to the storyteller.

Bruno continued. "After Michael popped open the cane he rested his body on it for a moment, like he was in terrible pain. But I knew he was faking—."

Michael's ears perked up. "Now just a minute," he broke in. "How would you know I was faking?"

"Easy, lad. You told us on your last visit that your leg was free of pain." Bruno smiled and nodded.

That's right, Michael thought. No one knew about his big fight in the alley with the bad boys the night before.

"Go on, Bruno," Nash said. "You were just getting to the juicy part. What happened next?"

Again, Michael felt like the invisible man. He looked at Bruno, "Yeah, that's quite a smart phone; what happened next, Bruno?"

"Well blimey; Michael swiped the cane at her legs and the woman didn't know what hit her. She had this crazy, surprised look on her face as she fell to the ground like a sack of bricks."

Michel blocked out Bruno's voice and looked over at his father. He was sure he saw a flicker of recognition in his eyes.

No, probably just your imagination.

When Bruno finished his story, Heoma made eye contact with Michael. "I'm so proud of you, Michael. You're our very own hero."

He glanced at his father. "Not really, just taking care of the folks I love."

Perry squinted as he gazed at Michael. "Don't I know you? You look so damned familiar to me. I've been trying to place you all evening."

Michael's heart quickened. In a flash, all the years of resentment, all the fear of rejection, the hate, and the frustration washed away in one clean sweep.

Perry's eyes grew wide. "Michael... is that you? That is you, isn't it?" He gazed over at Heoma and pointed to Michael. "That's my son, yes, that's my son, Michael..."

Michael smiled. He no longer felt invisible. "Hello Dad. I've been meaning to ask... how about we go out on the houseboat tomorrow and take in a little fishing. We've got a lot of catching up to do."

"Why, I'd love that, Son."

The smile on his father's face made it all worthwhile.

Also available in Paperback and Amazon Kindle

DANGEROUS PRESENCE

A Jacquelyn Kincaid Thriller

by M.G. Cronkite aka Marlene Cronkite

My blog:

http://story-gems.blogspot.com

www.ingramcontent.com/pod-product-compliance
Lightning Source LLC
Chambersburg PA
CBHW070857180626
46817CB00003B/809